HARPIST FOR THE BEAST

SUMMER HAYES

Chapter One

A shiver crawled up Jude's spine as he stepped through the gates of Harlock Castle. He shut his eyes for a moment, wishing as he had so many times before that he could wake up from this nightmare. He'd never believed in monsters until he'd first been summoned to Harlock, but now, every time the moon glowed bright, he came face-to-face with them.

The ruins of the castle were covered in a thin layer of fog. A fire had taken out most of the structure about a century ago, and left only the crumbling walls. Guided by the light of the full moon, Jude stalked through the thick weeds that surrounded the decaying stones. His destination lay beyond the lone archway at the back. He passed under the curved stones and stopped in front of the trapdoor nestled in the earth at his feet. Without a roof to shelter it, the oak boards had warped from the constant rain of the Scottish Highlands.

Jude bent down and threw the heavy door back on its

hinges. He drew in a deep breath and descended into the pitch-black stairwell. A few steps down, Jude stopped and removed his cell phone and car keys from his jacket. He tucked them into a wide crack between two stones and pulled out a flashlight he'd stashed there to help guide him down the rest of the stairs. The beam struggled to life. He made a mental note to get fresh batteries for next time. Jude took each step carefully. The weakened bulb did little to illuminate the dark abyss in front of him.

At the bottom of the narrow passage, behind a solid iron door, awaited his personal hell.

Before he lost his nerve, Jude pulled on the handle. A warm current of air rushed at his face. Candles lit the large chamber, their hot wax dripping from the sconces onto the stone floor. A black granite table with veins of gold dominated the center of the room. Cold beads of sweat trickled down his forehead at the sight of it.

"All these years and you haven't failed us yet," a voice said from the shadows.

Jude shone his flashlight at the figure standing across the room. The front of a human skull covered the man's face, but he knew the voice. It was the leader of the cult.

"Haven't you grown tired of this ritual yet?" The man stepped into the room. Shadows from the candlelight danced across his ruby cloak.

"Of course I'm tired of it." The hackles on the back of Jude's neck rose. Men in The Order rarely spoke to him when he came to Harlock. They only desired his blood. Why address him now? These rituals left him so weak. What more could they take from him?

"Why don't you relinquish your position and allow

another to feed the brotherhood?" The man withdrew a dagger and played with it in his hands.

Jude tried to hide his flinch. He stepped directly in front of the cultist. "Why would I allow you to torture anyone else?" Anger built inside him.

The cloaked man rushed forward and pressed the tip of the blade to Jude's bare collarbone. The dagger sliced open an old wound. Jude backed up, but the man was persistent, and kept the blade on his taut flesh until they both slammed against the granite altar, Jude bending backward over it. He grabbed the man's wrist to push the blade away, but his strength overpowered him.

"So noble, aren't we?" The man laughed and withdrew his steel.

Jude clutched to the bleeding wound as he stood up straight.

"The proposal I'm about to make might change your mind." The cultist went over to the table that held the instruments they used to extract the life from Jude. He picked up a clean rag, waving it in the air a moment to tease Jude, then tossed it in his direction.

He'd been cut countless times in the dungeons of Harlock, but the pain never lessened. Jude held the delicate cotton to his angry wound, hunched forward from the throb from his collarbone.

The masked man stood directly in front of him, looming over him like the Grim Reaper. "Join us, Master Rocoeurs. Join the brotherhood and continue the legacy of maintaining order in our empire. God has chosen us to rule the world."

Jude winced as he pressed on his wound, the rag now

soaked with his blood. The same blood the cultists drank when they performed their barbaric ritual, all in an effort to make them more powerful, to keep sickness and old age at bay for as long as they possibly could. Now they were offering him a seat at their table, so that he may feed off another poor soul. Could he ever do such a thing? Taking another man's life force would turn him into one of the monsters he'd dreaded for so many years.

Far off in the dungeons, iron doors creaked open.

They're here.

ELIZABETH STOOD IN THE NARROW FOYER OF HER London apartment, thumbing the check for two hundred pounds. Outside, a late summer rain flooded the streets, and her last student of the day ran through the torrent toward the SUV idling out front. She watched until the vehicle drove down the road and out of sight, then looked down at the check.

"It's not enough," she whispered to herself. Walking into the kitchen, she placed the check in envelope that held her rent money, added the amount to her tally on the back flap, and tucked the stash of checks and cash behind the empty biscuit tin.

Tears began to cloud her eyes. Sadness gripped her heart like a serpent smothering its prey. Hours and hours of practice had gotten her nowhere. All the hard work she'd put into building a music career felt so pointless now. Each month she barely eked out a living. She took every opportunity she got to play a gig, but her rent increased each year, and the struggle to stay afloat was breaking her down.

She stood in front of her harp and plucked a single string. How could she have been so stupid? Making a living as a musician was a pipe dream. If she hadn't fallen in love with the instrument as a teenager, she might have chosen a different path; one that didn't force her to scrape by, even now, in her thirties.

You're a failure, Elizabeth. Just accept it.

Trying to ease her woe, Elizabeth drew herself a hot bath. As she undressed, she accidentally knocked an old bar of lavender-oatmeal soap into the tub. She picked it up, feeling the oats poking out of the otherwise smooth bar. It was the last thing Gran had given to her before she died. Elizabeth rarely used it because she wanted to preserve it for a little longer, but the day had been a long, tiring one, and she deserved something special. After she submerged herself in the hot water, she rubbed the soap across both of her arms. The relaxing aromas of her youth brought back memories of Gran tucking her in bed after they'd stayed up late baking Christmas cakes. If she tried hard enough, she could even hear the sound of Gran's voice.

Elizabeth's phone vibrated against the linoleum countertop. The notification snapped her back to the present. She knew without looking that it was a reminder to pay the water bill. She groaned and plunged her head underwater. Beneath the surface, it was quiet and calm. Her head cleared until a distant memory of a little white cottage flashed in her mind. She broke through the surface and grabbed her phone to dial.

"Elizabeth, hon?" her mother said.

"Hey Mum, I was wondering if I could go up to Millie's cottage for a bit."

"You can. I'm not sure what sort of state it's in though. Your father planned on going there before the winter to shore things up."

"I can take care of it."

Could she take care of it? Elizabeth wasn't sure, but she didn't have much of a choice. It was either that or find another rat hole in London she could barely afford. To top it all off, her landlord was a complete asshole. He screamed if the rent was even one day late. She knew she had to be gone before that happened again.

Elizabeth said goodbye, tossed her phone to the floor and dunked her head under one last time to relish in the warmth. She wasn't sure if Millie's cottage even had a working hot water tank, since the place had been abandoned for so long. The thought of cold showers made her shiver, but there would be no angry landlords, and she could quit her frantic searches for posh gigs. The only thing the cottage needed was Gran's magic.

Oh, how I miss you, Gran.

In everything she did, from the soups she cooked to the dresses she made, and even the fantastic stories she told about fairies living in the woods and trolls hiding in the mountains, Gran made Elizabeth believe there was a magical force at work in the world. Some part of her thought if she could feel that spark, that small burning flame of enchantment, maybe she could believe in herself again.

§.

LATE SUMMER BROUGHT FRIGID TEMPERATURES TO Beauloch. Jude stood in the dining hall, gazing out of the tall arched windows framing a panorama of the woods. Outside, a grey mist hung over the tall pines. A sudden gale spun the drizzle in a dance until it reached the castle, drenching the windows and distorting the view of the forest.

You have a decision to make.

Feeling the hot flesh at his collarbone, Jude contemplated the offer The Order had made to him. If he joined them, he would be free from their torture. The only problem was, he would have to take part in enslaving another person to a life of agony. The thought of drinking human blood to gain strength and maintain youth sickened him.

He walked through the swinging doors to the kitchens without warning. Annie and Fiona, both kneading dough, shot worried glances at him.

"My laird?" Fiona said.

"I want to have a meeting after dinner," Jude said.

Annie, a young girl in her twenties, and Fiona, a woman pushing seventy, both stood frozen. Their faces twisted with fear and dread; a look Jude had become familiar with.

"I'm taking my meal in the dining hall tonight."

"Anything else?" Fiona said.

"No." He left.

Jude knew he had to make a decision. With every full moon, he grew weaker. He would be thirty years old in a few months, and his body ached more and more from the drain of the monthly rituals. This couldn't go on forever, and it was time to confront that fact.

Jude limped down the corridor, holding onto the wall for support. It felt like boulders were shackled to his wrists and ankles, making every step a struggle. He was forced to stop and catch his breath.

"Damn it all!" he roared, forcing even more air from his lungs.

A long time ago, his staff ran to help him if they heard him shout. Now they let him be. His howls of anguish and frustration had seeped deep into the crevices of Beauloch castle over the years. His despair surrounded them all. It clung to every corner and haunted every room.

He grunted, shaking off the pain. Determination pushed him forward. He continued to struggle until he reached the entrance to the staff office on the far east side of the castle. Walter, the gamekeeper for Beauloch, sat at his desk, marking something down on a map of the lands surrounding the castle.

"Dinner is almost ready. Come to the dining hall when you're finished here," Jude said.

Walter looked up at him, then went back to his map. "Is that all?" he said in his usual monotone voice.

"A fire would be good," Jude said as he turned to leave. Humility weighed heavy on him. He wanted to build his own damn fires, but he was too weak. It would be a fortnight before he regained enough strength for such a task.

When he reached the dining hall, he sat down at the head of the long table. The weathered oak had been carved from the forest behind the castle and brought up the back steps almost two centuries ago. His ancestors had used the exquisite piece of furniture to feast during holidays and other celebrations like weddings and births. Jude ran his hand over the scars carved into the surface from years of cutlery chipping away at the wood. Extra varnish had been applied to prevent any further damage. It felt smooth and cold against his palm.

Walter entered only to build and light the fire, and left without a word. Jude gazed into the slow-building flames doing their best to fight against the cold. An all-too-familiar loneliness crept up through the empty halls of Beauloch and into his icy heart. It was the same shadow of isolation he'd failed to escape for the last eight years. Nothing could chase it away. He'd accepted the unbearable solitude in the end. Somehow, he'd managed to freeze his heart like the ice that captured the summer blooms at the top of Ben Chross.

And yet, it ached.

Fiona brought out a bowl of homemade minestrone and a slice of hot sourdough laden with fresh butter.

He waited until she left to start eating. As soon as the kitchen doors swung shut, he picked up the soup spoon. His hand shook ferociously, the lack of blood in his wrist and fingers made it difficult to control the utensil. After a few attempts, he got into a steady rhythm of scooping and sipping and devoured the soup.

A little while later, Annie came in and draped a woolen blanket over his lap.

"I'm almost finished with my meal. Please let everyone know I'm ready to speak with them."

"Of course," Annie said.

Fiona, Walter, and Annie stood beside the table as he finished off his slice of bread. Jude wiped his mouth and stood up. The air grew thick with the lie he was about to tell. He cleared his throat.

"It has been a long time coming, but I will be leaving Beauloch soon," Jude said. The faces of all three of his friends remained still. No one said a word. They waited for him to go on, to explain this sudden decision. Jude continued. "Your services at Beauloch will not be needed come January."

Between the crackling of a log and the wind whistling through the tops of the old glass windows, silence consumed the room. Fiona twisted her face into a serious frown. Annie's eyebrows rose with confusion. Walter widened his stance and crossed his arms, and his eyes met the floor.

"You're leaving Beauloch?" Walter said.

"When the time gets close to my departure, I will let you know."

Fiona turned to leave the room, failing to hide her tears. Whimpers echoed through the vast dining hall as she walked out. Walter shoved his hands in his pockets. The grey stubble on his gaunt face accentuated the man's serious look.

It was, in fact, serious. Either he was going to kill everyone in The Order to rid the world of their scourge, or become the complete monster they wanted him to be by joining their cult. Both scenarios were horrible outcomes, and he had little chance of surviving either of them. It was highly unlikely he could take down every member of The Order in one fell swoop, and he would rather drown himself in the loch before subjecting another human to the tortures of the Harlock dungeons.

Chapter Two

Beauchross wasn't large enough to be considered a proper village. It consisted of a few essential shops and some abandoned storefronts. There was one lousy pub, the Cat and Crocus, on the main road. Inside the pub, stained tartan carpet covered the floor, the green wallpaper peeled at the seams, and a decades-old TV blared the local news. The air reeked of mildew and sour ale. Elizabeth leaned against the bar, a few adverts for her music services in hand.

The barman pointed to the bulletin board on the wall behind her. "It's not very full. We don't get a lot of traffic in here during the off-season. If I'm being honest, most tourists stop at the village on the other side of the glen. More shops and coffee places."

Elizabeth went over to the bulletin board. There was an advertisement for local, fresh eggs and a couple for old boats for sale. She pinned up her own flyer, offering to play the harp at parties, weddings, and funerals.

The old photo of her posing with her lever harp made her cringe. Most people wanted a young maiden to grace their events with beautiful music, not some thirty-year-old with more than a few grey hairs at her right temple. Still, she needed money for basic necessities, and she didn't have any other ideas for earning a living in this remote glen.

Elizabeth spent the rest of her morning in the pub eating a cold steak pie the barman had attempted to heat up in a microwave. Most of the time she wasn't picky, but his effort had been so minimal, she wondered if she should feel insulted or not. Not many people came in while she sat there. A middle-aged man stopped by and nursed a beer while he watched a football game. An older gentleman with a Scottish cap took a seat in the corner and ordered the same dismal pie she'd just choked down. The barman whispered to him when he brought it over, and they both glanced in her direction.

That's my cue to leave.

Elizabeth wrapped her scarf around her neck and shoulders as many times as she could and set out to Gran's old home. The footpath she took went over a few low hills, but the harsh wind didn't allow her to enjoy the view. She kept her head down. When she made it back to the cottage, she stopped for a moment, studying the exterior. Everything Gran had planted in the raised garden beds out front had been dead a long time, and the wild summer weeds had taken over most of the surrounding property, making the house look like an abandoned hut.

The fate of Gran was still a mystery. There had been a few signs leading up to her disappearance that indicated she'd been experiencing the onset of dementia. A few times she accidentally sent two Christmas cards instead of one. Other times she called Elizabeth by her mother's name. The worst incident happened when a bus driver picked her up eight miles from her home. She claimed she knew where she'd been going, even though nobody believed her. Not long after that, she vanished. The authorities assumed she'd hiked into the hills and gotten lost, but the details the police gave were scant, and no one could verify the last time they'd actually seen her alive.

Nightmares often plagued Elizabeth when she thought too hard about Gran's fate. Could Millie have wandered too far and fallen? Had she foraged too close to the river and gotten swept away by the currents? Did some sick stranger kidnap her and dump her body far away, where no one would find her?

The funeral her parents had held in London was the only closure she got. Since there'd been no body, her parents saw no reason to travel to the Highlands for a service, even though Millie had some close friends here. Elizabeth always felt guilty for that, but some part of her still held hope her grandmother would be found, and someday she would wake up from this terrible nightmare.

A large gust forced Elizabeth inside the cottage door. She cranked the radiator as high as it would go and took to the frayed chair next to the old bookcase. Thumbing through the titles within arm's reach, she landed on an old guide to wildflowers in the Highlands. Millie had been considered a very knowledgeable herbalist and was often sought out for remedies she made from the plants in her garden or things she foraged in the area.

Right as Elizabeth pulled the book off the shelf, a

knock sounded. She got up to peer through the little round window in the front door that looked out to the porch. Outside, an elderly woman stood wrapped in a shawl and rain cap. One of Gran's old customers? Elizabeth opened the door.

"Hello," she said.

"Well hello there! Rob said that someone had taken up residence in Millie's old cottage, so I thought I'd stop by and introduce myself," the woman said, beaming a bright smile. A gust of wind almost forced her over.

"Come in, please." Elizabeth held the door open.

The woman scampered inside, shaking off drops of rain that had just started to fall. "I'm Fiona, by the way." She looked around the place. "It's not changed much."

"You knew Millie?"

"Most of us around here did."

"I'd love to hear about what you know. Would you like some tea?"

"That'd be lovely."

Elizabeth went into the kitchen and fought with the old cooker. She'd fussed with it for an hour when she'd first arrived but had finally conquered the burners. She lit one with a match.

"Please, sit." She pointed to the small kitchen table, which was accompanied by only two chairs. Fiona took a seat in one of them.

"Can you tell me how you knew her?" Elizabeth said as she prepared a pot of Earl Grey.

"Och, I knew Millie for years. The best wise woman this side of the Beauchross River, she was. Anyway, wish we knew what became of her. Walter, our gamekeeper, thinks she just wandered a little too far one day and couldn't find her way back."

"Gamekeeper?" Elizabeth poured steaming water into the blue ceramic pot Millie always used when she made tea. The stain was still prevalent on the inside.

"I work at Beauloch castle. It's a bit hidden away in the old forest. Privately owned, so not too many people know about it. That's where I'd like for you to come tomorrow."

Elizabeth's memories of Scotland were a little fuzzy, but she was sure she would have remembered a nearby castle. She took the lid off the ceramic pot to check the tea. "What's at Beauloch?"

"Oh! Pardon me. Rob showed me the flyer you posted on the board. I'd like to hire you to play for the laird."

Elizabeth brought the pot to the table and poured the piping-hot tea into two cups, doing her best not to splash the elderly woman with the scalding beverage. She was surprised to get a response to her ad so quickly. Were the locals just being nice, since they'd known and loved Millie? Elizabeth was a little bit suspicious of this woman's motives, but she couldn't say no. Her bank account wouldn't allow it.

"You want me to play tomorrow? Is there something special going on? A birthday? Or anniversary?" Elizabeth set the blue teapot aside.

"Oh, no. It's just for the laird. He's, um, a bit sick at the moment, and we thought it would be nice to have music in the castle again."

"That's not a problem. I've done small gatherings before. I—"

"No. No. This is just for him. No one lives there but

him and a couple of domestics. I'm one of 'em." Fiona smiled. The lines in her cheeks and forehead that framed her sad, blue eyes seemed weighed down by something.

Elizabeth took a moment to think about the situation. "Is this end-of-life care?"

"Och, no! He's just in a bad way right now. He gets a little melancholy sometimes because of his condition, but he's not *dying*." She said the last words like they were a forlorn hope instead of the truth.

A concert just for one man? Elizabeth had never been in a situation like that. What would it be like to play for him? What if the man didn't like her music? It sounded like a disaster waiting to happen, but she had no choice. Her account balance was in the double digits, and she desperately needed firewood before the winter.

"I think I can manage a small concert for your laird," Elizabeth said.

"That's wonderful! Can you come around seven?"

"I can. It might take me a little bit to set up though. Do you have transportation for me and my harp?"

"I do. I'll send Walter around to fetch you at six."

After they drank their tea, Elizabeth walked Fiona to the door. The woman had a pep in her step as she left. It had been a strange encounter. Fiona hadn't gone into detail about the feeble old laird. What sort of music did he like? How much was he going to pay? What would she wear to the castle?

"Shit."

❧

A VIOLENT STORM ECHOED THROUGH THE GLEN, rattling the brittle windows of Beauloch. Jude stood in the ballroom, watching the torrential rain move in through the large bank of south-facing windows. It had come out of nowhere, as most storms did in this part of Scotland. They used to frighten him when he was a boy. Now he welcomed the wild winds like an old friend, because it linked him to the past, before he'd known the evils of man.

Despite the wrath of the sudden deluge, Jude felt peace with the unforgiving aspect of nature. A bolt of lightning struck the top of the mountain twice, illuminating the loch and trees below. This storm would not be a short one.

A knock came at the ballroom doors.

"Come."

Fiona scampered into the grand room, a tea tray in hand. "Will you not have your meal in the library so you may listen to the musician I hired?" she begged. The thin porcelain clinked as she set the tray down on the table near the fireplace.

"No. I do not wish to hear the cellist tonight." Jude went to the table for his tea. Fiona intervened, pouring it for him.

"It's a harpist, not a cellist," Fiona said.

"Doesn't matter. Send him home before the road washes out."

"May be too late for that," Fiona said, handing him the cup. She wrung her hands.

Something is bothering her, he thought.

A bolt of lightning struck a nearby pine, and they both jumped.

"Perhaps you're right. Anyway, I'll take my dinner by the fire," Jude said, and took a sip of his tea.

He looked out the windows again and admired the beauty of the storm. The ferocity of the wind and the power of the lightning mimicked how he felt inside. Every bit of him was firing, and he felt ready to finish what he'd started so long ago.

Anger filled him up as his fortitude gathered. It was the natural cycle of his affliction. The blood they extracted from his veins every full moon left him frail and weak, and as the days went by, he regained his strength and mind, and all the anger and torment The Order had left behind when they did their evil work. Slowly, month by month, year by year, Jude had transformed into the beast they'd wanted him to be. If there was any part of his old self left, he couldn't find it anymore.

Jude looked around the room, remembering how the cult had completely dismantled his life. Ever since The Order had gotten him in their grip, he'd had to make changes. The first thing he'd done was move from his old bedroom upstairs to the grand ballroom on the first floor.

The more blood they took from him, the harder it became to climb the stairs. His old canopy bed now stood in front of the long windows of the ballroom, the curtains pulled back to reveal the excess of blankets and pillows he used to warm himself on cold winter nights. Most of the floor of the entire room was covered in overlapping Persian rugs. A copper tub used for hot baths sat on the rugs in the center of the room. Old furniture from the library was scattered haphazardly around that. Stacks of books lay strewn here and there, most of them read. The small table and chair where he took his meals sat in front of the giant fireplace.

It hadn't always been this way. Memories of dancing across the parquet floors during weddings and sneaking in to watch his mother host big luncheons still echoed far off in his mind. Back then, the room gleamed bright with polish and fresh flowers his mother used to grow in the greenhouse. He tried not to dwell on the past, but moments of happiness did not come like they used to, and he wanted to cherish them before his mind became dull and forgetful.

Jude took a seat and continued to watch the storm until Fiona and Annie came to serve him his dinner. Fiona removed the lid of his tray to reveal chicken baked with honey mustard and thyme, one of his favorite dishes.

Ever since he'd announced his departure from Beauloch, Fiona had tried to do things to cheer him up, but in truth, his planned freedom was the only thing that tore him from his despondent thoughts. Still, he allowed her these small things since they seemed to make her feel better. While he ate, Fiona pestered him about butter, bread, and tea.

"Dessert?" she said, topping off his Earl Grey.

"No. I'm finished," he said, tossing his napkin on the table.

"I'll draw a hot bath for you. Can't let this chilly rain seep into your bones." Fiona removed the dishes from the table.

"Fine then." Jude went over to a faded green sofa and picked up one of his favorite books—*Kidnapped*, by Robert Louis Stevenson. Meanwhile, Fiona and Annie went back and forth to the kitchens, bringing hot water to fill the large copper tub in the center of the room. The sound of the water sloshing drew a yawn out of Jude. He placed the book back down.

"I'll put your medicine in the bath. It's almost ready," Fiona said, stirring some aromatics into the tub with a wooden spoon as Annie poured in the last pot of hot water.

As soon as they were gone, Jude approached the bath and stripped down. When he first climbed in, the hot water stung a bit, but the herbs helped him forget his pain. The bright, lemon scent mixed with earthy floral aromas made him feel like he was bathing in something only an enchantress could conjure up in one of the many stories he escaped into. All his muscles eased, and his blood flowed freely to his aching joints.

After he was settled, Fiona came in and brought him fresh towels. "Now, how about some music?"

"Yes, music."

Jude sank deeper into the tub.

Elizabeth was skimming book titles in the vast library when the door opened.

"He's just had his dinner, and we've drawn him a bath. Come with me," Fiona said, anxiously waving her along.

"I'm playing in a bathroom?" Elizabeth said, hesitating. She knew the old laird was feeble, but she thought he'd at least be dressed when she met him.

"No, he's in the ballroom. Come. We've put up a privacy screen. Don't worry, you don't have to look at him."

A privacy screen? She'd never been hidden away while she performed. The only scenario she could recall being concealed was when some posh old lady stuck her behind a large palm tree when she played at a tea room in London. Nevertheless, she tilted the dolly which held her harp, and wheeled it along behind Fiona, following her into a dark hall that seemed to go on forever.

When she'd first arrived at Beauloch an hour earlier, heavy rains had cloaked the castle exterior. The gamekeeper had ushered her through a set of massive doors, and once she'd been taken down a few corridors and peeked into a couple of rooms, Elizabeth concluded Beauloch was enormous. She'd never heard of it before she met Fiona and wondered how such a place had never been mentioned when she visited Gran. Who *was* this mysterious laird? No one bothered to give her a name.

Fiona stopped in front of a set of large double doors and urged Elizabeth to be quiet with an index finger to her lips. She carefully pushed the handle and held one door open as Elizabeth crept inside with her instrument. The privacy screen greeted her immediately, blocking her view from the majority of the dark room. Orange light from the fireplace flickered off the right edge of the screen. She pointed toward the hearth. "I need the light from the fire to play."

Fiona nodded and brought her a piano bench. Elizabeth positioned the harp to face the fire and sat down on the bench. She put her levers in place and looked to Fiona, who stood watching with interest.

"Ready?" Elizabeth whispered.

Fiona nodded.

Elizabeth started to play, beginning with a slow classical piece she'd conquered years ago, back when she thought she'd make something of her life. She supposed, at least now, she was doing something interesting.

The rain hammered against the windows while she played, adding to the strange ambiance. The vibrations of the harp echoed off the tall ceiling of the ballroom. On the other side of the screen, a distant splash could be heard. The setup felt awkward to her, but Elizabeth continued to play through her repertoire, and despite the bizarre situation, felt at ease with her music. The sound of the rain covered her mistakes, of which there were only a few. She was surprised at how well she was doing, until the crackling of a harp string and a boom that sounded like a gunshot made her stop.

Chapter Three

⚜

Jude felt like a cloud drifting over the mountains in late June. The herbs in his bath worked wonders for his pain, but something else soothed his nerves. A beautiful sound carried through the ballroom, echoing off the rafters. He could feel the vibrations in the air. His skin was tender from the warm water, making it extra sensitive to the vast range of notes being played.

Someone is here in the room, playing this music.

Fiona had tricked him by getting him into the tub and bringing in a musician while he was in a fugue state. He opened his eyes and saw the privacy screen that had been placed by the fire. The music came from that direction. At least the poor soul was hidden behind the screen and didn't have to look at him.

The melodies were too serene for Jude to be angry. Normally, he would push back against these intrusions, but this blissful serenade put him at ease.

The tune changed, and Jude felt his spirits lift even

higher. His mind woke to something new and joyous, like a child discovering a natural wonder for the first time. How could music make him feel this way? He'd heard many live performances before tonight. What made this one so different? He had an urge to peek around the screen and view the musician at work, but the euphoria of hearing the harp kept him in place.

Jude relaxed his neck and rested his head against the back of the tub. He wasn't quite asleep, but he wasn't awake either. It was as if time didn't exist, only the music. For once, he felt like things could be okay again, that the darkness had receded ... until the sound of a gunshot shook him from his trance.

Jude had stopped fearing death a long time ago, so there was no rush to take cover. He carefully stepped out of the tub and wrapped himself with a towel at the waist. The music had ceased. Intrigued by this strange development, he wandered over to the screen, and heard someone whisper faint curses.

He walked around the partition. On the other side, a woman stood beside the harp. She was beyond exquisite, with thick chestnut hair and a beautiful round face. She froze as soon as she saw him. Her dark-green eyes widened with fright. She released the broken string from her grasp and brought her delicate hands to her sides.

The swift motion drew Jude's attention to the soft curves of her breasts and hips, wrapped under a dress made with heavy green fabric. The frock hung loose on her petite frame and had to be cinched at the waist with a silver kirtle. It was like she had just emerged from a medieval tale and had been sent here to enchant him with her music. Where had this creature come from? Was he dreaming?

Before Jude had a chance to say anything, the woman turned and left the ballroom, the long skirt of her green dress and the tresses of her beautiful hair flowing behind her.

THE STRING THAT HAD BROKEN WAS A THICK, FOURTH-octave E.

"Dammit," Elizabeth whispered. She stood up from the bench and bent over to examine the flayed gut string jutting out from the pin. The sound of water sloshing and feet hitting the ground came from somewhere in the room. The laird must have emerged from the tub. She felt bad for disturbing the old man during his time of rest, but it couldn't be helped. The harsh climate of the Scottish Highlands had put too much stress on the harp.

Footsteps approached. On the left side of the screen, a tall man with shoulder-length, jet-black hair appeared. He was young, maybe in his thirties. Elizabeth's eyes wandered over his lean form; his sinewy arms and long, prominent ab muscles. When she realized what she was doing, her gaze snapped back up to his eyes, which were a deep dark brown, almost black.

The laird emitted a refined masculinity, but his eyes had a hunger in them that frightened her. The more she gawked, the more she realized he was, indeed, sick. Strange lines covered parts of his chest and forearms. They weren't so intentional as to be tattoos, but not so random as to be scars. The firelight created shadows, which danced around the circles under his eyes and in the hollows of his cheekbones.

Elizabeth could sense the demon behind the laird's gaze. An overwhelming presence of darkness surrounded him. Her knees quivered from the sudden chance meeting. Something caught at the back of her throat. She was in danger if she stayed, so she did the only thing she could think of and ran.

Elizabeth darted through the dark corridors, lit only by a few candles. A coldness gripped her. She went back the way she had come, heading for the library. Once inside, she closed the door behind her and stood there catching her breath. What had just happened? The laird wasn't some old feeble man. He was something else—a monster, a devil, a wraith perhaps. He exuded evil, but he also looked frail, like the shadows of the past weighed heavy on his shoulders.

Outside the castle, the strength of the storm grew. Lightning struck trees on the far side of the glen, causing flashes to bounce off the tall bookshelves in the room. Elizabeth tried to compose herself while she organized her music bag. She pulled the proper spare string out and held it in her hands. A knock came at the door. Fiona entered, a look of concern on her face.

"Is everything all right?" she said.

"One of my strings broke. I came to get a replacement."

"Oh, it's okay. You've played enough for tonight. Why don't we find you a room?"

"A room?"

"The road is washed out. You'll have to stay the night, I'm afraid."

"Oh, right." Elizabeth glanced out at the angry tempest. "What about my harp?"

"It will be fine where it is for now."

Fiona took Elizabeth up the grand staircase and down another dark hall. She lit their way with a single candle.

"Why are there so few lights in the castle?" Elizabeth said.

"The Lady of Beauloch wanted to preserve the authenticity of the castle, so not much electrical wiring was installed."

"The Lady of Beauloch?"

"The Laird's mother. She doesn't live here anymore."

"I see. Did she request you use candles to help you see in the dark as well?"

Fiona stifled a laugh. "We used to use flashlights, but the cold drafts seemed to drain the batteries faster than we could replace them."

How strange, she thought.

A cold shiver flitted up Elizabeth's spine. Being alone in this foreign place unnerved her. Thoughts about the mysterious laird flooded her mind as she followed Fiona. Why had he stared at her like that, and said nothing? Why did she think him so handsome, even though he appeared so menacing?

At the end of the hall, they stopped in front of an oak door. Fiona took out a key ring and unlocked the door with an old skeleton key. Inside the chamber, a fire crackled and illuminated the room. The dancing shadows highlighted silver vines stitched into the navy-blue curtains. The bed had been done up with a modern duvet, and beside it, a set of flannel pajamas sat folded on the edge of a vintage chaise lounge.

"The bathroom is through here. It's the best one we have." Fiona opened a set of doors, revealing a large room with white marble covering almost every surface. Windows lined two of the walls and looked out over the loch and mountains. "The shower is pretty basic, but the tub is a custom piece, quite luxurious. It was added about forty years ago by the Lady of Beauloch. Would you like me to draw a bath for you?"

Elizabeth trembled, partly from the cold brought on by the storm, but also from her encounter with the laird. "I ... yeah. That sounds lovely." She gazed down at the pit sunken into the floor.

The tub was so large it could have been mistaken for a swimming pool. The gaping circle had a set of stairs at one end leading into the interior. A wide curved bench ran along the back side and a combination of grey and white glass tiles sparkled over the inner lining. It was big enough for several people to fit inside and would take a long time to fill. Fiona twisted a knob on a bronze mermaid statue perched on the opposite end from the stairs. Hot water gurgled from her mouth and into the tub. Steam billowed up to the high ceiling.

"I'll be right back." Fiona disappeared into the mist.

Elizabeth approached the windows overlooking the loch. The storm put her into a trance as she gazed out at the rugged landscape.

How on earth have I ended up here?

Fiona came back with a tray of toiletries. "Millie sold

us some of these soaps. I couldn't bring myself to use them after she went missing. They were the last things I had to remind me of her. They've just been collecting dust in the linen closet downstairs. Maybe you're meant to have them," Fiona said. She turned the water off and laid out a towel on a bench by the tub. The lights in the room flickered every now and then from the storm, as if to remind Elizabeth she shouldn't get too comfortable here.

"Thank you," Elizabeth said. She picked up a lavender-oatmeal bar from the tray and brought it up to her nose. It smelled like home.

"Push this button if you need something," Fiona said. She pointed to the call button on the wall next to the light switch. A broad smile graced her lips, and she disappeared once more, gently shutting the bathroom door behind her.

Elizabeth carefully stepped into the bathtub, submerging herself in the scalding water. The experience was a big contrast to the cold rain falling outside. Another shiver crawled up her spine, but this time it was from relief. She was safe, away from the dangerous laird. Millie's soap filled the room with her benevolence. It felt like Elizabeth was back at her grandmother's cottage, surrounded by her love.

Thoughts of Gran and her disappearance crept into her mind. Elizabeth wondered if she'd ever come to Beauloch. Millie had never mentioned the place, from what she could remember. The castle wasn't very far from Millie's cottage; less than a couple of miles.

Elizabeth looked up at the mural of the loch painted on the high ceiling. How could she not have known this place was here? Fear of the unknown caused another tremor to shake her to her core.

There was something very strange about Beauloch castle, and she didn't want to stick around long enough to find out what that was. By the time dawn was on the horizon, she planned to be long gone.

JUDE PACED THE BALLROOM, HIS HEART BEATING RAPIDLY ever since his encounter with the harpist. Anger and confusion welled up inside him, creating a concoction of other emotions he hadn't felt in a very long time. Excitement? Desire? Intrigue?

"No more visitors until I'm gone!" he roared.

Annie hid her face behind the extra blanket she clutched in both arms.

"I'm sorry, my laird. I'll send her away right this minute," Annie squeaked.

"I'll go find her and tell her myself." Jude pivoted and headed for the door. He paused in front of the hearth for a moment, trying to quell his angered breaths. What had come over him? Why was he so intent on confronting her after he'd already embarrassed himself by approaching her in nothing but a damned bath towel? She'd been so frightened of his hideous form that she ran away without saying a word.

The memory of her racing out of the ballroom inflamed his anger and humiliation again. This time, he made sure his markings were well covered by his long-sleeved shirt.

Jude darted past Annie and went to the kitchens first,

hoping to ask Fiona where the woman had gone, but the room was empty. He growled and clenched his teeth. The deep rumble vibrated his chest. Fiona was to blame for this situation. She should never have brought the harpist here in the first place. He would have a word with her later. His focus now was on confronting the intruder.

Jude went up the stairs and down the hall where the main rooms were located. He caught Fiona near the end of the passage as she came out of the Blue Room.

"She has to leave," Jude said.

"Well, she can't leave right this moment. You said so yourself," Fiona shot back.

"At dawn then. Walter will take her."

"If the roads are cleared by dawn," Fiona said with attitude.

Jude stood there a moment, the heat from his body rushing up into his head. "If she is to stay, she must earn her keep! She must fix her harp and play tomorrow at dinner."

Fiona stamped a foot. "Uh! Which one is it? Is she to leave or stay?"

"Let me see her."

Fiona pulled her foot back. "Why?"

Jude opened his mouth to speak but couldn't find the words. He wanted to speak with her? About what? In truth, he was desperate to gaze into those green eyes again, to hear that beautiful music she made. He wanted to run his hands over her delicate curves and kiss her rosy lips. He turned away, shocked and ashamed by his own thoughts.

The memory of her was still driving him mad when he'd made it back to the ballroom. Jude took a few deep breaths. It didn't matter what he wanted, he told himself. In just a few months, The Order would have his body and soul forever.

❧

AFTER HER BATH, ELIZABETH PUT ON THE NAVY PAJAMA set Fiona had laid out on a bench near the tub. The fabric felt like an expensive cotton against her bare skin. The long-sleeve top had a large cursive B embroidered on the front pocket, and the hem of the pants had solid white stripes.

These weren't cheap.

The posh pajamas complimented the luxurious bed covered with a down duvet and tartan wools quite nicely. Elizabeth tucked herself underneath the covers and drew in a deep breath. The aroma of Gran's soap filled her nose, still as potent and warming as if her grandmother had made it yesterday.

Elizabeth looked at her phone. The battery was almost dead, and a single bar of service flickered on and off, but she was too tired to care. No one would be calling her anyway.

Right as she was about to close her eyes, she saw something strange. In the dark shadow of the far corner of the room, a wall panel moved. It looked as though it was swinging outward, like a door. Elizabeth sat up and blinked a few times. The panel moved again; she was sure this time. It swung as if it was on hinges and revealed a space behind it. From that black void, a figure emerged.

"Who's there?" Elizabeth shrieked. A deadly fear

consumed her. Her heart hammered against her ribs, as she expected the laird to appear.

The floor lamp in the corner flipped on, revealing a petite, ash-blonde woman in a powder blue polo and starched khakis holding a bundle of folded clothes. "It's Annie, the housekeeper. I'm sorry to have frightened you. I was hoping to set out some extra clothes for tomorrow. They're from the old gift shop and might be a bit stale, but at least they're unworn." She set them down on the chaise lounge.

Elizabeth took in a deep breath. "You scared the life out of me, Annie. Is that a door over there?" She pointed to the corner where the panel remained open.

"It is. Beauloch was built with a bunch of secret passages. This one goes all the way underneath the castle and connects to most of the rooms on the ground floor, even the kitchens."

"The kitchens?" Elizabeth became aware of her churning stomach. It growled and twisted in agony for food. "Are there any snacks in the kitchens? I'm dying for a bite to eat."

"Of course! There's plenty. Come with me," Annie said. She lit a thin wax candle, revealing the narrow doorway of the passage. "Take this, since you don't know your way around." She gave the candle to Elizabeth.

They descended a tight spiral staircase. The stones underfoot were wide, but uneven. Elizabeth took them one at a time. When they reached the bottom, they stood in a cramped hall with no windows. The original masonry of the castle had to be older than the stonework she'd seen in the foyer when she'd first arrived.

"Where are we?" Elizabeth said, holding the dull light up to the wide cracks in the walls.

"Servants used these passages centuries ago. I guess things don't really change that much over time. The kitchens are this way," Annie said, and pointed to the left.

"What's the other way?"

"More rooms. This hallway goes all the way down past the ballroom and into the library."

"Fascinating."

Annie turned left. Elizabeth noticed how quiet it was in the tight passage. Surrounded by the thick stones, she couldn't hear even a single drop of rain. The padding of their feet against the floor was the only audible sound. At the end of the hallway, they rounded a wide curve with a short door at the end. Annie pulled the iron latch up and guided them into the wine cellar, then through the pantry.

"Watch your step," she said.

Warm air hit them when they finally emerged in the kitchens. Annie sat Elizabeth down at a table and brought her a tray with bread, cheese, and fruit. Elizabeth scarfed the food down like she hadn't eaten in days. In truth, she hadn't had anything good since she'd arrived in Scotland a week ago. Neither the pub's poor fare nor whatever she'd scrounged up in the cottage had satisfied her.

"I made some tea," Annie whispered as she poured from a kettle.

Elizabeth sipped the warm chamomile, reminded again of Gran. She cherished the warm and fuzzy feeling.

"Thank you for the snack, Annie. I better be off to bed."

"Do you know which way to go? The castle is pretty big," Annie said.

"Actually, do you mind if I take the servants' passage back?"

"Of course not. Just remember to stop at the first stairwell, otherwise you might get lost. Do you have a light with you?"

"No, I don't."

"Here. Take this candle," Annie said, and handed her another candle.

Elizabeth went back through the pantry and past the cellar. She trod softly through the stone corridor and stopped at the foot of the winding stairs. The dull light of the candle danced over the steps that led up to her room. Then she studied the way straight ahead of her.

The passage looked as if it went on forever. Elizabeth was curious to explore, but she hesitated, remembering the fear she'd felt when the laird set his eyes upon her.

He's asleep by now though.

Chapter Four

❦

Jude couldn't sleep. Thoughts of the beautiful harpist had been tormenting him ever since he'd gazed upon her enchanting form. Every time he shut his eyes, he imagined touching her perfect skin, kissing her pouty lips. For the past few hours, he'd fought a raging erection. He hadn't been so aroused by a woman in years.

Frustrated, Jude got out of bed and wandered to the fireplace. Embers were all that remained. He tossed a log onto the grate and sat down on the sofa. He picked up *Kidnapped* again but couldn't focus on the story for more than a paragraph. Irritated, he tossed it on the floor. The book made a *thwack* when it hit the rug. Someone gasped, and Jude sensed a presence. He stood, scanned the perimeter, and his eyes landed on a dull light coming from a vent in the shape of a fleur-de-lis at the bottom of the wall near the baseboards.

It was an inconspicuous detail most people would overlook, but Jude knew what lay behind the grate. The candlelight flickered, moving away. He watched it until it was completely gone.

"Annie," he growled, and raced off once again. This wasn't the first time he'd had to reprimand her for skulking around Beauloch. More than once, he'd found her in restricted areas of the castle, like the section that had flooded some years past, or his father's old study, which had been locked away after his death. Jude went through the swinging doors of the kitchens, ready to enter the old servants' passage, but he stopped at the sight of Annie elbow-deep in a bowl of dough.

"Where have you been, Annie?" he said.

"I've been here, making the bread for tomorrow," she said.

Jude's stomach dropped. If Annie hadn't been the one in the secret passage, then it must've been *her*. Heat flared up deep inside him. He groaned in frustration, leaving the kitchens and heading up the stairs. Annie shouted something at him, but his rage deafened his ears to her words. He took the steps two at a time, his blood surging through his veins. Darkness met him at the top of the landing, but he knew his way around. Jude went to the last door on the left and pulled the handle.

ELIZABETH JUMPED WHEN THE DOOR SWUNG OPEN. SHE had just returned from the passageway and was holding out the clothes Annie had brought from the gift shop. She'd been inspecting them, lost in thought, when she was interrupted.

"You think you have a right to spy on me?" the laird said, his black brows furrowed, an evil scowl framing his dark eyes.

Elizabeth was too stunned to respond. She thought she had snuck through the hidden passage undetected. Had the housekeeper ratted her out? Was it all some sort of setup?

"I'm speaking to you! Answer me!" the laird roared, causing Elizabeth to tremble. Fear now gripped her even worse than before. Whatever ideas she'd had about the laird being a brute were nothing compared to this. This man was a monster.

"I'm sorry," she said, feeling as helpless as a child.

"Sorry? That's all you have to say?" The laird approached. Elizabeth stepped backward toward the hearth. The fire had gone out and this demon that towered over her blocked the light from the floor lamp. His tall shadow consumed her completely. Elizabeth's back hit the mantle.

The laird had her cornered. He leaned in, stopping only inches from her face. "Why did you come downstairs? What were you looking for?"

"Nothing, I was just—"

"You want to see my scars? Come on then," he said, and took the hem of his shirt in both hands. He pulled the garment over his head. "Look!"

Elizabeth glanced down at the horrible marks on his chest, arms, and stomach. Some were dotted in red and black ink, like tattoos; others looked like newer wounds, still trying to heal from some trauma he'd recently endured.

"I'm sorry about your illness," Elizabeth said, trying to be genuine to this monster who dared to come in her room and intimidate her like this.

"Illness? Is that what you've been told?" The laird's hot breath grazed the front of her throat. "This is a curse, and it consumes everyone that gets close to me. This is what you're in for if you keep coming around."

"Stop it! I didn't ask to come here." Elizabeth could feel her fight-or-flight response kick in.

"You weren't asked to lurk in the secret passageways of my home either." He leaned in even closer. His lips stopped mere inches from hers. "You're going to pay for your intrusions."

Elizabeth couldn't control the surge of adrenaline rushing through her veins. It came on so swiftly that it forced her to raise a fist and punch the laird square across the jaw. He staggered backward from the hit. Elizabeth took that as her sign to flee. She rushed out of the room and down the stairs. The castle was dark, but she remembered where the front doors were. She felt her way through the shadows and hurled one open the moment her fingers grasped the iron handle.

The rain had slowed to a soft mist, and the storm clouds had scattered to reveal a bright, waning moon. Elizabeth let the light guide her down the drive and toward the footpath Walter had pointed out when she'd arrived. It led straight to the village, and to the safety of Millie's cottage.

She started down the path and stopped when she reached the edge of the forest. Dense pines blocked out the moonlight, leaving the way shrouded in darkness.

Elizabeth pulled her arms tighter across her chest for

warmth. "I'm not going back in that castle," she declared, and forged on. She would have to send for her harp later, once she felt safe again.

The pea gravel on the old trail squished into the fresh mud under her bare feet. The tiny rocks hurt to step on, but the pebbles assured her she was on the right path. A lonely owl hooted in the distance, as if declaring to the other forest creatures a poor soul was on the run. A sense of doom crept up into the recesses of her mind, but she pushed it away. Fear would not stop her. She just needed to get back home, back to Millie's cottage.

After about a mile on the path, she stopped at a break in the trees. Moonlight shone down, revealing a long meandering section of the forest trail ahead of her. She was still going the right way. Elizabeth breathed a sigh of relief, but as soon as she did, she stepped into a giant hole and twisted her ankle. She fell to the ground and landed in a crater that had been hidden under a pile of dead limbs and pine needles. Her leg screamed with pain. She tried to move, but even the slightest flinch caused an electric shock that ran up to her thigh.

"Dammit."

Elizabeth pressed around her leg with her fingertips, feeling for any broken bones. Nothing poked out. As soon as she pulled her hand back, something cold and smooth slid over her foot. Black scales shimmered in the moonlight as the thing slithered up to her knee and then her thigh. Elizabeth stilled her breathing—there was nothing else she could think to do. Her weakened ankle couldn't accommodate sudden movement, and the giant serpent had crawled over half her body by then.

The black reptile flicked its tongue at her arm and smelled her. Her shivers of terror shook the creature as it crawled across her torso. Elizabeth stretched out her arms and clutched at the wet ground on either side of her. A pair of glowing, green eyes met her face.

Before she had time to take another breath, the creature whipped its angry head and planted its fangs into her shoulder.

❧

"WHAT DID YOU SAY TO HER?" FIONA SAID.

Jude was at the front doors, putting on his hiking boots. "Nothing but the truth," he said, heading out before she could berate him about his manners. He stopped on the last step and turned back around. Fiona stood like a sentinel, her arms crossed in anger at his behavior.

"I don't know her name," he said.

"Elizabeth. Her name is Elizabeth," she said.

Jude rushed out into the night. He shone his flashlight on the gravel in the drive. Elizabeth's tracks veered left, toward the woods.

"Dammit."

Jude wasted no time starting down the old footpath. Walter only kept parts of it up when he was out doing work on the property, which meant the way wouldn't be clear to an outsider. On top of that, steep drops, large boulders, and felled trees made the area a hazard. It was dangerous for Elizabeth to be out there at night on her own, not knowing where to go. Something horrible could happen. He knew he had to hurry.

Jude ran through the woods, the needles from the dense fir trees dripping rainwater onto his head and back. He swung the flashlight back and forth, hoping for a sign of the poor woman he'd terrified with his harsh words.

He stopped at a clearing where lumber had been harvested a few years ago. On the ground, near the roughly hewn stump of a pine tree, was the harpist. She lay in a deep ditch, her arms splayed above her head. Jude's heart sank. Was he too late? The sight of her so helpless wracked him with guilt.

This is all your fault, you monster.

Jude made his way down into the ditch and knelt beside her. He placed his hand in front of her mouth. She was still breathing. Relief stole over him like a cold chill in winter. What would he have done if she hadn't been alive? He shook his head and buried that thought while he dug his hands underneath her back and legs. His strength waned, but Jude fought hard and lifted her off the ground.

"Elizabeth? Are you all right? What happened?" he said.

"Who's there?" she said, her voice weak.

He could tell by the way she curled up in his arms that she was hurt. "Shh. It's okay. You're safe now," Jude said, trying to be careful as he carried her through the woods, back to the castle.

Normally, it would have taken another whole week for him to have the strength for such a task, but something powered him forward. He had to be strong, and brave, for her. Despite all she had done—showing her blatant disgust for him when they'd met, being a voyeur in his home, and not to mention the mean right hook she'd given him—Jude couldn't leave her out in the elements.

"I probably deserved that punch," he said to her as he walked.

"Oh, it's you," Elizabeth muttered, her eyes still shut.

He chuckled. "I wouldn't be happy to see me either, but it's cold and wet out here. I need to take you back inside."

Elizabeth nuzzled her head in his chest. He felt the small, tender act through his entire body like a salve to his wounds. This beautiful woman, Elizabeth, was in his arms, at his mercy. Ancient instincts awoke in him. Never in his life had he felt the need to care and protect something so precious.

Fiona's expression turned to astonishment when she saw him walk up the drive. "What happened?"

"I found her like this in the forest. Help me get her to bed."

Fiona went into the foyer and pushed a call button on the wall. "Annie, start a large fire in the ballroom and bring some dry towels. Hurry!"

"We are taking her to my room?"

"It's the closest one. Come on."

Jude followed Fiona to the ballroom.

"Lay her down over here first," Fiona said, and pointed to a spot on the floor near the hearth. Jude didn't argue, not after his foul behavior. He carefully placed Elizabeth on the edge of the rug.

Annie came running in with an armload of towels. "What should I do?" she said.

"Start on the fire. I'm going to dry her off," Fiona said.

Jude took a seat on the sofa to catch his breath. The strain of carrying Elizabeth hit him all at once. How had he managed such an activity? He had been drained of so much blood only a few nights ago. On days like this, he was lucky if he could take the grand staircase without getting winded.

"You too. Take your clothes off. They're soaking wet," Fiona said to him.

Jude hadn't noticed the dampness. All his focus had been on Elizabeth. He raked his gaze over her small body, lying prone on the floor. Her muddy bare feet stuck out from one end of the blanket Fiona had wrapped her in. She must have fled without her shoes.

What have I done?

Fiona set out to remove Elizabeth's nightclothes. He turned away, knowing he would become aroused if he saw her without her clothes. Clenching his teeth, Jude grabbed a towel from the pile on the sofa and went over to his chest of drawers on the other side of his bed to change into a dry long-sleeve shirt and a pair of sweatpants.

"It's still so damn cold down here," Fiona said.

"We should take her upstairs," Jude said.

Fiona shot him a doubtful glance.

"Don't worry, I can carry her."

Jude knelt and scooped her back up in his arms. Fiona had wrapped her in a clean wool blanket, but Jude knew she was naked underneath. His mind fixated on the curves of her waist and the long strands of her chestnut hair. Dammit. She was so beautiful, even in her pitiful state.

Jude laid her down on the bed in the Blue Room like she was a delicate, porcelain doll. Fiona removed the blanket and tucked her under the covers. Annie built a large fire that quickly banished the cold air. This room held the heat better than the drafty ballroom. He hoped it would be enough to keep her from falling ill.

The rain had ceased, but the wind picked up and howled through the glen.

"I'm going to make some soup for her. Annie, you keep an eye on her. Jude..." Fiona said.

"I know. Go rest."

Chapter Five

⚶

Elizabeth awoke, her naked body tucked under a thick layer of blankets. When had she taken her clothes off? The sheets surrounding her were buttery soft, not like the rigid ones from her old bed, nor the scratchy ones at Gran's. She moaned with pleasure at the warmth of the bed.

"You're awake," Annie said.

Elizabeth opened her eyes to see the petite maid sitting on the chaise next to her bed.

"I am, but I don't remember how I got here. The last thing I remember is ... running. Did I hit my head?" Elizabeth felt her scalp, but there were no bumps. When she tried to sit up, her ankle stung. "Oh, yeah. I fell in a hole."

"You did?" Annie said.

"Then there was ... a giant snake."

"A giant snake?"

"I remember now. It bit me." Elizabeth ran her hand across the spot where the fangs had sunk deep into her shoulder, but there was nothing there. "I swear it struck me right here."

Annie took her hand. "Jude brought you back to the castle."

"Jude?"

"The laird."

Elizabeth remembered then what had driven her to run away. Jude, the Laird of Beauloch, had come into her room and threatened her. Yet there was another memory, or at least bits and pieces of one, about a man who had rescued her after she fell in the woods. Could those be memories of the same man? One was a monster driven by anger and the other a warrior, warm and full of compassion.

"Oh." Elizabeth sat up and pulled the sheets with her to cover herself. She swung her legs out of the bed and rested her feet on the floor. She tried to stand, holding onto the bed frame, but a stabbing pain in her left foot stopped her. "*Dammit.*" She sat back down. "I forgot I twisted my ankle."

"I will get you something for it." Annie hopped up and rushed out of the room, leaving through the panel that led to the secret passage. Elizabeth carefully rose to her feet and limped to the chaise, where a fresh set of clothes—weathered jeans and a thick cable-knit sweater—had been placed. She got dressed.

Annie came back in no time, a first aid kit in her hand.

"What time is it?" Elizabeth said. Daylight crept into the room from underneath the thick embroidered curtains.

"It's almost noon. Jude brought you back a little after midnight last night. You've been asleep since then," Annie went to the curtains and pulled them back, revealing a stunning scene. The glen was bright with sunlight glittering off the loch. The trees on the other side of the water were already turning red and brown for the fall. From where she stood, she could see everything. Whoever built Beauloch had picked the perfect spot to view the wild nature of the Scottish Highlands.

"This place, I had no idea," Elizabeth said as she hobbled to the window. "I didn't get to see this when I arrived."

"It's breathtaking, isn't it?"

Elizabeth turned around and caught Annie staring at her. The young maid blinked a few times, pulled her gaze away, and faced the chair.

"Please sit so I can wrap your foot," Annie said.

Elizabeth did as she was told. Annie knelt in front of her, took out some bandages from the kit, and started to wrap her ankle.

Why had Annie been staring like that? Elizabeth's curiosity got the better of her.

"What were you looking at earlier?" Elizabeth said.

Annie glanced up, feigning ignorance. "Oh, you mean outside?"

"No. I mean just now, when you were staring at me," Elizabeth persisted.

Annie sat back on her heels. "You're just very beautiful. I apologize for gawking."

Elizabeth laughed. "I like your honesty, even though I'd have to disagree with you. Anyway, I want to know more about the laird."

"Jude?" Annie corrected her again. She took great care with the wrappings, unrolling the bandage a fare distance before making another gentle wrap around Elizabeth's heel.

"I've seen his scars. What is his affliction exactly?"

Annie finished pulling the bandage tight around Elizabeth's ankle. She sat back on her heels and looked out at the loch. "I don't know. None of us do."

"All those marks. Is he doing it to himself?"

"No."

A quick response. What was the maid hiding? Elizabeth got to her feet and put on the flats she'd left behind before she ran out of the castle.

"He really likes you. I can tell," Annie said, smiling.

"What? That monster who threatened me last night likes me?" Elizabeth tried not to laugh at the notion. Jude was a complete maniac who had barged into her room and shouted at her. Even if she'd committed some transgression against him, that hadn't given him the right to confront her like that.

Annie looked disappointed. "It was my fault. I shouldn't have taken you into the secret passages."

Elizabeth drew in a deep breath and went to the window again, surveying the unyielding beauty. The sun beamed its glorious rays over the mountains across the loch. "I shouldn't have wandered off by myself. This is his home."

Annie folded the extra blankets on the bed and took them in her arms. "The road is still washed out. Walter can't take you back until tomorrow." She came up to Elizabeth and stood beside her. "Would you have dinner with him? I know he wants to apologize."

Elizabeth was relieved to hear Jude had a softer side,

but she still didn't trust him. The entire situation was so bizarre. Her stomach had had a perpetual knot in it since she'd arrived, but that didn't mean hunger didn't gnaw at her. She really needed a good meal, and if she was being honest, she wanted to see him again. Darkness might have filled his heart, but she felt drawn to him in some weird way. Being attracted to someone like him seemed unthinkable and filled her so full of shame she could hardly acknowledge it.

"I have something you could wear." Annie set the blankets in a chair, walked to the wardrobe, and pulled out a blue velvet dress. It was a modern piece, with flutter sleeves, a surplice neckline, and a full gown that went all the way to the floor.

"This is lovely, but I have my other dress," Elizabeth said. She reached out to feel the soft velvet fabric of the gown. She'd lived in London long enough to know designer wear when she saw it.

"No! I mean, this is..." Annie shook the garment, frustrated. She took a deep breath and slowed down her speech, articulating her words very clearly. "My mother bought this for me a long time ago but it's not my style. It will never see the light of day unless you wear it," Annie insisted, holding out the dress on the hanger.

Elizabeth grew skeptical. "If this is your dress, why is it in this room?"

Annie smiled. "Beauloch has a moth problem, and they're partial to the ground floor. They've made little holes in almost all of my shirts."

Elizabeth took the hanger from her. A part of her wanted to wear the dress, to have the dangerous laird see her as something beautiful, delicate, and refined, but another part of her was frightened, and the frightened part won every time.

"After dinner, will I receive my payment?" Elizabeth said, trying not to sound desperate.

"Of course. Certainly," Annie said, nodding.

Enduring the brutish laird for another evening sounded like perilous work, but Elizabeth knew if she pretended to be pleasant, it would make it easier for her to get paid. She wasn't leaving Beauloch without a check in her hand. That she was certain of.

JUDE WAS WELL RESTED WHEN EVENING ROLLED AROUND. He threw on jeans and a blazer and slicked back his hair. Standing in front of the mirror, he surveyed his looks. Something about his appearance made him frown. Jude was never the conceited type, but he wished he ate more, and maybe left the castle more, at least to find some sunlight. He didn't think himself ugly, but his face lacked the vitality other men his age had.

Fiona chimed in on the wall speaker to announce dinner.

It'll be okay. Just be nice. Apologize.

He tried to remain calm, but thoughts of Elizabeth flooded his brain. Everything about her excited him. Her face, her hips, her beautiful hair, her legs. He hadn't left anything out when he'd undressed her in his dreams last night.

When he made it to the dining hall, he took a seat at

the end of the table, where a few candles and two place settings were laid out. The room felt warmer than usual. Walter had made a gigantic fire in the massive hearth beside the dining table and the radiators had been cranked to full blast. He tugged on the collar of his shirt and looked out the windows at the stars twinkling in the night sky. Annie had pulled back the curtains, revealing a beautiful crescent moon glowing over the tops of the pines behind Beauloch. Sometimes he forgot he lived in such a remarkable place.

The door rattled. Annie held it open for Elizabeth, who slowly walked into the room, even more beautiful than before. Her dark-brown hair flowed past her shoulders in giant waves. The velvet dress she wore featured a collar which revealed her delicate collar bones. The fabric hugged her breasts and hips. She glided forward on her flats and took a seat beside him at the table. Her eyes avoided him as she unfolded her napkin and placed it in her lap.

"You look lovely, Elizabeth," Jude said, He kept his voice down so as not to startle her. She snapped her gaze to him.

"My name is—"

"Jude. I know."

He paused and cleared his throat. "I wanted to apologize for the scene I made last night. There's no excuse for that type of behavior. It won't happen again."

Elizabeth raised a single brow in response. "No one has mentioned payment for my concert, and I believe some recompense is in order, on account of my injury," she said, her back ramrod straight, her tone serious.

"Of course. Send the bill to Fiona."

"I'll have my payment before the evening is over." She looked away from him to stare at the candelabra set directly in front of her.

Everything he'd said so far only seemed to irritate her. Before he could open his mouth and make even more of an ass of himself, Fiona brought out the appetizer.

"Potato leek soup. It's an old recipe," Fiona said as she ladled the hot purée into their bowls.

"This looks wonderful, Fiona, thank you," Jude said. He dug in, slurping it down quickly. He was more than halfway through his serving when he realized Elizabeth had barely touched hers. "You're not hungry?"

She kept her eyes down. She clinked her spoon against the side of the bowl without ever raising it to her mouth. "Last night, you said I would pay for my intrusion. Now you say your conduct was unwarranted. Which one is it?"

Jude sat back. "My affliction complicates things sometimes, but I assure you—"

"Complicates things? Fiona hired me to come here and play for you, even though you refused to greet me. The next thing I know, you approach me in your bath towel. Then you come to my bedroom and ... well, you were so aggressive that I thought I was in danger! I tried to run for my life in the middle of the night during a thunderstorm! And all you've offered is a diplomatic apology, and what? A free meal?"

She trembled with anger, but never once raised her voice. Every word she said had been thoughtful and genuine. Her emerald eyes bore into him like an adder homing in on its prey. Jude had never seen a creature who made him feel so inane. Her words and presence commanded the room, as much as her beauty enraptured him.

"Elizabeth, please sit down," he said, trying to keep her calm.

"No. I won't sit unless you offer a true apology, because I don't think you feel you've done anything wrong. Your type never does."

"My type?"

"Yes. You're born with so much privilege you think you can do anything, can get away with anything. I'm not a lesser person just because I don't live in a big castle or have loads of money."

Jude got to his feet. He was losing control of the situation. The dinner had been meant as an apology, but also an invitation. He wanted to learn more about Elizabeth and her music, but it was turning out to be a disaster. "Please, you don't even know me."

"That's just it! And you came bursting into my room without permission!"

"Permission? What about when you were watching me from the hidden passage? Did you ask my permission then?"

Elizabeth crossed her arms in defiance. "I didn't know where the passage led."

She was lying, and Jude knew it. His blood surged with anger again. The heat from the kitchens and the hearth made the air too warm. He released the top button of his shirt for relief. "Please, just eat. I cannot explain everything you want me to, not now anyway. You have to believe my apology is sincere."

"I don't believe you. You've been nothing but strange

and cruel since I arrived." Elizabeth uncrossed her arms and allowed them to hang by her sides.

Jude wanted nothing more than to take her hand. If only he could hold it in his own and comfort her, maybe she would listen to what he had to say. He took one step in her direction. She turned her gaze away from him, as if to punish him for how he behaved the night before. Jude reached his hand out to her, not only to touch her—his legs had begun to falter and he needed stability.

"Elizabeth, please..." Jude lost all control of his body and fell to the floor.

❧

"HELP!" ELIZABETH SCREAMED, AND KNELT BESIDE JUDE.

The doors to the kitchen swung open. Fiona and Annie came running.

"He just fell. I don't know what happened," Elizabeth said. Something forced her to take his large palm in her petite hands. Would the small gesture comfort him?

"Annie, call Walter. Tell him we need to get the laird to his room," Fiona said, and Annie ran off. "He's usually not this weak."

"Will he be all right?" Elizabeth said. A pang of guilt shot through her chest. She'd been very forward about the way she felt, how she'd been treated. But perhaps it had been too much for him.

"I don't know," Fiona said. She placed the back of her hand on Jude's forehead. "He's a bit warm. Maybe he caught a fever last night in the rain."

Elizabeth squeezed Jude's hand and placed it in her lap. His fingers felt cold.

Walter came in with Annie, and they lifted Jude off the ground and placed him in an ancient-looking wheelchair. They whisked him away before Elizabeth had time to think, to ask questions. Fiona followed behind them, leaving Elizabeth alone in the dining hall. The sound of the fire crackling and the wind whipping through the pines sent shivers up her spine. He'd turned ill so suddenly, without any warning at all. Was it something she'd said?

Elizabeth waited for a moment, then decided to take action. If she was going to stay at Beauloch for another night, she needed some answers.

She darted through the kitchen and down to the pantry. The long storage room was dark, but she descended the steps with confidence, the layout still vivid in her memory. She took off her flats when she got to the bottom and crept through the secret passage until she reached the corridor under the ballroom. Once there, she couldn't see anyone, but she heard the voices of Fiona and Walter. They stood in a blind spot, behind the giant poster bed.

"He needs rest." Walter's deep voice echoed in the large room.

"I know, but he likes the girl. That's why he went out in the rain last night. I'm surprised he hasn't caught his death," Fiona said.

"Don't speak too soon," Walter said.

Annie appeared beside the hearth with an armful of logs. Suddenly, she turned as if she were looking straight at Elizabeth, through the vent grates. Elizabeth stepped back into the shadows.

"Do you think he'd change his mind about everything if Elizabeth stayed?" Annie said as she stacked the logs to build a fire.

"God knows none of us can turn him from the depraved path he is on," Fiona said.

Elizabeth's breath went out of her. What had Fiona meant? Their words were too vague and confusing to make any sense to her.

"Do you really think The Order will release him of his bonds? There's something more he's not telling us," Walter said as he paced the floor.

Elizabeth kept her back to the wall, staying in the shadows.

What is The Order? she wondered.

"I don't know, Walter, I just don't know," Fiona said.

The knot in Elizabeth's stomach clenched her insides. An urge to flee stirred in her bones again, but the pitiful look on Jude's face when he'd collapsed tugged on her heartstrings. He had been trying to apologize the entire evening and she'd pushed back at every turn.

Why did Annie think she could help him? What could she do? She was just a broke musician running away from her old life in London.

Elizabeth rushed back to her room. She threw on the stale-smelling jeans and puffy sweater Annie had brought up. She looked out at the silhouette of Ben Chross and wondered how such a beautiful place could exist under such a bleak shadow. What should she do now? Her heart told her to stay, but her gut reminded her it was dangerous to be here. A knock came at her door, breaking her train of thought. Annie stepped inside.

"He came around. He wishes to see you," she said.

"Is he angry with me?"

"No. I think he wants to apologize."

Elizabeth went down the grand staircase and carefully walked through the set of ballroom doors. She looked around the vast, strange room she had been forbidden to see the night before. Now she understood why. It was as if someone had taken all their favorite things and threw them together with no thought as to how it might look. Old furniture sat haphazardly around the room; towers of books were stacked in random piles on the floor, and a large canopy bed stood against the wall of arched windows overlooking the forest. Her harp still sat in one corner of the enormous room.

She approached the bed with caution. Jude lay on his side, facing away from her.

"Jude?" she whispered.

There was no answer. She went around to the other side and bent over to get a better look at him. He was asleep, but his face was twisted as if in pain. Something gripped Elizabeth's heart. She reached out and brushed a strand of his long black hair away from his face.

Jude startled awake and seized her wrist. He set his deep, chestnut eyes directly on her. Elizabeth's heart raced. She tried to pull away, but he brought her hand back to his face. When Elizabeth realized what he intended to do, she relented.

Jude closed his eyes again and rubbed the back of Elizabeth's hand along the scruff of his jawline. The prickle of his beard against her soft skin felt sensual. Heat flared within her, reminding her of those parts of her that had been dormant for a long time. His hot breath against her fingers sent an icy shiver up her back.

He opened his eyes. Elizabeth gulped, wondering if he was delirious, if maybe his bad spell in the dining room had confused him, or maybe he performed this gesture in a state of sleep. Jude brought his lips to her knuckles and kissed them. Elizabeth's legs trembled from the sudden intimacy.

"Jude?" she said.

"Will you play for me?" Jude released her hand.

"I, um ... Yes. Let me go get a new string," Elizabeth said. She made her way back to the library, where her bag and string remained. She took her time, her mind racing with wild thoughts about the laird. Why had she been so reactive to his touch? He was dangerous, wasn't he? She should be more careful. When she came back, she reached out to grasp the handle of the ballroom door but paused. She debated if she should return to him. He had been so cruel to her before. Did he deserve her kindness?

It's either stay or run. Make your decision now.

Elizabeth grabbed the handle. The entire time she replaced the string and tuned the harp back up, she had her thoughts entirely on Jude. She delighted in being so close to him, in feeling the warmth of his hand, his face. His stubble had scratched her skin and left it red and irritated, but she'd give anything to feel it again. What had come over her?

Instead of going through her usual repertoire, Elizabeth played some traditional Celtic tunes. They were simple, but endearing pieces that had captured her heart many years ago. The ancient melodies drifted through the air.

I doubt this is the first time Celtic music has filled these halls.

The thought stirred something deep inside her. Ever since Elizabeth plucked her first note on a harp as a child, she had never felt a connection to her music like she did now. It was as if everything fell into place at this moment in time. Something new stirred in her soul, something she didn't have words for.

When she finished a couple of pieces, she glanced at the bed. Jude's eyes were closed.

"Don't stop," he said.

Elizabeth didn't want to stop. The music carried her on throughout the night. Some of the pieces she improvised; the deep-seated memory of the notes came back to life through her hands. The music echoing throughout the ballroom helped too—a sound so grand and lively kept her playing on.

Elizabeth smiled. When she finished the last song, she stood up to leave. Looking back, she saw Jude fast asleep, his face no longer twisted in pain.

Chapter Six

❧❦❧

Fiona dropped her dish towel on the floor. "You want to throw a ball?"

Jude shifted his weight from one foot to the other. He thought Fiona would be excited to host a large gathering, but her vexed expression made it clear she wasn't enthused about the idea. "Well, not a real ball. That term is so archaic."

Fiona picked her towel up and removed the whistling kettle from the stovetop. "So you want to throw a party. Who are we inviting?"

"Oh, you know, people who love to come to parties at castles. People of high society, and other try-hards. They shouldn't be too difficult find."

"Two weeks from now?" Fiona held out her hand, counting the days on her fingers. "Won't that be after your next meeting with The Order?" she whispered.

"Let me handle the brotherhood." Jude reached for a plate and filled it with eggs, waffles, and fruit. After his weak spell, he was determined to get his strength back in full. Fainting in front of Elizabeth had been a huge embarrassment, and it probably only confused her even more about his situation. It was all he could think about since she'd left three days ago.

After he ate his meal he went outside, where Walter was chopping firewood. The old man gave him a sideways glance mid-swing. He placed the ax on the stump and stood up straight.

"You need something, my laird?" he said, his tone coarse.

"I'd like to go into the village, but I want to take the footpath," he said.

Walter picked a splinter out of a finger, acting almost disinterested. "It's still there. Might be a little muddy in some spots. Just tread carefully. I'll put some fresh gravel down if you want."

"No. I'll manage," Jude said. He took off in the direction of Beauchross village.

He couldn't remember the last time he'd been there. Childhood memories threatened to surface as he traversed the damp path. Jude suppressed them, knowing they would only bring him heartache. Instead, he thought about what it would be like to have children of his own—to take them to the bakery and go with them to browse the little bookshop on the corner. What was the name of it?

Jude stopped dead in his tracks. What was he doing, dreaming of a future with children? Deep down, he knew it was all because of Elizabeth. He could think of nothing else but her ever since he'd first fallen asleep to her beautiful music in the bathtub. The second time had been more captivating than the first. He'd watched her play that glorious instrument until his eyelids couldn't stay open. The peace she'd conjured anchored his heart and gave him hope for a future he didn't believe could exist.

When he emerged from the trees, Jude stopped. Beauchross was desolate. Not a single person was on the main street that cut through town. It had never been a buzzing metropolis, but usually during the fall, the locals were out, doing a little shopping. Where had they all gone?

Jude stepped down the hill and went into the Cat and Crocus pub. He sat at the bar and ordered a coffee. The bartender gave him a cold stare.

"Not a lot of traffic today," Jude said, searching for answers about the village.

The barman grunted. "It's quiet on this side of the mountain."

"Is the bakery around the corner still open?"

The barman straightened up and crossed his arms. "The bakery? That hasn't been there for ages. You from around here?"

"No," Jude said and took a sip of coffee. He winced, not used to the taste of cheap roasts. The barman gave him a look of suspicion.

"There used to be a lot more foot traffic around here when the castle was open for visitors. People stopped in town for lunch before they went up. Some came back for drinks after hiking to the loch, but harpt road hasn't been open to the public for years. The Rewcores, or however you say it, closed off the road."

"Why?" Jude said.

"Everyone knows the old laird offed himself for some

insurance money. Left the wife and two boys without a husband and dad. Place hasn't been the same since."

"That's a shame. Do you have any cream?"

The barman went to the fridge for cream and returned, pouring it into Jude's coffee. "We kept afloat for a while when the herbalist was here. People came from all over for her remedies. Such a sad thing, her going missing like that."

Jude remembered an old woman his mother used to take him to near the village. He'd heard stories about her being a witch, which used to frighten him. The first time his mother took him to the woman's cottage, he shivered from a mixture of fear and a fever. It wasn't until he was sitting in her small house next to a basket of yarn and knitting needles that he realized she was just an old lady; someone's grandmother who knew her way around plants. She'd given him a syrup that made him feel better almost instantly.

"What happened to her?" Jude said.

"Went missing about five years ago. The police said she probably just got lost, on account of old age, but I knew her. She came in here to visit some of the old duffers that were too stubborn to seek her help. She wasn't going fuzzy."

Walter had helped search for someone who had gone missing in the village some years ago. But he'd been too deep in the throes of his own suffering to recall any details on the matter.

"I thought since her granddaughter moved here, people might come back, but she's not into herbs. She plays music," the barman said, his disappointment apparent.

Jude's heart did a flip. He hadn't realized Elizabeth was staying so close to Beauloch. Fiona never told him where she'd found her. He just figured she'd looked on the internet.

The barman turned the volume up on the television. The weatherman was emphasizing a nasty storm on its way in from the north.

Jude stood up and dug out the petty cash he'd shoved in his pocket before leaving Beauloch. He tossed a few quid on the bar and gave the wood a couple of knocks. "Thanks for the coffee. And it's *Rocoeurs*, not Rewcores," he said, emphasizing the proper way his last name was pronounced. He didn't stay to see the barman's reaction. He'd had enough village gossip. When he left the pub, he headed up the hill, veering slightly from the path, and down the weathered trail that led to the little white cottage.

THE SOUND OF SOMEONE RATTLING THE BACK DOOR OF the cottage made Elizabeth bolt upright in bed. Her heart hammered against her ribs. The light of dawn crept through the curtains, but Gran's tiny bedroom was still dark.

Who in God's name could this be?

Elizabeth had departed Beauloch a few days earlier, and not a single soul had called on her since then. Beauchross village remained a ghost town and no cars had come up the drive to the cottage.

The moment she put her feet on the cold floor, she heard the weathered old door creak open. "Hello?" she called out as she stole into the sitting room. From there, she could see a wide figure standing in the kitchen. It was short and shapeless, with no details apart from the single piece of fabric covering it.

"Hello?" Elizabeth called again.

The figure froze and turned around slowly. "Elizabeth?" an old, tired voice said.

"Gran?" Elizabeth took a step forward and turned on a floor lamp.

The specter was illuminated, revealing a bundle of a person with long, white hair and glassy green eyes staring back at her from the hood of a weathered black cloak. It was Millie, but all her liveliness was gone. The pretty silver jewelry she used to wear, her colorful garb, and the rosiness of her face and lips were absent.

"What are you doing here?" Millie said, her face contorted with confusion.

Elizabeth rushed to embrace her, ignoring the question. She needed to make sure what she was seeing was real, and not some wild, lucid dream.

"Oh my God, it's you," she whispered.

Millie pulled her into a tight embrace like she always had. The bony protrusions of the woman's wrists and elbows pressed against Elizabeth, as if trying to hold on for dear life.

"I know. I'm sorry I've been away for so long, but I couldn't tell anyone where I've been staying," Millie said.

"What do you mean? What's happened?"

"Come, sit. I'll make some tea," Millie said. She commanded Elizabeth like she'd been around all this time, and not presumed dead for the last five years. Elizabeth followed Millie's direction and sat down in the frayed chair next to the bookshelf. She watched Millie move around in the kitchen, but had to blink and pinch herself a few times to be sure she wasn't dreaming. Millie brought two cups of warm herbal tea to the sitting room. She took up her old spot in the green leather chair across from Elizabeth.

"I'm so sorry, child, for making it seem like I've been dead, but I only did it to protect everyone." Millie took a sip of her tea. Her fingers jutted out through a pair of tattered, fingerless gloves. They were frayed and covered in dirt. She smiled at Elizabeth, but a look of pain enveloped her features.

"Where have you been? Are you well?" Elizabeth said, ignoring the tea. Her nerves were still rattled from the sudden encounter with her presumed-dead grandmother.

"I've been out and away, living among the fairies," Millie said, flitting her hand toward the wilderness.

Elizabeth's heart sank. Had her grandmother gone completely mad? If she wasn't all there, how had she survived five years on her own? Elizabeth pressed her. "The fairies? Why did you leave in the first place, Gran? We've missed you."

Millie set her cup of tea down. "I know, I know. But I told you, it wasn't safe. I'm sure you'll think I'm bonkers, but you have to trust me. There were some people who were after me. I think they still are."

Elizabeth tried to sort through different scenarios in her head. Maybe Gran was just too deep into her dementia to realize mythical forest creatures weren't real and that nobody was out to get her. Then again, Elizabeth had witnessed the bizarre situation with Jude at Beauloch, and still couldn't find the mark the serpent had left behind after it bit her. She didn't know what was real anymore.

"What sort of people are after you?" Elizabeth said.

Millie shook her head. "Oh, the worst kind. Men who are so rich and powerful that their hunger for youth and vitality is beyond that which I can satisfy. I know what they're doing, and it goes against everything I've ever stood for. I refused to help them do their dark magic, so they threatened me. I tried to play the part of a declining old woman, but I'm not sure they bought it. I come back here every so often to get some things I need, but also to see if they're still watching me." She leaned over to peer out the narrow window looking out at the front of the house.

Elizabeth picked up her cup of tea and brought it to her nose. It was a blend of nettle and raspberry leaf, Millie's favorite. A flood of old memories came rushing back when the aroma penetrated her lungs. Something deep inside her knew Millie told the truth.

"I believe you, Gran."

Millie smiled. "Just like that?"

"I was at Beauloch castle two nights ago. Some strange things happened while I was there. I overheard the cook say something about some cult; I forgot the name of it. The Guild?" Elizabeth couldn't remember the specifics of the conversation because the rest of the evening had over-shadowed it. The touch of Jude lingered on her skin long after she'd gone to sleep. Heat rose to her cheeks. She hoped Gran didn't notice.

The deep lines around Millie's mouth pulled her smile into a frown. "You went to Beauloch?"

"Yes, your friend Fiona asked me to play for the laird. I

thought it was just another gig. She told me he was sick," Elizabeth said.

"The laird is part of the brotherhood who have been trying to hunt me down. Fiona should know better than to bring my granddaughter to that awful place. Elizabeth, you have to be careful. Don't ever go back there."

"I'm sure I won't. Jude is very sick."

"Jude?"

"The laird, I mean. He's very sick, Gran. Are you certain he's part of this brotherhood?"

Millie stood up. "Without a doubt. He is practicing that dark magic we've been taught to never go near, to never touch. He's dangerous, Elizabeth."

A hard knock at the front door startled them both. Elizabeth hopped up and pulled the sheer curtain back from the front window. "It's him," she whispered.

"What does he want?" Millie said.

Elizabeth thought she knew, but she didn't want to let her grandmother know what had passed between her and the laird. "No idea. I'll send him away."

"He might not be shooed off so easily. I'm going to hide in the back," Millie said, and sauntered down the hall to her old room. She went in and shut and locked the door behind her.

Elizabeth's legs did that funny trembling thing again. She tried to shake off the nervous tingling as she walked up to the front door.

JUDE CLEARED HIS THROAT AND RAPPED ON THE DOOR OF the cottage. He took a step back, trying to seem casual, but his heart rate increased with every beat. Waiting to see her again was killing him.

Elizabeth opened the door. "Hello Jude, may I help you?"

Jude flicked a half smile at her, unsure of how his presence made her feel. "Good morning, Elizabeth, I've come to speak with you about another job."

Elizabeth didn't move from the doorway. "Playing music?"

"Yes, of course. May I come inside?"

Elizabeth looked behind her, still holding onto the handle. "Yes, of course." She swung the door open wide.

Jude nodded and followed her into the cottage. She went straight to the kitchen and readied a kettle. She looked back over her shoulder at him as she lit a burner. "Would you like to take a seat in the living room? I'll bring you some fresh tea."

Something about her demeanor felt off, but Jude couldn't quite place it. He sat in an old chair by a window and looked out, trying to seem calm. Out of the corner of his eye, he noticed the bedroom door swing open. A crone stepped into the room with a paring knife held high above her head. She looked at Jude and screamed something in Gaelic before she rushed him. Her frizzed white hair and damp black cloak flew back as she took two big strides in his direction. Right before she reached him, Jude hopped up and stopped her blade from coming down on his chest.

"Gran! Stop!" Elizabeth screamed.

The old woman was strong. Jude had to use all his

strength to keep the knife from making contact. Their arms shuddered, locked in a battle. Elizabeth ran to the enraged woman and tried to pull the knife away.

"Get back!" the woman shouted.

Jude felt the old hag's grip weaken. He planted his right foot, and using the leverage, forced her back into the chair in the corner. She yelped as she sat heavily. The chair tipped onto two legs and hit the bookshelf behind it, causing dust and old titles to fall to the floor, along with her knife.

"Millie! What are you thinking?" Elizabeth said.

While the woman caught her breath, her black hood fell back, revealing the old wise woman Jude remembered from when he was a boy. Her hair was whiter, but the glint of her green eyes was the same.

"Agh!" She grunted and held up her arm. Drops of blood raced down her forearm and dripped off her elbow. She bundled the sleeve of her cloak up against the wound to stem the bleeding.

"I'll look for some bandages," Elizabeth said, her face going pale.

"No need," Millie said. She gave Jude a hideous scowl, then got up and walked gingerly into the kitchen.

"Does someone want to tell me what in the hell is going on?" Jude said.

"Gran, why did you do that?" Elizabeth said.

Millie came back to the chair with some first aid supplies and began dressing her wound. "I think I actually nicked myself on this damn chair." She pressed fresh gauze on her cut and paid no mind to their questions. "Here, Elizabeth. Hold my skin together while I tape it up."

Elizabeth said nothing as she helped her grandmother wrap the slice on her arm. As soon as she was done, Millie pulled out a vial of red liquid and put a few drops on top of the bandage. Then she carefully placed a poultice on top of the liquid and wrapped another layer of cotton around her arm.

"Answer me, witch," Jude said, aiming the tip of the small knife at the woman's face.

"Take the knife away and sit, Rocoeurs," Millie pointed down to the green chair.

Jude lowered the knife. "How do you know who I am?"

Millie got to her feet. She listed to one side and clutched the chair's armrest for stability for a moment before straightening back up. She shuffled across the floor and stood in front of Jude. "Look to the right, to the window."

Jude challenged her with a glare. Millie took him by the chin and forced his head to the side before making him look at her again. She stared into his eyes as if she could see his past laid bare like a woven tapestry set into his head. He tensed until she finally let go.

"The darkness in you is not of your own choosing, is it?" She flopped back into her chair and poked at the armrest. Jude darkened his gaze at the mad woman sitting across from him. What did she know about it all?

"Your blood is weak, that much is certain, but your spirit is also broken. It will take a multifaceted approach to get you back to normal. Young men heal quickly, so you've got that."

"Back to normal?" Jude said.

"My apothecary is back at my home. You'll have to come there if you want my help."

"Come *where?* Gran, you can't run off again. We thought you were dead!" Elizabeth said, shaking with ire.

"What makes you think I want your help?" Jude said, his glower still fixed on the old woman. Why would he go anywhere near her? She had just tried to stab him!

"I have a place in the woods now. It's hidden away from evil. Come find me if you want." She got to her feet and said some words in Gaelic again.

Millie looked at Elizabeth. "You, my dear, cannot stay here. I fear the eye has been on this place for some time now."

"She can stay with me," Jude said, knowing full well his intentions were selfish. He didn't want to see Elizabeth harmed, but he also enjoyed the thought of having her close by, her music and her beautiful figure floating through the castle, bringing it to life again.

Millie huffed. "I guess it's a good place to hide. The Order would never think to look for my kin at Beauloch." She chuckled and secured the knot on her poultice, making sure it wouldn't move. "If you want help, come to the big flat stone." Millie smirked. Her green eyes glistened like two bright emeralds, like something otherworldly, not human.

Chapter Seven

Elizabeth clutched Millie's hand. "Please, don't go. I need to call my dad and let him know you're alive."

"Absolutely not. It's safer for them to think I'm dead. Listen, my dear, go back to Beauloch and remain hidden. Don't leave the castle for anything." Millie broke free from Elizabeth's grip and left through the back door.

Elizabeth turned back to Jude. "I'll pack my things, but I'll need Walter to take the harp again."

Jude pulled out his phone to make a call. Elizabeth left him in the living room while she went to the bedroom to change her clothes and pack her things. She stuffed both of her suitcases with everything she could. If she couldn't come back to the cottage, she didn't want to regret leaving something behind.

As soon as she was done, she carried everything to the front door.

Jude stood in the corner with his arms crossed. "This is

all my fault. You should have never come to Beauloch," he said. The look of despair was carved into his face like a greedy sculptor had taken too much granite from his subject.

"You haven't told me how this is your fault. In fact, you haven't told me anything. So until you do, it remains to be seen who got us into this mess," Elizabeth said, going to the kitchen where she gathered teas, soaps, oils, and tinctures she thought were still good.

"Walter is here," Jude said, and carried her bags to the Land Rover idling out front. He spoke to the old gamekeeper, who came in to help load the harp.

"Same as last time, Walter. Lever side up. Thanks," Elizabeth said, throwing her purse over her shoulder. She climbed into the vehicle.

They rode to Beauloch in silence. Elizabeth kept her eyes glued to the tree line, hoping to catch a glimpse of Millie, but it was wishful thinking. The woman had appeared out of nowhere like a specter and disappeared just as fast. How had her grandmother survived on her own all this time?

Fiona stood waiting on the front steps when they arrived. "We're glad to have you back," she said as Elizabeth approached. "Is the same room okay?"

Elizabeth smiled, realizing she'd missed the warmth of Fiona's hospitality. "Of course. Do you mind if I take a bath and have something to eat?"

"Oh, that'll be no problem at all. Come on." Fiona ushered her back into the long, shadowy halls of Beauloch.

Elizabeth didn't hesitate to strip down and climb down into that luxurious bath with the outlandish mermaid.

While water rushed from the statue's mouth to fill the tub, Elizabeth studied the fangs in its mouth and the spikes on the tail. Someone had paid extra attention to detail when they'd casted the strange creature.

She couldn't believe she was back at Beauloch, submerged in this massive bathtub again. The last time she was here, she'd thought her grandmother was dead due to some tragic accident on account of her dementia. Now, Elizabeth found herself entangled in a strange web spun by some secret brotherhood. If Millie really had been forced into hiding, the stakes were higher than she thought. Elizabeth could tell by the look in her grandmother's eyes that she worried for her safety, and if the scars on Jude's body gave any indication of what these men did to their own, she couldn't imagine what they might do to their enemies.

Elizabeth knew her wits would only get her so far. Her methods of learning more about this secret society would have to be quieter, more cunning and discreet. She needed, more than anything, to get closer to the laird.

Cozying up to Jude wouldn't be hard to do. Like most women, she knew how to manipulate a man into giving her information, but going down the path of pretending to be coy and vulnerable could be a slippery slope. She had to be on her guard. Despite his feral behavior and severe features, Elizabeth thought him very handsome. She dreaded to think what might happen if she accidentally developed feelings for the man.

He's dangerous. Don't forget that.

The image of Gran trying to stab him seared itself into her memory. Millie had thought he was a threat until the moment she looked into his eyes. What had changed? What had Millie seen that she couldn't?

A cold shiver wracked her body. She submerged herself in the scalding water until Annie came up to her room with a plate of sandwiches.

"We're so glad to have you back," Annie said from the doorway. Elizabeth got out of the tub and wrapped herself in a towel. She approached the young housekeeper with a smile.

"Unforeseen circumstances have brought me back for the time being. I missed this beautiful room, too, if I'm being honest." She sat down on the edge of the bed and picked up a sandwich. "The view of the loch from the bath is so relaxing."

"I wish we had a lady about the castle. You know, the laird has never married," Annie said, keeping her voice to a whisper as she sat down beside Elizabeth.

"Why not?" Elizabeth took another bite of the egg sandwich.

Annie's shoulder slumped. Her gaze fell to the floor as she thought. "I'm not sure."

"That's a shame. He's quite handsome," Elizabeth said. She didn't have to lie. Jude was more than handsome, he was absolutely striking, even with his bad temper.

Annie flashed a cheesy grin. "You think so? He's so self-conscious about his looks, you know, because of his condition."

"Oh yes, I've seen his scars, but they're not so bad. His face makes up for all that anyway. I've never seen a man with such noble features."

Annie seemed overcome with joy. She scooted closer to

Elizabeth. "He thinks you're beautiful, I just know it. Other women have come around over the years, but they were sent away without another thought."

"Sent away?" Elizabeth said. She didn't understand.

"Don't worry. Those other women were nothing like you. Ever since you came and played your music, the laird has been held captive by you. You're beautiful, and so talented and smart."

Elizabeth took a moment to think as she chewed. She needed more answers. "What were they like?"

Annie huffed and waved a hand dismissively. "They were just dense creatures who were only here for the money." Her face flushed red with embarrassment.

Now we're getting somewhere, Elizabeth thought.

"What are you talking about? Those women were musicians like me?" Elizabeth wiped her mouth with a soft cotton napkin.

"Um, well, Fiona found them through some service. She paid them a lot of money to come and visit the laird. I saw the receipts before she threw them away." Annie shrunk down, lowering her head.

"If they had been paid well, they must have rendered some service beyond coming to Beauloch for tea," Elizabeth said. Had she been played? She would *not* be taken advantage of.

Annie coiled up and remained rigid. Elizabeth needed to make her feel at ease. She stood up and dropped her towel, trying to seem careless. She wanted Annie to keep talking. The maid gawked at her figure again for a moment, then tore her eyes away and continued.

"It was all Fiona's idea! She's tried to get him to leave The Order for years, but nothing ever worked."

"I see," Elizabeth said.

The Order. That was the name of the cult, she thought.

Annie got to her feet and became frantic. "It's not what you think! They weren't some cheap whores you find on the street. They were *very* expensive, and some were even beautiful!"

Elizabeth bent over to put her wool socks on. "And none of them stayed? Were they sent away after he was done with them?"

Annie clutched at her khaki pants with tiny fists. Elizabeth almost felt sorry for her. "Most of them left of their own accord, if I'm being honest. After one night with the laird, most of them fled as soon as they were able. There were one or two who tried sticking around and we had to send them away."

Elizabeth didn't blame them. Hell, even she tried running away after her first night.

Annie came closer and faced her. "He's really not that bad. You have to believe me."

Elizabeth smiled. "Don't worry. I won't run off again, if that's what you're afraid of."

She didn't have a choice. It was either suffer Jude's bad behavior or risk being found by the men who dealt in black magic. The mysterious laird seemed the lesser of the two evils, for the moment, at least.

❧

FOR THE NEXT FEW DAYS, JUDE KEPT TO HIMSELF. SINCE his last attempt to dine with Elizabeth had ended in disaster, he thought it best to give her some room. He tried to stay out of her way but often found himself looking for her over his shoulder. One evening, just before sunset, they locked eyes in the corridor outside the library. Her presence overwhelmed his senses to the point that he froze and said nothing until she turned on her heel and walked away. Her poise and grace had made a fool of him!

She spent a lot of her time in the library with her harp playing music. The notes echoed throughout the castle, bringing a sense of life back to the old stones. Annie, the ever-persistent gossip of Beauloch, had informed him that when she wasn't practicing new songs, Elizabeth read or slept. He hoped she would ask for him, but that was wishful thinking. He knew she wouldn't come to him after he'd treated her so poorly that first night. Jude thought hard on how to make amends, but he was at a loss for ideas.

After a week had gone by and he still hadn't mustered up the courage to approach her directly, Jude asked Fiona to invite her to dinner. He didn't want to make Elizabeth uneasy since she'd be stuck at Beauloch for the foreseeable future, and he thought she would be more comfortable accepting his offer this way, even though he didn't expect her to. When Fiona informed him after his breakfast that she'd like to join him for dinner, Jude smiled for the first time in a long time.

That evening, he paced back and forth in the ballroom, looking at himself again and again in the mirror. A knock came at the door.

"What is it?" he said, a little frustrated by the interruption.

Annie came into the room with her head down. "The dinner is ready, but there's a problem," she said, staring at the rugs, never meeting his eyes.

"What's the problem?"

"Well, we can't find Elizabeth anywhere."

Jude's heart dropped into his gut. "What? How long has she been missing?"

"We last saw her this morning after breakfast, when she accepted your invitation to dinner."

Jude rushed from the ballroom and into the kitchens. Fiona had the landline up to her ear, talking to Walter about performing another perimeter sweep.

"Why wasn't I informed our guest was missing?" Jude said with a raised voice.

Fiona put the phone back on the receiver. "We just discovered the door to the servants' stairs in her room was left open. She might have gotten lost."

Jude growled in response. He hated when things were out of his control, especially when they involved something in his own home. During full moons, when he went to Harlock to make his blood payment, he knew he was vulnerable, but at Beauloch, he was the master, and that meant he was in control of everyone and everything.

He threw off his dinner jacket and shot through the pantry and into the underground tunnels. At first, he headed to her room, but she wasn't there. Then he went down toward the ballroom and library. There was no sign of her in the narrow passage, and he checked the library twice, looking for clues as to where she could have gone.

Did she flee like she had the first night? Had his dinner proposal scared her off?

He went back underground and continued through the long corridor until it reached the end. Jude stopped at the door that had been sealed off after a terrible flood. It was slightly ajar, allowing cold air to rush through. He pushed it open. It had become so warped over time that it scraped against the floor and got stuck halfway.

The space on the other side was pitch black. Jude took out his cell phone and shone the light down the corridor. The way reached deep into the east wing, and the weak LED light didn't reveal much. He started down the hall very slowly and stopped at the bottom of a steep, winding stairwell. Something about this place haunted him. Memories of playing hide and seek with his brother flashed through his mind.

He turned a corner and kept going. Another set of stairs met him at the end of the hall. Light seeped in from the top of the steps.

Where does this lead? I can't remember.

He carefully climbed the stairs and pushed the weathered oak door open that had been leaking daylight. Memories of a lush garden came racing back as soon as he saw where he was. Elizabeth was at the far end of the conservatory, bent over a clay pot. The setting sun shot a powerful beam of gold through the greenhouse glass, illuminating everything. Jude stood back and admired Elizabeth in the ray of sunshine. Her beauty radiated so brightly that it incinerated everything else around her. Jude stepped closer, drawn to her divine nature.

"This wing of the castle flooded about five years ago.

We had to seal off the halls leading to the greenhouse," Jude said.

Elizabeth stood up and turned to him. Her curious green eyes looked him up and down.

"It's sad that the plants have been so neglected, but I found some things that continue to thrive on their own." She held out a large pot overflowing with weeds.

Jude approached her. She placed the pot on a worn planting table beside her.

"There are cleavers, red raspberries, and even a large aloe vera plant back in the corner," she said, thumbing the leaves of the plant on the table.

"My mother used to come here and read when it was sunny," Jude said. He glanced at the old wicker chair in the corner, now rotting and falling apart.

"What happened to her?"

"She went a little mad after my father died. My brother looks after her now." Jude was surprised by his forthrightness about his family. He often avoided the delicate subject.

"I'm sorry," Elizabeth said. She picked through brittle limbs in another pot to reveal a stubborn sprout looking for sunlight underneath the decay.

"She's doing better now. Especially since she's far away from here." Jude leaned against the main pillar supporting the roof. The steel was rusted and covered in mildew. He didn't realize how run-down this part of the castle had become. Walter had stopped delivering reports about the repairs Beauloch required some years ago.

"Can I ask you something?" Elizabeth said as she continued to throw the crumbling leaves onto the ground.

"Of course."

"What happened to your father?"

Jude straightened up and his muscles tensed. "He was found dead in his car in London."

"He killed himself?"

Jude drew in a deep breath. "No. My father joined The Order when I was a young boy. He threatened to leave them and ended up dead."

Elizabeth quit messing with the shriveled stems of the plant and looked up at him. "You think they killed him?"

"No. I know they did. They told me so when they came to recruit me."

"I don't understand. What is The Order? What do they do?" Elizabeth took a step closer.

Jude clenched his jaw. He hated talking about it, but she needed to know the truth if he was going to protect her from them. "They're a group of powerful men who feed on blood to preserve their youth. They find a young man and use him for their ceremonies until he becomes too weak or too much of a liability. Then they find another to drain the life from."

Elizabeth twirled a stick in her fingers. Jude thought she could make anything look beautiful when she touched it. He tried his best not to stare but was failing miserably.

"And they feed on you?" she said, her voice low, as if she was afraid to ask.

"They do. It was either me or my brother. I accepted the punishment. I knew if I ran, I would end up like my father. Then they would come for Jamie, and I couldn't allow that to happen. So I stayed."

Elizabeth took a step closer and placed her hand on his

forearm. Her soft fingers felt like warm silk against his skin. Jude came to life at her touch.

"What do they want with Gran? What's going to happen?" Her eyes trailed up to meet his, her green orbs glassed over with fear.

"Let me handle the brotherhood," Jude said, placing his hand on her shoulder. Her delicate frame underneath his palm acted like a lightning rod, attracting him with electricity. The current was so strong it overtook him. Before he had time to think, Jude leaned in and kissed her.

Instinct took hold. Jude gently placed both hands on the back of her neck and pulled her in closer. He was gentle at first, laying soft kisses on her supple, wet lips. Their velvety texture awoke a level of arousal in him he had never known before. He opened her mouth with his tongue, prodding and tasting her as much as he wanted. She moaned with pleasure, causing his blood to go hot with desire. He picked her up and set her on the weathered potting table.

Jude moved one hand down her throat, tracing a line to her breast. He ran his palm over it and kept going until he reached the hem of her sweater. His hand slid up her stomach to the thin material of her bra. As gently as he could, he caressed her while kissing her wondrous lips.

A slight moan from deep within her chest almost made him lose control. She leaned back on the table, allowing him to touch her soft skin from her collarbone down to her navel. Clearly, whatever reservations she'd had about him were now gone. Jude tightened his muscles to try to keep his composure.

He pulled away for a moment to look into her eyes,

needing to see the desire in her face. Her eyes gazed up at his, two emerald stones glimmering with golden sunlight. Jude felt his heart hammering in his chest as he studied her. Elizabeth slid her hand under the hem of his long-sleeved shirt, running the tips of her fingers over his abs. Jude was ravenous and went for her neck, biting and sucking the sensitive skin beneath her ear.

"Hello?" a timid voice called out from the dark, underground corridor. It echoed off the glass around them.

"Shit," Jude said, and helped her off the table. The moment Elizabeth planted her feet on the ground, Annie emerged from the servants' stairs and walked into the conservatory.

"Oh, there you are! I saw the old door left open and…" She stopped rambling for a moment and studied them both. Jude felt blood rush to his face. "Dinner is getting cold. Fiona wanted me to tell you." She scurried off as quickly as she'd come.

Jude turned back to Elizabeth, who hid her smile behind a fist. "What's for dinner?" she said.

They laughed.

Chapter Eight

In the time it took Elizabeth and Jude to reach the dining hall, the mood had shifted between them. She kept her composure, but her hands still shook from the unexpected encounter. Jude said only a few words to feign politeness as they sat down for their meal. He acted as if nothing had happened between them in the conservatory, but that was the farthest thing from the truth.

Every chance she got she glanced in his direction to admire his high cheekbones and chiseled jawline. It took a lot of effort to not make her gazes obvious. After Fiona brought out their soup, Elizabeth turned her focus to food, even though her subconscious was still occupied with Jude, going over every touch and every kiss they had shared. The heat between her legs never dissipated, forcing her to readjust herself for relief.

"Have you decided what you'll play?" Jude said.

Elizabeth's mind remained elsewhere. "Play?"

"For the party. You still want the job, I hope?"

"Of course I do. I'll play a set list I used when I worked parties back in London."

Jude left his spoon in the empty bowl and sat back. "What did you do before you came to Beauchross?"

Elizabeth had known the question was coming. She just wasn't sure how much information she wanted to give him. Her old life had left a gaping wound in her heart.

"I gave harp lessons and played some gigs from time to time."

Jude laced his fingers together and set them on the edge of the table. He had long, muscled fingers and knew how to use him. Her left nipple still tingled from his warm embrace.

"Why did you leave?"

Elizabeth put her spoon down. "It was difficult making it as a musician. I wanted to start over, and I missed coming up here."

Jude smiled, revealing his dazzling white teeth. His canines looked sharp. "I could see why you missed Scotland. This is one of the most beautiful places in the world. It's a far cry from the noise of London."

Fiona brought out the roasted lamb on a cart. She said nothing, probably so she wouldn't intrude. Any good impressions Fiona had made during Elizabeth's time at Beauloch were overshadowed by what Annie told her about hiring escorts. The thought made her stomach drop, and her hunger left her. Could it really be true? Annie claimed Fiona had arranged for the women to stay with the laird. How many had there been? Annie never gave her a solid number.

"Is something wrong? You're not eating." Jude stopped cutting, and his fork and knife remained in the lamb.

"May I leave? I feel a little bit sick," Elizabeth said. A cold shiver wracked her body.

"You don't have to ask me for permission to leave," Jude said, revealing a tenderness in his eyes she hadn't seen before.

Still, he unsettled her, which was why for the last few days, she had avoided him at every opportunity, keeping to herself in her room or in the library.

A whirlwind of emotion consumed her as she stood up to leave. At once, she was frightened of Jude, of his strange situation and his intent isolation, but she also longed for him to hold her, to kiss her like he had as the sun set, when the golden hour had pulled them together. Jude had felt like a dormant tree seeking out the first sunlight of spring in her arms. His rigidity softened at her touch.

"Elizabeth?" Jude said.

Elizabeth paused at the door. "Yes?"

"Thank you, um, for having dinner with me."

His words stirred the confused thoughts in her head. She flattened her lips, too scared to say something lest it come across as discontent. On her way back to her room, the feeling that she'd been manipulated and used consumed her. It sucked the air out of her, and by the time she arrived at her bedroom door, tears fell down her face.

She lay down and tried to keep her sobs low by crying into the pillow. A fragile humiliation ravaged her nerves, making her shiver with fear, sadness, and an entire host of other things she'd never experienced before. It felt like desperate yearning but stung like cruel rejection. What were these novel emotions? Were there even words for the way she felt? Deep in her mind, where her forbidden thoughts lay, she craved Jude, but, she didn't *know* him. Could she trust him? The most hopeful part of her wanted to, but she had been used and deceived once before.

Annie didn't knock before creeping into the room with a tray of food and medicine. When Elizabeth lifted her head from the pillow, the maid stopped in her tracks.

"Jude said you weren't feeling well," she said and placed the tray on the table before rushing to her side.

"I'm sorry, Annie. I'm just upset with myself. It's nothing. Really," Elizabeth said as she wiped the tears from her cheeks.

"I brought you food since you didn't finish your meal." Annie sat on the edge of the bed.

"Thank you. I'll eat it once I've had a bath," Elizabeth said. She took a moment to catch her breath.

Annie stayed beside her. "Do you want to talk about it?"

Elizabeth sat up and looked out the window. Darkness had fallen over the glen.

"I was married once, to a really awful man." She moved her gaze to the flame of the single candle that sat on the food tray. It flickered in response, as if validating her claim. "We tried to have a child, only to discover he was sterile. He was too ashamed to admit it and told everyone we couldn't get pregnant because of me. When we got a divorce, he took everything, and I was too scared to ask anyone for help. I tried so hard to make it on my own, but everything started to crumble around me. All our friends stopped talking to me, and my parents demanded I return to him, so I had to distance myself from my own family. Even when I thought Gran had returned from the dead, she disappeared again like a ghost." Tears started anew, their hot droplets forming in the corners of her eyes.

Annie took Elizabeth's hand and squeezed it. "You're afraid of being hurt again. I promise I won't let that happen."

Elizabeth nodded; her tempest of emotions prevented her from speaking.

JUDE RAN A HAND THROUGH HIS HAIR AND LOOKED OUT at the overcast morning. Sleep had evaded him for the first half of the night. He couldn't stop thinking about her. Had he done something wrong? His advances had been forward, but she'd relented so easily beneath his touch.

Fiona came in with his eggs and tea.

"Is Elizabeth awake?" Jude said. He hopped out of bed and dug through his dresser for a warm shirt and a pair of fleece-lined pants.

Fiona crossed her arms. "No, but you could have told me her grandmother was still alive. Annie filled me in last night," she said.

Jude sat at the table and scarfed his food down. "You knew her?"

"We were close friends! You know, I had some thoughts after she disappeared. One of which was that she ran away. I suppose that was sort of what she did. But living out there?" She nodded toward the windows. "That's daft. Even for her. Millie loved her creature comforts."

Jude sipped his tea. "Do you think I'll find her out there?"

Fiona uncrossed her arms and paced the floor. "I don't know."

Jude laced up his boots and stood in front of the mirror. His face was not the one he remembered from years past. This curse, this affliction, had changed the core of who he was so much that he barely recognized himself. The witch at the cottage had gazed into his eyes and saw something in him, something he'd hidden away a long time ago. Jude knew he had to find her if he wanted a chance at life again.

Walter drove him to the head of the trail on the far north side of the mountains. They parked on a gravel patch, next to a compact car. Beside it, a young couple bickered over a map and pointed in the direction of the trailhead. Jude kept to himself as he got out and put on his raincoat.

"Hello! Do you know where this trail leads?" the woman said.

"The trail is closed. Some grouse have taken to that area and it's my job to protect them. You'll need to head south to get to the loch," Walter said with a gruff.

"We're going to have to tell that guide she was wrong." The woman crumpled up her map and stuffed it in her backpack. The couple said nothing as they got back into their car. They sped down the road.

Walter shook his head in frustration. "I thought all the old maps were destroyed. The new ones shouldn't have the old footpaths on them. Half of the trails have been washed out anyway."

"Has this one really been overrun by game?" Jude said, looking down the opening that led into the forest.

Walter chuckled. "No. I just don't want tourists back here. It's hard to keep up with everything else I have going on right now. Don't need to spend extra time on maintenance in places that don't need it."

"You think I can find her back there somewhere?" Jude nodded in the direction of the mountains.

"Aye," Walter said. He leaned against the vehicle and stared at the ground as he bit off a piece of dried venison.

Something about Walter felt off. Before Jude had been enslaved by The Order, Walter never got so frustrated with visitors. He enjoyed his job, for the most part.

Jude ran his hand through his hair. It was still wet from his shower. He stepped sideways to put himself in front of Walter. "You've seen her, haven't you?"

Walter shot him a stoic glance.

Jude continued. "I mean when she was practicing her arts in the village. You'd know what she looks like, if you saw her?"

Walter thoroughly chewed the venison before responding. "Yeah, I know her."

Not good enough. As much as he respected every member of his staff, he was sacrificing more than his life to protect those he loved. If Walter knew something, if he was keeping something from him, Jude would get to the bottom of it. "What aren't you saying? I won't be angry. This could be important, Walter."

Walter met his demanding gaze. Jude had always known the man was tight lipped. It came with the territory. A good gamekeeper protected all life in the forest, regardless of whether they were animal or human.

"Head north when you reach the fork in the path. You'll find her," Walter said, and gave him a solid nod.

That was as much Jude was going to get out of him, and he knew it. He gave his old friend one last look and set off. When he was about fifty yards into the woods, he heard the Land Rover drive away.

He felt odd at first, being so deep in the wilderness on his own. He never left the castle much since joining The Order. When he was younger, he was always with his mother or brother when they wandered the land.

Jude stopped for a moment to listen to the sounds of the forest. Little birds chirped their morning songs, and a light breeze danced through the trees. Up above, the sun tried its best to poke through the clouds, but grey mists overtook the skies bringing with it a wintry current.

Jude zipped up his coat and continued to wander the woods, taking his time to survey the landscape. If the wild woman lurked in the trees, he wanted to be sure to spot her. Two hours had gone by when he came to stand before the large boulder she had mentioned at the cottage. Jude and his brother always used it as a landmark when they were playing in this part of the woods. How had she known that he would remember it?

Jude did a complete three-sixty, making sure he didn't miss anything. Walter said he would find her, but Jude saw no indication of the witch. Had he overlooked something? He ran his palm over the trunks of the trees surrounding the boulder, hoping for some sign of her. His efforts only led to disappointment. But this *must* have been the rock she spoke of. It had fallen down the mountain in a landslide hundreds of years ago. He knew of no others like it.

Waiting seemed like the best option, at least for a little bit. It was a quarter past noon, which meant he had plenty of daylight left to get home. He walked up and down the path, constantly checking his watch.

Defeated, Jude sat down on the rock for a moment, considering the situation. Maybe this had been her way of luring him out here to humiliate him.

Why should she help me, anyway?

"Took you long enough," a woman called out.

Jude snapped his head around, nearly throwing out his neck. It was as if the woman had appeared from thin air. He hadn't heard her footsteps come up behind him, although she stood a mere four feet from him! He hopped off the rock and faced her.

"Follow me," she said.

Jude studied the strange witch as he trailed her. She wore the same weathered cloak from the day she tried to stab him. Daylight revealed it had been patched many times, likely from the harsh elements of the Highlands. Her hiking boots, on the other hand, were in good condition. Someone had been helping her.

"How did you know I would be here today?" Jude said.

Millie turned around to give him an amused look. "I divined it from the birds," she said, and pointed to the pair of black crows perched on a branch above them. They cawed in response. She laughed. "No, I'm only teasing. Walter told me you were coming."

"I knew he was involved," Jude said.

Millie led them out of the trees and into a narrow

opening between two giant stones. Behind the twin monoliths, other tall rocks formed a tight maze. They weaved through the labyrinth of boulders until they came upon a waterfall. Icy water gushed from the steep side of Ben Chross and into a shallow stream. Millie used her long walking stick to keep herself upright as she traversed a series of large stones to get across the water. Jude followed her across the wet rocks until they reached the rocky face of the mountainside. A large crack formed an opening at the base. Millie slipped into the gap.

Jude had to duck to enter the cave. Just inside the entrance, a small fire crackled in a pit on the floor. Smoke billowed up from the flames and rose high into the recesses of the cavern, where a small opening allowed it to flow out. Jude didn't know if the hole in the ceiling was the result of a natural formation or if it had been altered by some ancient pagan tribe centuries before.

Beyond the fire, the cave went deeper into the mountain. Jude crept down a narrow passageway. The tight space grew wider and gave way to a hollowed-out formation. Under his feet, the uneven floor had been padded by layers of hand-woven rugs. They lined a room containing a twin bed and sitting chair. The ugly orange striped recliner matched the piece of furniture the witch had cut herself on in her cottage. How had she managed to move such large items to such a remote area, and moreover, how had she squeezed them through the narrow passage?

A formation of stalactites hung down from another opening on the far side of the large room. Lights flickered off the long fingers of limestone. Jude ducked and went through the narrow cavity. On the other side, a vast chamber thirty feet wide glowed brightly from an opening above in the mountain. The room itself must have been formed by an ancient waterfall because a rivulet still flowed from the ceiling, down a sluiceway, and into crack near the floor. Plants that had no business thriving in the isolated cavern bloomed in bright pinks and blues around the steady stream of water. On the wall to the right, shelves had been fashioned to hold bulk foods like oats, beans, and sugar.

The witch had her back to him. She tended a steaming pot on an old stove fueled by a small propane tank. "You may sit," she said.

To his left was a table no more than two feet tall. Jude sat on one of the large woolen cushions beside it.

"How long have you been living here?" he said.

"Too long. I miss my cottage," Millie said. She brought over a piping-hot mug of tea and took a seat across from him at the short table.

"Why did you leave? What did The Order threaten you with?" Jude said as he wrapped his fingers around the mug.

Millie groaned. "They threatened me with employment."

"They wanted you to work for them? Doing what?" Jude took a sip of the tea, but nearly spat it back out. His dislike of the sour taste must have been apparent on his face, because the witch got up to fetch some honey. She added a large spoonful to his cup.

"I treated one of their wives about six years ago. Helped her beat breast and liver cancer without the harsh medicines her doctor prescribed. Once her husband caught wind, he came to my cottage to extend an invitation to some gathering. He made it sound like it would be a meeting for other druids like me, but that wasn't the case. His fraternity asked for secrets regarding everlasting youth. I told them I could remedy their deficiencies of strength and vitality with my herbs. Most men their age do well with some of the treatments I've created over the years. But they wanted more. In the end, I declined to give them access to the black magic they sought. I've lived a long time, and I've seen some strange things, but what those men wanted, only a demon could provide."

"What happened when you refused them?" Jude said.

"Most of them laughed at my other offerings, but one glared at me through that hideous mask he wore. I knew he would continue to harass me, or set some trap for me to fall into, so that I would be forced to help him with this fantasy of eternal life."

"Who's home did they bring you to?"

"I have no idea. They hid their identities from me, but the home wasn't far from here."

Jude took another sip of the tea. The honey muted most of the tart overtones. "So you thought your best option was to disappear?"

The witch sighed. "It sounds mad, but I know evil when I see it. The wickedness dwelling in that manor knew no bounds. I pity any soul that crosses the threshold of The Order, for I barely escaped with my own soul intact."

Jude knew well what the witch meant. Every time he left the Harlock dungeons, a tiny piece of him stayed behind. He'd survived this long on his own, but things were changing. He'd be crossing that threshold very soon, and what little of his soul remained, he wanted to preserve. Not for himself, but for another.

"Don't fret. You've already taken the first step on your return home." Millie pointed to the tea.

Jude peered into the hot mug. "My return home?"

"That's what we call it. When someone has an illness like yours, and we attempt to heal it, we call it returning home."

The more Jude sipped the tea, the more pleasant it tasted, like sweet water that clung to the earth after a long rain.

Millie got up and removed the lid of a larger pot on the stove.

"What's in there?" Jude said. His curiosity had piqued after hearing The Order sought her for her healing powers. What could the witch brew that might erase all the years he'd spent feeding the brotherhood? He still held doubt anything could return him to the man he once was.

"Dinner," Millie said, and stirred the simmering pot.

Jude caught a whiff of something that could have been venison, but it smelled more wild, more feral. "Should I tell you what I'm suffering from?" He said.

"No. I already know the cost of the rituals your sacred brotherhood practices, assuming you aren't on the receiving end of those holy blessings."

Not yet I'm not, he thought.

"You're right. I'm the sacrifice," Jude said, hating the way the words sounded as he spoke them. His frustration went deep, and he knew the witch could sense it. How could she not? But she made no mention of his delicate state.

Millie ladled the dinner into a bowl and brought it over to the short table. Jude peered down into what he thought was stew, but the liquid shimmering around the chunks of meat looked red, like blood.

Millie handed him a well-worn silver spoon to eat with. "I was wrong about you, son. I apologize for attacking you."

Jude chuckled. "I would've done the same thing if I thought The Order was in my home."

Millie flattened her lips in a line. "Go on, eat."

Jude tried not to think about what was in his bowl and slurped up the stew. He thought the witch might have added too much salt, but he didn't dare offend her by saying so. After they ate, Millie got up and weaved her way through the limestone teeth.

"Come," she said, waving him in.

Jude ducked underneath the stalagtites with his mug of tea and joined her in the spacious bedroom. The witch retrieved something from underneath her bed and laid it across the floor.

Jude recognized the pattern on the blanket. The quilt was one of his grandfather's. "How many things has Walter stolen from under my nose?" he said.

"*Borrowed.*" Millie held up a crooked finger.

Jude laughed. "Excuse me. How many things has he borrowed over the years?"

The witch ignored his question as she pulled out other blankets of varying material to form a pallet on the floor. "You take the bed," she said.

He sat on the edge of the creaky twin bed. "Do you believe in curses?"

Millie let out a high-pitched laugh. "We're all cursed, son." She continued to giggle as she smoothed the pallet she'd made on the floor and propped herself up on a large feather pillow.

Jude took another sip of tea and placed it on the rickety nightstand beside the bed. He removed his boots and crawled under the blankets. His body shivered.

"Ah, you're cold. That's good. The life is coming back into you. Now lie down and rest."

He had no choice. The food and drink she had given him released all the tension in his muscles and sleep called to him. Outside, the cold winds howled over the rocky giants. Thoughts of Elizabeth soothed him while the witch's potions took hold of his body.

Chapter Nine

Elizabeth turned the pins on her harp with her tuning key. The old castle constantly shifted from warm to cold, which meant her strings went out of tune more than usual. She stood on the tips of her toes to get a better handle on her pin while she twisted it. Once the instrument was in tune, she put the key aside and sat down to play.

The library echoed with her scales and chords as she warmed up. The notes were the only man-made noise she'd heard since she woke up, and it was already half past six in the evening. She stopped to listen to the eerie sound of air whistling through the flue of the fireplace beside her. The mound of ash left behind from the last fire dusted the rusty andiron. No one had come to light a new fire or clean out the remnants of the old one.

Where is everyone?

After a short practice session, Elizabeth wandered into

the kitchens. Annie stood behind the counter hammering a slab of dough with her hand.

"Annie, where is Fiona?" Elizabeth said.

Annie startled at the sound of her voice. "Dinner will be late tonight. I apologize," she said.

"You're making dinner? Doesn't Fiona normally prepare dinner?"

"What?" she said.

"The castle has been deathly quiet ever since I woke up. What is going on? Where is Fiona?" Elizabeth said.

Annie dropped the mound of overworked dough on the counter and huffed. "I don't know, and I'm frightened." Her arms trembled with fear. She wiped a bead of sweat from her brow and took a deep breath.

"Why? What's happened?" Elizabeth said. She placed her hands on the counter.

"Fiona received a phone call about two hours ago. She said something happened with Jude and she had to meet Walter right away. She hasn't phoned since, and she never told me what was wrong." Annie peered at Elizabeth with alarmed doe eyes.

Elizabeth sensed the fear in Annie's voice. It made her own heart skip a beat or two. What could have happened to Jude? When was the last time she'd seen him? Two days ago?

"I'll go find out. Don't worry," Elizabeth said, squeezing Annie's tiny arm to try and console her. "Where can I find Fiona?"

"She went to Walter's cabin."

Elizabeth left the kitchens, meandered through the rooms on the first floor, and exited Beauloch out the back doors. The night sky glistened with stars above. Elizabeth shut her eyes for a moment to clear her head. The dread that had filled her when she heard Annie say Jude had gone missing wouldn't wane, and she feared what that meant. She pressed on, not ready to confront her emotions.

The overgrown brush of the neglected gardens hid the flagstones that led to Walter's cabin. From Beauloch's porch, she had to feel around with her foot until she found the first one. Once she did, Elizabeth set off right away. She fought rogue vines as she tramped deeper into the woods. Walter's cabin wasn't far, and the forest soon revealed a small light, the lamp that illuminated his front door. A knot formed in her gut. The alarm in Annie's voice had left her rattled, and every step she took brought her closer to discovering the truth, making the acid in her stomach churn.

Elizabeth waited outside the cabin for a moment, listening to the sounds within. She couldn't catch much, but when she heard Fiona and Walter's muffled voices, steeped in worry, she couldn't wait any longer and knocked on the door. Walter answered immediately.

"Missus," he said and stood aside for her to enter.

Fiona sat at the wooden table in the middle of the room with a cup of hot tea in front of her. She straightened up when she saw Elizabeth.

"Annie is out of sorts. She's worried about Jude. Has something happened?" Elizabeth said. Walter pulled out a chair for her and she sat down. He seated himself at the other end of the table.

"We don't know. Walter informed me just a few hours

ago he took the laird out yesterday and dropped him off in the woods. He's been gone ever since."

Elizabeth looked between them. "We need to search for him. He's afflicted, isn't he?"

"Maybe not," Walter said.

"What do you mean?"

"Jude went out into the woods to look for your grandmother," Fiona said and rubbed the sides of her neck. She closed her eyes and shook her head in disapproval.

"Millie? He went out looking for her?" Elizabeth said.

"I'm sure she's found him by now." Walter hunched forward, placing his elbows on the table. He wrapped his weathered fingers around his own steaming mug. He avoided eye contact with both of them.

"How can you be so sure?" Fiona challenged. She threw a hand up in the air. "I mean, you won't even tell us how you get in touch with her."

Walter slammed a palm down on the table. "We didn't know who could be trusted."

"That means you don't trust me, Walter. *Me*," Fiona said, her mouth twisted into a snarl.

"How long have you known she's been living out there?" Elizabeth said.

"Ever since she left her home." Walter seemed comfortable enough to take a sip of his tea, but Elizabeth's gut muscles remained tensed. Everything felt surreal. Ever since Elizabeth had left her Gran's cottage to stay at the castle, she'd been trying to convince herself that her grandmother had landed somewhere safe. Maybe Millie had been staying with a friend, and that her talk of fairies had been nothing more than a flight of fancy brought on by her dementia.

Elizabeth's head swirled with too many thoughts. There were so many unanswered questions. "You knew I was kin, and you still didn't tell me. If she hadn't come back to check on the cottage, I might have lived the rest of my life thinking she wandered off and froze in the cold."

Walter looked at her with his usual stoic gaze. "And who do you think it was that told her to go check on her house?" he said, lowering his voice to emphasize his point.

Elizabeth's mind continued to reel. "We have to go out there. He may be in danger."

"What sort of danger?" Fiona said.

"Gran tried to stab Jude when he came to the cottage. She knows he's part of The Order."

"Walter. We have to go find him," Fiona said, her voice frantic.

"No. If someone comes to Millie with an ailment, she helps them. Jude didn't tell me why he was looking for her, but there's only one reason people do. She's a healer."

Tears welled up in Fiona's eyes. She dabbed them with the hem of her cardigan. Walter leaned over and placed his hand on her back to comfort her.

"You may be right, Walter. Gran said something about coming to find her if he wanted help breaking the curse." Elizabeth said.

"I'll look for correspondence from Millie in the morning. Right now, we should all try to get some rest," Walter said.

"Correspondence?" Fiona said through a sniffle.

"Look. Millie trusted me with keeping her presence in

the forest hidden. I've kept that promise for five years now. We have methods of communication which are only known to us. She's remained unseen all these years and I'm not going to break my promise now. Be patient."

"He's right," Elizabeth said as she helped Fiona from her chair.

Walter handed Elizabeth a flashlight. The two women walked back to the castle through the dark trees, with Elizabeth holding tightly onto the cook's bony hand. Her mind ceased running rampant with wild scenarios about what might have happened to Jude.

They stopped when they reached the back doors of the castle. The tall grasses surrounding the grounds of the estate rustled in the breeze. Elizabeth glanced up at the behemoth that was Beauloch looming over them. Now that Jude was gone, the high stone walls of the castle seemed like an empty shell. Elizabeth shuddered at the thought of being alone in the giant fortress.

"I'm worried about him, Elizabeth. Time is growing short," Fiona said.

"What do you mean?" Elizabeth said.

"The Order meets in five days. What's going to happen if he's not there? What if…"

A sudden rush of autumn air sent shivers up Elizabeth's spine. She didn't need Fiona to finish her sentence. The brotherhood had already taken the life of one Rocoeurs.

JUDE LINED UP HIS WEAPON WITH THE TARGET AND TOOK aim at the stag. The glorious beast turned its head, listening for sounds of danger. The midday sun glided across the woodlands, creating a serene, dappled light on the forest floor. Jude didn't want to kill the majestic beast. It deserved to live the rest of its life in the purity of the forest, away from man, and his rifle.

Millie leaned in, her voice barely a whisper. "Channel your anger. Harness it."

He left fly the tension that had been building up in him for the last few days as he pulled the trigger. The bullet hit the stag. Jude lowered the rifle and took a deep breath.

Millie motioned for them to approach the animal. The creature still gasped for air, clinging to life, when they came upon it. Millie pulled out her knife and handed it to Jude. "Finish the job."

Jude knelt beside the stag and pushed the knife into its neck. He took a moment to stroke the beast's side.

"No need to apologize to it. You honor him by giving him a quick death. Come here," she said, and reached for the knife. Jude stepped back to watch the old woman. She withdrew a vial from her coat pocket and dripped some sort of oil across the deer's back. Then she started cutting it up.

"When you go to The Order tonight, you must be prepared for anything. They need to believe you mean to join the brotherhood, that you're not just posturing. Otherwise, they might become suspicious," Millie said while she peeled the deer's hide back. She dug her hands into the carcass to reach the vital organs.

Jude helped her bag the heart, the liver, and some other pieces of the animal she sought out. "The invitation I received to join their ranks wasn't a friendly one. I'm still not sure this whole thing isn't some sort of ruse. Do you really think they will let me join them?"

Millie looked up at him briefly. "We better hope so. The closer you get to them, the easier it will be to kill them. And if you join, you'll have access to the brothers in a way you don't now."

Jude got to his feet and stepped into a patch of warm sunlight. He remembered how he'd felt just days ago when he was in the conservatory with Elizabeth. Thoughts of her kept him strong and pushed him forward on this path. He wanted so badly to return to her, but the witch was being thorough with his transformation. Every day he woke up with an old memory he had buried, remembering times when he had been strong and vital. He needed to continue.

"Will you tell me more about Elizabeth?" Jude said as he looked up at the clear blue sky, wondering what she was doing right then.

Millie chuckled. "My Elizabeth is not who most people think she is. She's strong, unyielding, like me. That's why she had to leave her husband." The witch pulled her final piece from the stag, her hand covered in blood.

"Her husband?"

"A real prick, that one. I told her father that idiot was no good, but he and his wife didn't listen to me. They were the real uptight, cared-too-much-what-other-people-thought-of-'em type. Anyway, he was sterile, but he blamed their inability to conceive on Elizabeth." Millie laughed and got to her feet. She wiped the stag's blood on the hem of her cloak and looked over her work.

Jude clenched his fists, making his knuckles turn white.

Millie noticed his reaction and patted him on the back.

"Remember, channel your anger. The emotions that come back will be stronger than what you remember from before."

"Why would anyone hurt someone like Elizabeth?" He didn't let his fists go.

"Forget about that right now. We need to prepare for the meeting." Millie shoved him along in the direction of the cave.

Later that evening, Jude approached the ruins of Harlock a different man. He wasn't the same as he'd been before, considering all he had been through. He felt stronger, surer of himself. The herbs and tonics the witch had given him had brought all the color back to his face, and the diet rich in game meat and wild vegetables had filled out the hollowed spaces on his abdomen.

He approached the trapdoor wearing modest clothing —a pair of warm corduroy trousers and two layers of plain thermal shirts. Jude felt strong and sure of himself, but he had to shake any false sense of security he might've gained from spending time with the witch. He couldn't screw this up, because going back to his old life wasn't an option.

Steeling his nerves, he threw the door back and descended the staircase.

BORIS LIT THE SCONCES ON THE WALL, ILLUMINATING THE dark chamber. The Order gathered in the dungeon, awaiting their new recruit. The bright flames cast long shadows against the cardinal-red cloaks the brotherhood wore—a vow to their blood oath.

"Remove your masks, brothers. The young Rocoeurs laird will be joining our ranks very soon. Let's greet him with our true faces," Boris said.

The iron door swung open. The brothers watched the tall man standing in the doorway. Boris smiled at the young Rocoeurs, remembering when he'd first brought him to Harlock to fulfill his late father's role in The Order. Jude had resisted every step of the way, but Boris broke him down over the years. No other man could have endured what Jude had for as long as he did. Now, Boris would have him in his grasp forever.

"Please, take a seat," Boris said, and motioned to a chair beside him. The young laird sat down, and Boris presented a red cloak to him. Rocoeurs looked uneasily at the offering in front of him. Before he could refuse the garment, Boris whipped the cloak over his shoulders.

"Let us begin right away," Boris said. He took up an ancient manuscript and recited a passage in Latin. The brothers repeated his words, which were an ancient call to power. They filled a copper chalice with wine and passed it around. Boris kept his eye on the young man when the cup came around to him, making sure he drank.

"Don't worry. We fast during initiations. It's only wine," Boris said when the cup got to him. The young buck took a few big swigs.

At the end of their chant, Boris went to the table filled with old torture devices. He pulled out an iron used for branding from a felt sheath and placed it in the hot coals burning in a stove in the corner. "Come forward and receive the mark that shall never fade," Boris commanded.

This was his favorite part. Each one of them had to

endure the pain of the brand, and he loved to inflict pain. He knew Rocoeurs could take it, which was why he had modified the iron.

"Remove your cloak and shirt," Boris said, holding out the glowing rod. The young man did as he was bid. "Hold him."

Two brothers moved to stand on either side of the young man and held his arms.

Boris had told the smith to add tiny spikes to the brand, with the intention to maim in such a way that the scar would be deeper than usual. He put some force into it and pressed the glowing iron against the boy's shoulder. The young Rocoeurs screamed before clenching his teeth together as he tried to withstand the pain. Boris wanted so badly to push it into the flesh farther, to give it a little twist to make sure the young laird knew who owned him, but he resisted the urge. He needed the image of the skull to scar well.

Boris's blood surged when he pulled the spiked brand out of Jude's flesh. He always felt the ultimate pleasure when he subdued one of his inferiors. "You are now one of us! A brother is born this night!" he declared.

The brothers clapped.

Boris motioned for the sconces to be put out and the chamber put back in order. Now it was time for the real test.

After Jude's shoulder was wrapped up, everyone followed Boris through the back entrance of the Harlock dungeons. Several SUVs waited on the other side of an iron gate on a path that led away from the side of the hill. They got into the vehicles and drove the few minutes it took to reach his estate. At the mansion's entrance, his staff welcomed them with drinks, and women he'd bought for the evening waited for them in the dining room, looking bored.

Going to have to punish them for their insolence later.

His cock grew hard at the thought of whipping one of the little sluts.

Boris kept his eye on Rocoeurs as the evening wore on. Most of the brothers went off with a woman for a quick fuck, but the young laird stayed back and conversed with the remaining men. He ate very little and drank even less.

Boris went over to the young blonde woman he'd set aside for a special assignment. This morning, he'd given her clear instructions on what she needed to do.

"It's time," he whispered in her ear. She nodded and sidled up to the laird. Rocoeurs remained stiff and unresponsive to her flirtations until a quick glance toward his master changed his mind. The blonde pulled him away from the party. Boris waited a couple of minutes, then went down the hall and into the room he'd designated for voyeurs. He pulled back a curtain to reveal a one-way mirror looking into Rocoeurs' room. On the bed, the blonde straddled the laird. She'd rushed to undress herself, but the stupid dog wasn't responding to her perky tits. She bent over him to kiss him on the neck, but he was clearly uncomfortable. The moment she reached into his pants, he grabbed her wrists and moved her aside.

Boris shook his head. He looked at Dr. Brenner, who was seated next to him and often enjoyed studying women while they were in various stages of undress. "He hasn't committed to us. His vows were superficial."

Dr. Brenner stood and stepped closer to the viewing window. "You may be right."

This would be the last time the arrogant young laird defied Boris. He was going to pay Jude Rocoeurs a visit very soon.

☙

THE DRESSING ON HIS SHOULDER STUNG AS JUDE PEELED it off for the third time. Three days had passed since initiation night, and the burn had already started to form new skin. Millie had crafted such a powerful poultice that the brand of the skull wouldn't be noticeable. The mark left behind would just like any other he had. Jude believed the witch had real healing powers after she helped him gain so much of his strength back, but now, he would have a permanent reminder of her work.

Millie helped him tie off the new wrappings then went over to the stove. "You're quiet," she said, as she threw rice into the daily pot of stew.

"I'm wondering what this woman might have said to Boris after my initiation."

"What woman? You never mentioned women were at the meeting."

"They were hired escorts. One of them tried to seduce me, but I couldn't go through with it."

Millie tossed the ladle back into the pot of venison stew she'd been tending. "You idiot! Why didn't you sleep with the dumb whore? Boris gave her to you because he was trying to test your loyalty."

Jude pushed off the wall he'd been leaning against. "I'm

not going to fuck some random woman they throw my way every time I'm at a gathering." His heart raced and his body readied for a fight.

She was right. My strength as well as my emotions are coming back stronger than ever, he thought.

Millie sat on a cushion next to the low table, ignoring him. She crushed herbs in a mortar to prepare a poultice for his wound. He didn't like her silence because it meant what he'd done was a serious problem. She was probably working out ways to try to fix the mess he'd put himself in. He sat down on the cushion across from her, shirtless. The witch moved behind him and gently placed her remedy over the oozing wound on his shoulder.

"Well, your actions are your own. My work here is done," Millie said.

Jude didn't know what to say. He knew he'd messed up at the meeting. All his physical strength might have returned, but the mere thought of one woman left him weaker than if he'd been drained of every last drop of blood. The wind blew into the opening of the cave and swept over the pink foxgloves and baby-blue forget-me-nots on the stone wall. In that moment, he felt magic might truly be real. If beauty could exist in such a dismal place, maybe he could hope to revive his decaying heart. It fluttered at the prospect of seeing Elizabeth again.

A pang in his right shoulder snapped him back to reality. Jude felt like these new emotions would sunder him in two if he let them. He stood up, determined to finish what he started—The Order needed to be taken down no matter what. Everything else could wait. No more weakness.

"Take this with you to help keep your strength up." The

witch shoved a hide bag to his chest, which she'd stuffed to the brim with all the special teas, tinctures, and capsules she'd prepared over the last few days. Jude took it by the strap and hoisted it over his good shoulder. "And bring me this herb if you get a chance." She held out a charcoal drawing of a plant.

"Where will I find this?" Jude said.

"Flip it over."

The other side of the paper was a map. A small area had been circled in red ink.

The witch slipped through the limestone fangs and through the short vestibule. She crouched beside the firepit near the entrance to add some fresh logs to the flames. Jude followed behind her. He stopped in front of the fire to warm his hands.

"Thank you. For everything," he said.

"Don't thank me yet. You still have to take care of the brotherhood. Remember, neither of us are safe until they are all dead."

Her words echoed throughout the cavern like an eerie omen. Jude said goodbye and left the place where he'd spent the last week coming back to life.

By the time he reached the castle grounds, it had grown dark. He walked past Walter's lodge and saw him inside, reading a book by the fire. Jude thought differently of the old groundskeeper after discovering how much he'd helped Millie the last five years. He'd always been a little brute and standoffish at times, but the man had a heart of gold when it came to helping those in need.

Jude vowed to do more now that his strength had returned. With the witch's help, he felt more powerful than ever. His heart blazed with a heat he'd never experienced before.

The moment he crossed the threshold of Beauloch, he heard harp music. He paused in the foyer for a moment to listen to the alluring sound. Knowing she was close sent a quiver through his legs. The moment they'd shared in the greenhouse had tormented him while he'd been away, but now he felt excited. She would finally see the real him, the Jude that wasn't so hesitant and fragile. The only thing he had left to do was wash the muck from the forest off his body.

Jude snuck into the ballroom, but he didn't remain undetected for long. As he removed Millie's bag from his shoulder, the door opened without warning.

"It's you," Fiona whispered.

"It's me, and I'd love a hot bath if it's not too much trouble," Jude said.

"We have no hot water on the ground floor. Walter has called someone to fix it, but they can't come for a couple of days." Fiona remained planted by the fireplace.

Jude approached her.

"You look different," she said. Tears formed in her tired eyes.

"I know." He placed a hand on her shoulder. "Have you seen Elizabeth?"

"She's in the library with Annie again. You can use the mermaid tub undisturbed. They've been going to bed late."

"Thank you." Jude embraced his old cook and crept up the stairs. The harp continued to resonate through the castle. He wanted to stop and listen, but the Highlands had left him with more dirt under his nails than he could stand.

Jude tiptoed up the stairs and into the Blue Room. Elizabeth's clothes were scattered across the chaise and her personal effects sat on the vanity in the corner. A smile formed on Jude's lips.

She's getting comfortable here.

He proceeded to the bathroom. To conceal his presence in case Annie or Elizabeth came back early, Jude lit only a few candles on the toiletry tray to give him light. The constant flicker glinted on the shiny bronze mermaid. When Jude turned the faucet handle, she retched out hot water. Steam filled the round chamber and billowed up to the ceiling. A deep, resounding sigh left his chest. Damn, he was glad to be home.

It didn't take long for the giant tub to fill. Jude kicked off his boots and sat on the edge to soak his feet for a moment. Bathing in the shallow brook by the witch's cave had made him long for modern comforts like indoor plumbing. He would have settled for a quick shower, but this felt even better. Jude gripped the edge of the tub to lower himself into the hot water.

New blood rushed to the surface of his skin.

On the first night in Millie's cave, he had asked her what he would be once she brought him back to life.

"A person who goes through trials like the ones you've endured doesn't return to themselves as the same man. You'll still have a darkness in you, but you'll be powerful. The scars of your past will fade, and the beast they created when they practiced dark magic will come to devour them in the end."

He'd thought, when he first met her, she was mad, living in the wilderness and speaking nonsense about earth gods. Jude never believed much in the divine, but her bizarre beliefs grew on him. She gave him hope in some strange way.

The soap on the tray next to the bath was still damp from earlier use. He picked it up and smelled it. The scent of Elizabeth filled his nostrils, causing his blood to throb and his mouth to water. All his senses were now heightened after his time with the witch. Thoughts of Elizabeth naked, bathing in the same spot he was sitting in now made him hard.

Fuck, I've missed this. I've missed her.

Jude only had two options. He had to deal with his erection right then and there, or go find Elizabeth and try to seduce her. The latter option was out of the question. After what he'd put her through, he knew it was best to handle things himself.

Chapter Ten

Elizabeth plucked as fast as her fingers could go. Sweat formed on her brow as she played the last two measures of a lively Spanish piece she used as a finger exercise. After the final chord, she sat back and took in a deep breath.

"Whew! That's always a tough one," she said.

Annie continued to dance and sing as if the song hadn't ended. She twirled around with a half-empty bottle of wine in her hand, singing something in German. Elizabeth laughed at the drunk housekeeper's antics and hopped up to dance with her. They spun around in circles in front of the roaring hearth, holding hands and going as fast as they could go until Elizabeth's grip slipped and Annie fell backward onto the sofa. The bottle flew from her hand and cartwheeled through the air. Elizabeth reached out to catch it at the last second. She snatched the neck of the bottle, but it was upside-down. A few splashes of wine escaped the mouth with a *glug* and spilled onto the front of her nightgown.

Elizabeth righted the bottle and looked down at her chest, now soaked with expensive Burgundy. She burst into uncontrollable laughter. "Better me than the books, I suppose."

Annie got up from the sofa and took the bottle. "Ah no, that was the last of it. Where did that other bottle go?" she said.

"Let me see that thing," Elizabeth said, walking on unsteady feet to where Annie stood with the empty bottle. She snatched it up and licked the rim. "Yep. We're definitely out." She placed it on the coffee table and stretched her arms high above her head. All that playing had invigorated her. The last time she'd felt this good performing was at a wild party back in her early twenties.

"Wine and music go so well together, don't they?" She giggled.

"What?" Annie took hold of her wrist and pulled her down on the sofa beside her.

Elizabeth turned her head to face Annie. Their glazed eyes met. "I mean, I'm having a really good time. Thanks for keeping me occupied while I'm imprisoned."

Annie smiled. "I like having you here."

Elizabeth got up and turned the knob on an old radio from the seventies. Heady jazz music echoed through the room, bouncing off the high ceiling of the library. She twirled to the erratic beat of the slow song. Annie hopped up and caught Elizabeth's hand, pulling her into another dance.

"Do you know this piece? I was never any good at

playing jazz," Elizabeth said, shutting her eyes as they swayed back and forth.

"There it is!" Annie released Elizabeth's hand and scurried over to some old food trays on the floor in the corner. "This one's from last night's dinner, so Fiona won't suspect anything. Good thing I left the dishes out." She removed the cork and took a swig.

Elizabeth ambled over to the fireplace to warm her hands. Annie held the bottle out to her.

"One last drink, then it's water." Elizabeth took a small sip of the cabernet. As soon as she lowered the bottle, Annie's face was directly in front of hers. Before Elizabeth realized what was about to happen, Annie pressed her lips against hers.

Elizabeth was too drunk to know what to do. She allowed Annie to finish her delicate kiss, then took a step backward. "Oh, that was, um..."

"I'm sorry! I don't know what came over me. I've had too much to drink," Annie said, the embarrassment in her voice almost palpable. She dashed off to clean up the dishes on the floor.

Elizabeth stepped behind Annie and squeezed her shoulder. "Annie, I'm sorry. I never meant to mislead you. The kiss was lovely. It really was. I'm just not..."

"I know. You like the laird," Annie said, her arms full of plates and empty wine glasses.

Elizabeth studied the girl, realizing the hurt she had caused by not returning the passion she had received.

"I'll bring some water to your room. It's getting late." Annie smiled and forced a giggle, but Elizabeth knew it was to cover the mortification she felt. The young girl raced to the door and vanished into the dark halls of the castle.

Elizabeth sat on the floor and groaned, releasing the frustration that had built over the last few days. Being trapped in Beauloch had been more difficult than she had anticipated.

The melancholy of this place must be driving Annie mad, she thought.

Elizabeth waited a few minutes to give Annie time to hide before going up to bed. As she climbed the stairs, she examined the extent of the wine stain on her gown. It had seeped through the thin fabric and made the surface of her chest wet and sticky.

When she reached the Blue Room, a tray containing a glass and a pitcher of water had been placed on the table by the window. Elizabeth chugged a few glasses and looked out at the glowing moon reflected in the shimmering loch. The sudden sound of water splashing in the bathroom gave her pause. She thought it might be Fiona or Walter.

No, that would be ridiculous. They have their own living quarters.

Her adrenaline surged. Who on earth could be in the bathroom? She tiptoed to the door. It was slightly ajar, revealing a lean figure with shoulder-length black hair reclining in the giant mermaid tub.

The thought of seeing Jude again made her almost dizzy with excitement. Staying on her toes, Elizabeth snuck into the room. The chamber was dark, with only a couple of candles for light. Seeing the silhouette of Jude reclined in the tub warmed her cheeks.

He's back.

She knew she was invading his privacy. He'd been bathing in the dark to remain discreet, but this was *her* bathroom. At least that's the excuse she would use if he decided to retaliate again.

The water splashed and a quiet groan escaped from his mouth. Elizabeth paused, wondering is she'd been detected, but then she realized what he'd been up to. A tight grin formed on her lips as she crept to the tall windows to stand in the moonlight.

She waited a moment, looking between the laird and the fragments of moonlight dancing across the water in the loch. A half-suppressed laugh broke free from her lips, but Jude continued on his path of pleasure, not once noticing her presence.

"Your maid tried to kiss me," she said, causing Jude to start. The bath water splashed, and he reached for a towel to cover himself, submerging it just above his lap.

"Elizabeth."

"Well, she did kiss me, I believe, and I'm flattered, truly. All this time I had no idea." Elizabeth approached the edge of the bath. The rush from the red wine made her bold. She stepped down, placing one foot into the water.

As she got closer to him, she could see the outline of his features in the dim light of the candles sitting on the soap tray. The light flickered across his eyes and cheekbones. They were no longer hollow.

"You're different from before," she said. Her gaze wandered first to the thick muscles on his chest and continued down his abdomen. His scars were still there, but he'd filled out considerably since last she saw him. The reflective surface of the water prevented her from discovering anything else about his appearance.

She put another foot into the tub, taking the steps one at a time.

"Are you drunk?" Jude fought with the towel he'd used to cover himself. It floated to the surface, forcing him to pull it back down to his lap.

"I am. You know, there's not a lot to do when you're trapped in an ancient castle. Drinking alone sounded boring, so I convinced Annie to join me." Laughter escaped her lips.

Jude followed her movements with his rich, chocolate gaze as she sank deeper into the water. She was waist-deep now and her nightgown floated to the surface. She took another step closer to him, wading through the tub until she was directly in front of him.

"Are you well, my laird?" Elizabeth said. Despite her playfulness, she had been worried about him ever since he'd wandered into the woods to search for Millie. How long ago had that been? Eight, nine days?

"I am myself again." Jude's face remained stoic, his eyes never leaving her.

"I'm glad." Elizabeth reached across him to pluck the bar of soap from the tray. The movement placed her breasts right in front of Jude's face. Once she had the soap in her hands, she submerged it in the water.

"Did you say my maid *kissed* you?" Jude said.

"She did." Elizabeth rubbed the soap across her collarbones. Suds dripped in between her breasts, which she kept right at the surface. Jude shifted in the water, still clutching the wet towel. She set the soap aside and splashed water on the front of her thin white gown. The delicate fabric clung to her skin and revealed the soft curves of her breasts. "It was a lovely kiss."

"Oh yeah?" Jude's smile pierced through the dark.

While Elizabeth teased him with the soap, she noticed how relaxed he seemed. Before, any chance meeting they had, Jude tensed up. His eyes darted away to avoid looking at her. Now, his posture was relaxed and his eyes widened with curiosity.

"Should I be jealous of my housekeeper?" Jude's hands moved through the water to grab Elizabeth's hips.

He really is different from before, she thought.

Oh, how she was looking forward to finishing what they had started in the conservatory. She put both hands on his shoulders to steady herself and placed her knees atop the bench on either side of him. "Maybe you should."

"Mmm. I think I'd have done the same thing if I were her." Jude seized the back of her neck and pulled her in for a kiss. Their lips met, warm and hot from the bath. His mouth gave sweet caresses at first, then he prodded with his tongue and entered her mouth.

Elizabeth moved her hands up to his neck, which was slick with sweat, and dug the tips of her fingers into the back of his head to hold him in place. She licked and nibbled at his lips. Jude made a low growl, and his frame rumbled underneath her palms.

"What were you doing in here before I came in?" Elizabeth said.

Jude grabbed her ass and drew her in until their torsos touched. "You know, thinking."

"Oh? What were you thinking about?"

Jude raked his hand around her waist and up her chest. With delicate fingers, he pinched her nipple, making the hard peak sting with pleasure. "I was thinking about this." He brought her in close again. This time he grazed his lips right beneath her jawline. Elizabeth's body shivered with an aching pleasure she'd never felt before. She'd been so drawn to Jude that she'd intruded on him and offered herself up to the beast of the man. Did she care?

She let out a soft whimper. "Is that all you were thinking about?"

Jude released her nipple and gently placed his hand on her sex. "And this." He continued to suck and nip at her neck, making his way down to her collarbone. Elizabeth let out another moan, louder than the first. Jude carefully stroked her folds with his fingers, feeling her arousal.

Frustrated from the tease, Elizabeth reached down to feel his erection.

"Fuck..." Jude grasped Elizabeth's gown with both hands as she stroked him.

"Why don't we?"

Jude caught her hand and pulled it away. "Because you're drunk, and I've already gone too far."

Elizabeth climbed off him and stood up. "Too far? Do you regret our time together?"

"No. It's just ... You don't know what you're getting into, and I'm afraid I won't be able to control myself."

Disappointment felt like a heavy weight pressed against Elizabeth's heart. She went up the stairs of the bath and sat on the edge, leaving only her calves and feet dangling in the water. "I'm a grown woman you know, not some stupid little girl. I know what I'm doing."

Jude waded over to her and put himself directly in front of her, his face meeting hers. "I know you are." He forced himself in between her legs. "I just want to wake up tomorrow happy, not regretting something we did."

Elizabeth turned her head away and looked out at the loch. She started to unfasten the buttons on her gown. "Maybe I already regret coming here. At least Annie was bold enough to make the first move. I can be sure of what she wanted. You, on the other hand..."

Jude gripped her outer thighs and squeezed them tightly. "Now you are trying to make me jealous. If my maid has proven to be better at courting you than I have, then I've failed miserably." He smiled that vicious smile.

"Courting?" Elizabeth burst out into laughter. "Just because you live in a castle—"

Before Elizabeth could finish her words, Jude ripped the top of her nightgown down to her elbows, revealing her breasts. He clutched the back of her neck and bit her right nipple with just enough force to make her yelp. Without warning, he changed intensity and gently sucked and kissed her puckered flesh while he slid his hand up her thigh. Elizabeth panted, her breath heavy with need. Jude pulled her butt closer to the edge of the ledge, causing her to gasp.

Before she had time to register what was happening, Jude plunged a finger deep inside of her drawing a cry from her lips. His mouth moved up to her collarbone as his fingers stroked her soft, wet flesh.

"Do you like that? Or do you think my maid could do a better job?" Jude whispered.

Elizabeth was too far gone to respond coherently. All she could do was feel the thrusting of his hand and his soft lips, which worked their way along her breasts. He lightly sucked and bit her nipple and she cried with courses of pleasure.

Jude tore away the rest of her soggy gown and placed both hands on her ass, gently cupping it while he kissed the skin between her breasts. He was in no hurry and teased her with his tongue against her wet skin, trailing it down past her belly button. As he got closer to her swollen sex, she leaned back on her elbows to allow him full access and he took it, kissing and sucking the sensitive area that had bloomed just for him.

Elizabeth collapsed onto her back from the intensity of his touch. Jude placed her knees over his shoulders as he licked and stroked her over and over. His own moans made her realize he was enjoying it as much as she was. He pinched her nipple while he fully engaged her clit with his slow, teasing approach.

"Jude," Elizabeth managed to force out between heavy breaths.

The wine and the euphoria of Jude's touch all came to a head and Elizabeth felt the tension in her core begin to rise. The hot rippling began, causing her to moan in ecstasy. Jude moaned too while he kissed her flower with tenderness. The earthquake inside her made it seem like the world stood still for a moment. Maybe it actually had.

Once she caught her breath, Elizabeth sat up on wobbly arms. Jude kissed the inside of her thighs, his dark eyes filled with something she couldn't describe. Power?

Control? Satisfaction? His hands were slippery with his semen, and he rubbed it along her calves.

"You sent me over the edge," he said.

"Me? But I didn't do anything," Elizabeth said.

"You didn't have to. Just feeling you writhe underneath me was enough." Jude stood up, caressed her face with both hands, and kissed her.

It was a different kiss than before. This one was strong and intentional, a solid message he was trying to send to her. He drew back to look into her eyes and studied them for a while. Elizabeth was too drunk to be shy and peered back at him. He leaned in for another kiss, this one a little more tender. Elizabeth met his lips with dignity and grace, digging through the trenches of his soul. She sensed the man he once was long ago, and the kisses he gave her signaled he felt more than lust. Much more.

It was early in the afternoon when Elizabeth finally came around. She woke to the sound of a tray being placed on the nightstand. She sat up and saw Jude sitting beside her.

"What time is it?" she said.

"A little after three. I brought you some breakfast," he said.

"I slept that long? It must've been all that wine." She brought her fingers to her temple.

Blood rushed to her face when she realized her breasts were on display. She quickly pulled the covers up, reached for the orange juice, and took a big gulp.

"Oh, that's good juice." Elizabeth dug into the toast and jam. "Did you bother Fiona with this? Isn't she getting dinner ready?"

"I made it. I gave everyone the day off," Jude said.

Elizabeth built up enough courage to look him in the eye. His face glowed with vitality. He appeared more confident and seemed to have the disposition of an entirely different person. She blushed again, admiring just how handsome he was.

"If you feel up for it, I'd like to take you somewhere," Jude said.

Elizabeth didn't slow down the pace of her eating; she was absolutely famished. "I will be once I get dressed. Where are we going?"

"You'll see. We better hurry though, before it gets dark." He checked the time on his phone.

"I'll be ready in twenty. I just have to bathe and change. I mean, put some clothes on," she said, letting out a nervous laugh.

Jude laughed too. "I'll leave you to get ready," he said, then got up and left the room.

Elizabeth rushed to the shower, brushed her teeth, and put a bit of makeup on. She looked a little less like the walking dead and a little bit more like herself when she was done. Jude waited for her at the bottom of the stairs, a set of car keys in his hand.

"You look lovely," he said.

She felt more confident with her thick sweater and denim covering her vulnerabilities.

They went out the front and around the side of the castle to the garage. Jude raised one of the overhead doors to reveal a smart-looking SUV. He opened the passenger door, and she hopped in.

"Where are we going?" Elizabeth said.

"Someplace I think you'll like to see."

For the first few minutes, they didn't speak and instead enjoyed each other's presence. The sound of the engine and the wind whipping across the glen was all that filled the air between them.

"Do you want to talk about last night?" Elizabeth said.

Jude gave her hand a firm squeeze. "Do we need to?" He kept his eyes on the winding road.

"I feel I may have been too aggressive. You'd just gotten back home."

Jude chuckled. "It was the perfect coming-home present." He brought her hand to his lips and placed a kiss on top of it.

"What did you do while you were with my Gran? Where is she living?"

Jude concentrated on turning the wheel safely as they drove past the loch. "Your grandmother is living in a cave. Mind you, it's well furnished, and Walter looks after her, so she is comfortable. As far as what I did there, well I mostly ate, slept, and roamed the wilderness."

Elizabeth could barely believe it. Millie lived in a cave? It was the stuff of fairytales, but after the last couple of weeks, she wasn't surprised. "I know my Gran was always good at helping sick people. I'm glad she was able to help you too." She paused for a moment, thinking of a good way to phrase her next question, but all her options were poor. "So, the affliction you suffer from...?"

Jude gripped the steering wheel a little bit tighter. "We

can talk about that when we get to where we're going." The tension in his body was noticeable.

Continuing the conversation didn't seem like the best option, so Elizabeth rested her head against the window. Jude took her hand and held it for the rest of the drive.

Chapter Eleven

✿

The evening sun was shrouded by clouds, heralding the coming winter. Jude parked the car in an overgrown lot. He shut the engine off and turned to look at Elizabeth. She was fast asleep, like a small child hunkered down against the window. She looked at peace, which gave him some comfort. He felt it almost a shame to rouse her from her dreams.

"Elizabeth? We're here," he said, rubbing her knee.

Her long lashes fluttered as she woke. "Oh, I must've dozed off. Where are we?"

"Nowhere yet. We have to walk up a path to get to it." Jude unbuckled, got out, and went around to open her door. He took her hand and helped her out of the vehicle. Instead of letting her go, he hauled her into his arms and kissed her.

It wasn't a sultry, erotic kiss like they had shared the previous night. This one was sweeter, a little more tender. When he pulled back, her cheeks were nice and rosy. The response she had to his touch made his heart swell. He'd never felt this way with a woman before. In fact, he couldn't think of another woman he had ever cared about more. He was struck by her elegance, her refined beauty, and her talent for brightening a situation when it seemed all was lost to the darkness. If it were up to him, he'd never let her go.

Jude placed his hands on Elizabeth's face. He held her still.

"What? What is it?" she said.

"I care for you. Do you know that?"

"Me? You barely know me," she said. Her words stung like the hot iron The Order had used to brand him. Jude tried his best to hide his frown.

Her face went from disbelief to sorrow once she realized the hurt she had caused him. "I'm sorry, It's just..."

"Don't worry about it. We should get moving, before it gets too dark." He released her from his arms. It took every ounce of strength he had to keep his hands to himself.

That's what you get for making yourself vulnerable, he thought.

Jude forged ahead on the muddy, overgrown path. They tramped through the wild heather up a steep hillside. When they crested the top, Elizabeth stopped. "I know this place," she said.

"I had a feeling you might."

They paused to survey their surroundings. Low hills of umber dotted with grey boulders surrounded them in every direction. The fading grasses beneath their feet were tall and damp. It was a savage, unyielding landscape.

"They say these are the oldest rocks in Scotland." Elizabeth crouched down to touch one of the stones.

Jude pulled out the drawing of the plant Millie had asked for. "Do you know what this is?"

Elizabeth took the paper. "It's a drawing of bog myrtle. Why?"

"Your grandmother wants me to bring some to her. She marked it here on the map." Jude flipped the paper over in her hand.

"I know what she is doing. Come on." She handed the drawing back to him and trampled down the path and through the rocks.

Jude followed her until they reached the top of another hill. On the other side was a dense copse of firs and a shallow loch that held unnaturally still water. Elizabeth continued down the sparse path into the trees.

Tucked amid the firs, a primitive-looking dome made of rocks stood twenty feet high. A narrow tunnel led inside. Elizabeth went in without any hesitation. Jude stayed right behind her.

From the dark shaft they emerged into the main chamber. Light coming through a wide, circular opening in the ceiling illuminated a tall stone in the center of the room.

Elizabeth approached the stone. "I haven't been here in ages."

Jude stepped closer, studying the rock. The tall pillar had been sculpted into the form of a hag. The long hair and watchful gaze of the old woman sent a shiver up his spine.

Elizabeth knelt in front of it. "I wonder how long this has been here," she said in a low voice. At the foot of the pillar was a grouping of half-melted candles. Elizabeth found a match on the ground near her feet and used it to light them.

"Who is she?" Jude said.

Elizabeth got to her feet. "You don't know the Cailleach when you see her?"

"The what?"

"It's the Cailleach. The old hag of winter. The goddess of death. It's why Gran led you here." Elizabeth handed the map back to him.

Jude studied the carving a little closer. "Your grandmother asked me to come here and collect some bog myrtle."

Elizabeth laughed. "That sounds like Gran. Send you to look for an herb so that you could find the gods." She went to him and nuzzled her head against his shoulder. His heart soared at the warmth of her touch. "I remember the stories Gran used to tell when I was little. She loved talking about the old gods when I came to stay with her. My mother was raised a catholic, so she always convinced me Gran's stories were just that—stories and nothing more. But something about the tales stuck with me, like how in many legends, the Cailleach had three faces."

She let go of him and went around to the back of the stone. The sudden release of her warmth was like a bolt of frost through his chest.

"Come look," she said.

Jude joined her on the back side of the stone. The pillar was multi-faceted, with three sides in total. Carved into the second face of the stone was a beautiful young woman with a crown of flowers and on the third was a woman swollen with child, a serpent at her feet.

"She embodies the cycles of nature, but the Cailleach herself is the crone, which is associated with winter. In ancient times, they said she also brought death," Elizabeth said.

Jude had learned many local myths, but never applied them to real life. Every time someone spoke to him of the divine, it had been to subdue him in one way or another. He didn't know what to believe, but after the miracles of the last few weeks, he knew there was magic in the world. Elizabeth practiced it when she played music, and her grandmother conjured it when she plucked the oldest of medicines from the earth.

Elizabeth ran a hand down the carving of the mother, tracing the lines of her hair and the tail of the serpent. "You are different than before. Is it over, then? Are you free from The Order?" She kept her gaze on the goddess.

A tightness formed in Jude's chest. He wanted so badly to be done with The Order, but they still had him in their grasp. "Once I've dealt with every member of the brotherhood, I won't be bound by their tethers anymore. I'll be free again, one way or another."

"Then Millie will be able to go home, and I can tell my parents she is still alive."

"Yes." Jude brought her hand to his lips and kissed it. He hoped to keep her believing things would go as planned, that he would make it out of everything unscathed. "Are you ready to go back?"

Elizabeth sighed. "I don't want to return to Beauloch

yet. It's stifling when you're trapped in there all by yourself."

Jude laughed. "Is that why you started hitting on my housekeeper?"

Elizabeth ripped herself away from his clutches and peered up at him with her deathly beautiful eyes. "That's not fair. I had no idea she favored women."

He approached her with caution, holding out his hands. "I know, I'm only joking. What do you say to some dinner? There's a pub just up the road with decent food."

"I like the sound of that."

&

ELIZABETH'S MOUTH WATERED WHEN THE WAITRESS SET the massive plate of fish and chips in front of her. She hadn't had any junk food since she'd left London. "This looks amazing!" she said, and took a bite of the crispy filet and then ate a hot chip. Jude laughed at her reaction. Elizabeth didn't think she'd ever get used to that devilish smile. She still felt her cheeks blush ever so slightly when he used it on her.

After she had torn through most of her food, she sat back and took in a deep breath. "I'm curious—what did Millie say when she asked you to bring her the bog myrtle?" She pulled out the bundle they'd collected from the edge of the car park and twirled it in her hand.

Jude had just taken a bite of his venison burger and had to swallow before he could answer. "She didn't tell me why she needed it." He took a sip of ale to wash it down. "Although, she may have mentioned the Cailleach in passing. One day, we went foraging for berries and the wind turned cold. Millie said something like, 'Winter is upon us. Soon the tree spirits will go into hiding and the hag will wander the glen to seek out her next victim,' I'm still not sure what she meant."

"She has always followed the old ways," Elizabeth said.

He's so talkative right now, she thought.

Elizabeth couldn't be sure if she was just a novelty to him like the other woman had been, or if there was something more between them. He'd had every opportunity to shove his cock inside her last night, to fuck her brains out, but he chose to pleasure her instead. It had been the last thing she'd expected, based on what she could guess about his past exploits.

Thoughts of his naked body did not belong at the dinner table. Elizabeth needed to get back to what they were talking about. "What can I do to help now?" she said, as she sipped her hot tea.

Jude furrowed his brow and shoved another fry in his mouth. "What do you mean?"

"I mean with The Order."

He took another chip, seeming reluctant to respond.

"I want my freedom back. I'm tired of being locked away. I know I can't really complain, since Gran has been hiding out for years, and they may still be looking for her. If someone was watching the cottage—"

"No one saw you. You're safe now," he said, cutting her off. His tone had softened, and his mood darkened.

"I'm not completely helpless," she said.

Jude put his burger down and looked at her, deconstructing her with his harsh gaze. "I'm not involving you in any of this. These people are dangerous." He took a sip of his beer. "You have to understand what I'm trying to tell you when I say these people are evil. They're foul. One brush with The Order and all the light you had in your life dwindles to nothing. I don't know how vast their network is or how great their influence may be. Anytime I've tried to investigate, I got nowhere. They're completely hidden. They've destroyed eight years of my life. Do you think I would risk something like that happening to you?" Jude reached across the table and took her hand.

Elizabeth's heart leapt at his words. She squeezed his rough palm. Her hand fit into his like a long-lost piece to a puzzle.

No. You cannot do this. It's too dangerous, she thought.

Fear gripped her, twisting her guts, but it wasn't fear of Jude. Elizabeth was afraid of what her heart felt in that moment. Somewhere deep in her soul, where all the love and comfort had been ripped away before, now felt warm. She never knew she could feel this way with a man. She and her husband had just gone through the motions, but with Jude, she felt alive.

"No, I wouldn't want someone getting hurt to be on my conscience either, so I understand," she said.

In the corner of the pub, a traditional Scottish group had set up to play a session. They turned the mics on and introduced themselves. She didn't catch their name. Things were a little fuzzy because all Elizabeth could think about was being with Jude. She never wanted to leave the pub. If there was some alternate universe where they could stay forever, eating greasy food and holding hands and kissing, she would jump there with him and never come back.

"Come on, let's have a dance." Jude scooted from the booth and held out his hand to her.

"If you insist, but don't go too fast, lest all my dinner ends up on the dance floor," she said.

Jude responded by giving her a few venison-infused kisses on her lips and bringing her into him as tightly as he could. "I'm not making any promises."

Up close, it was too difficult to ignore how handsome he was. Elizabeth always considered herself average looking, but she wondered now if her measurements of beauty were solely based on how she'd been treated before. She was Jude's sole focus when they were together. He couldn't keep his hands off her, and she couldn't get enough of it.

The band started to play a jig and Jude swept her onto the dance floor. A few other patrons joined in, fueled by food and ale. The pub grew warm. Heat emanated from the music, the fire, the food, and the people, but Jude didn't look ill like he had the night he fainted.

In fact, his constitution radiated good health.

Gran is a real witch after all.

Jude looked so happy, so at ease, that for a moment, Elizabeth's heart sunk. She wondered if he often had evenings like this with other women. Annie had mentioned that other girls had come around to give him pleasure he couldn't get by himself. Maybe this was just his way of life, and come morning, she would be discarded.

The music stopped and the audience clapped. Elizabeth stepped back and took in a deep breath. The band started another jig. Before Elizabeth could protest, Jude scooped her up and spun her around.

"Whoa!" she exclaimed as the world around her whooshed by in a blur.

Jude planted a kiss on her lips. He didn't let her up for air for a long time. "Sorry, love, it's just that you're driving me mad. Now dance with me some more."

Elizabeth held on for dear life as Jude led them back and forth across the timbers, which bounced underneath their feet.

"That one's not gettin' away from 'im anytime soon," an old woman's voice said behind her. She looked back to see a lady with silver hair being led by her man gawking at them. Her partner looked in their direction.

"Better keep that one close," he said.

"I plan to." Jude squeezed her hand.

Elizabeth felt that gaping pit in her soul start to mend. It was as if hot new skin was forming over some ancient wounds in her chest. Then she remembered the actual scars Jude hid beneath his shirt. He had experienced much worse and had still managed to come out of it with a fire in his heart, so it *must* be possible for her to have something good, something real—a love that could feed her like nothing else ever had before.

Her thoughts drifted away with the music.

Chapter Twelve

❧

Jude had barely greeted dawn when the sound of a dish breaking and a shrill voice echoed through the halls of Beauloch. He quickly dressed and headed to the kitchens. The moment he pushed through the swinging doors, he met with a chaotic scene.

"That's not how you fold it! You'll ruin it!" Fiona said, pushing Annie out of the way so she could fix the trays of unbaked baguettes. "Go and cut the tomatoes."

Annie went to her station and caught sight of Jude, but said nothing.

"What's going on here?" Jude said.

Fiona startled and turned around. "Ah, you're awake. You can help advise us on what the bloody hell we should do about this evening." She snatched a piece of paper off the counter and held it out to him. Fiona never cursed. Something was very wrong.

"This evening?"

Fiona planted a hand on her hip and bored into him with her determined blue eyes. "The party you were so enthused about a few weeks ago is tonight. Annie here had been confused and posted the invitations that were on my desk without my permission. She just informed me we've been receiving RSVPs all week! That's what I get for letting someone else handle the mail. Now, which appetizers do you wish to serve?"

"The invitations already had stamps on them," Annie said.

"Hush! Keep chopping!" Fiona snapped.

Jude was dumbfounded for a moment. He had completely forgotten about the party. It had been a desperate ploy to get Elizabeth to stay a little longer at Beauloch, but it was no longer needed now that she was forced to be his guest. He'd thought of only her the last few days, keeping to the perimeter of where she often dwelt to speak with her about a book or a piece of music. They'd even shared dinner together in the library two nights earlier. The last thing he wanted was for their blissful moments to be interrupted by strangers.

"Pick what you feel is best." He handed the paper back to Fiona. "How many people did we invite exactly?"

Annie looked up from her tomato chopping, her cheeks blushed.

"Go on, tell him how many you invited," Fiona said.

"Well, I invited most of the people who came to your brother's graduation party, minus that weird guy with the greasy beard."

"How many is that?" Jude said.

"A little less than two hundred, but not everyone confirmed they are coming," Annie said, holding the knife still as if waiting to see what his reaction would be.

Jude pressed his fingers into his closed eyes and rubbed them until the stars vanished from his vision.

"We can send them away if you're ill," Annie said.

"No we can't," Fiona called from across the kitchen.

"I'm not ill, Annie, just a little bit surprised is all."

Fiona finished placing the last of the baguette trays into the hot ovens. She came back and stood in front of Jude, studying him. "You look well." She rubbed his arm.

"Thank you," Jude said.

Fiona leaned into Jude. "Do you think *they* will come tonight?" she said, her voice so low that Annie couldn't hear. She looked over her shoulder at the frantic maid before continuing. "Should we expect trouble?"

A hot flame rose up in Jude. He tried to calm himself, to remember what the witch had taught him in the forest—how to channel his anger—but the thought of a brother from The Order in his home was almost enough to make him sick.

"If they show up, I'll handle it. Don't worry." He placed his hands on Fiona's shoulders and gave her a kiss on her sweaty forehead.

He left them to their work only to pass Walter working with a couple of scruffy locals in the dining hall, moving furniture around to accommodate the large crowd they expected later that evening. Normally, Jude was hesitant to have outsiders in the castle, but he trusted Walter's judgment and could count on him to keep any bad actors away from Beauloch.

The bigger problem was going to be the partygoers. He knew many of the people Annie had invited were extended family members and other try-hards who liked to cozy up to him because of his ancestral seat. Many were probably eager to see how the laird was handling things after the tragic passing of his father.

The details surrounding his father's death had never been revealed to the public. Only those closest to the family knew a pistol had been involved. Jude hated guns, but even he had to admit a firearm was the best protection he could afford, which was why he removed his father's old handgun from the study and kept it close.

Jude arrived in the ballroom. With much care, he opened the hidden compartment in his bureau and unlocked the drawer with a small key he kept hidden in an old book.

It was a rare .9mm handgun issued to intelligence agencies back in the '90s. His father had acquired it during his work for the British government. On paper, he'd been investigating fraud and tax evasion, but Jude always thought there was more to the story. Nothing could be done about it now though. Whatever links his father had had with anyone of consequence were gone. He stood alone in this fight.

Jude inspected the firearm and tucked it into the holster he had put on underneath his dress jacket. He went to his mirror to see how well he had concealed the weapon, only to be haunted by the image of his late father. Nausea roiled in his gut.

How dare they take my father away.

Thoughts of his mother and brother began to surface.

The pain they'd endured after his father's death was more than anyone should have to go through. His parents were so in love with one another that his mother had broken down to a mere shell of her former self, and his brother hid himself away in his school studies. Still, he was proud of the man Jamie had become.

If only I could take pride in myself. But The Order has turned me into a monster.

Jude couldn't dwell on the past. His sole focus was on Elizabeth now. Her beauty, her talent, and her soul were beacons of light in a hideous world. Her presence alone could chase any demon away. If he couldn't escape his bonds of The Order, he would at least make sure she was safe.

Jude checked the ammo in his pistol one more time and descended into the tunnels under Beauloch.

"Are you sure it's today?" Elizabeth said, throwing a shawl over her shoulders.

"Aye, it's today," Fiona said, laying out a few options for her to wear. "You'll need to change soon. The guests are coming in a couple of hours."

Elizabeth had gotten up early and wandered the castle looking for Jude. She never found him and got back in bed as soon as she saw the weather had turned. Outside, the north winds rushed through the tops of the trees, throwing heavy droplets of rain onto her window facing the loch.

"I had no idea, otherwise I would've gotten up."

Fiona held out a hand to silence her. "It's better that

you had your rest. By our last count, there are close to two hundred guests confirmed to arrive."

"Where's Jude?" Elizabeth said, asking as if it was a technical question, but really wanting to know the whereabouts of the elusive man.

"He's wandering around somewhere," Fiona said, flitting her hand in several directions. It wasn't the answer Elizabeth had wanted.

Elizabeth got to her feet and stretched. "I'd like to warm up a bit before I change. Where am I to play?"

"I think by the hearth in the dining room will do nicely. I'll have Walter move the harp there. I know you'll need light, and by the looks of it, warmth too." Fiona shivered as she gazed out the windows at the increasing wind.

Elizabeth thought she could feel the frigid gale as dead leaves slapped and stuck to the ancient leaded glass. As much as she enjoyed the view, the old windows didn't do much to protect the room from the old hag of winter. Her icy hands were naked branches reaching out to tap on the panes of Beauloch, letting everyone know she'd arrived.

"I'll move the harp myself, no need to bother Walter," Elizabeth said. She got dressed in a sweater and jeans and left the room, going downstairs to explore the castle, and to see if she could find Jude before she had to perform.

As soon as she descended the steps, Elizabeth saw the castle had come to life. Candelabras lit the dark corners of the stairs and foyer. Vintage lamps she never noticed before buzzed with warmth in the long hall leading to the library. She kept her eyes peeled for Jude but found him nowhere. Instead of pining after him like a dumb schoolgirl, however, she got to work, strapping her harp to the dolly and rolling it from the library into the dining room. She checked and double-checked her tuning.

She warmed up by playing chords and arpeggios. The sound of the harp sung against the background of the winter storm. The curtains had been pulled back to reveal the forest being drenched in Highland rain. The old radiators combined with the warmth of the fireplace did a good job of keeping winter at bay, but she couldn't shake the chill that was in the air.

Elizabeth rushed back upstairs to change. She didn't call on Annie for help, seeing as her last encounter with her had been an awkward one. Still, she wanted to clear the air between them before the night was over, preferably after a glass of warm whiskey to ease any tension between them.

Considering the weather, Elizabeth wanted to wear something warm, but the sleeves on two of the dresses in her wardrobe could be cumbersome while playing. The only thing left was a long black dress with a halter neck and no sleeves. It was her favorite dress to wear to events. The form-fitting bodice flattered her chest and hips, and a narrow slit to the knee gave her just enough room to straddle her harp.

There were no heels to go with it, but Elizabeth hated wearing them anyway and slipped on a pair of pointy black flats she'd bought for such occasions as this. After she dabbed on a bit of makeup, she made her way back down the grand staircase. The sound of Jude's voice echoing in the foyer made her heart skip a beat.

The moment her foot reached the bottom step, a man

with bright-blond hair turned toward her, revealing a face almost identical to Jude's.

"Elizabeth, this is Jude's brother, Jamie," Walter said.

"Oh, it's a pleasure to meet you," Elizabeth said, holding out her hand to him.

Jamie took it and planted a kiss on top of it. "Same to you, Elizabeth. I hear we are in for some spectacular music this evening."

Elizabeth blushed, reacting to Jamie's warm kiss much like she had when Jude first took her hand and kissed it the night she'd put him to bed. She worried that her feelings for Jude could be seen on her face, and she felt embarrassed. It didn't help that Jamie's eyes remained on her long enough to make her uncomfortable.

"Forgive me, Elizabeth. This is my mother, Irene," Jamie said, holding his hand out to the woman beside him.

She was tall, like her sons, with silver hair pulled back tightly into a wavy ponytail. Irene kept her arms in close, wrapped up in a blue tartan shawl. Nothing about her was welcoming. She forced a smile and turned away to examine her surroundings, her diamond earrings glittering in the warm light of Beauloch.

"You're the harpist?" Irene said, looking back at Elizabeth.

"I am," Elizabeth said.

"I'm going to see if that old crack is getting any worse. Excuse me." Irene took off down the hall. There was a moment of awkward silence.

"I hope the weather doesn't interfere with the party. Won't the road by the loch get washed out from all this rain?" Elizabeth said as she watched the storm through the open front doors of the castle. Mist from the downpour swirled up from the gravel drive and into the foyer.

Walter laughed. "A washed-out road isn't going to stop people from coming to Beauloch, lass. This place has been a tomb for the last decade or so. They'll be wanting to see what's become of the paintings and statues. But don't worry, I've rerouted the road since the last storm."

"They'll be wanting to see Dracula too, not just his castle," Jamie said, with a condescending tone Elizabeth didn't like. "Where is my brother? Is he still holed up in that old ballroom?"

"Aye, he is, but last I saw him he was crawling through the dungeons," Walter said.

Elizabeth left them to their conversation and receded into the castle, hoping to remain scarce until more guests arrived. She held her head low as she went to the kitchens.

Annie almost ran into her with a tray of hors d'oeuvres. Her abrupt stop caused two bruschetta pieces to fall off her tray. They splattered onto the floor at their feet. "Oops! Looks like I'm headed back to the kitchen."

Elizabeth bent down to help her wipe the tomatoes up. "I'll walk with you. I need some water."

"Let me get it. Fiona is a basket case right now." Annie quickly had the mess cleaned up with her dish rag.

"I can handle a basket case. Greeting strangers is the much scarier option."

Annie shrugged. Elizabeth followed her through the kitchen doors. She took a glass from the cupboard and filled it up.

Fiona rushed in from the cellars, holding a couple of

bottles of wine. "I swore we had another Burgundy down there. It was an expensive bottle too, I remember."

Annie shot a glance at Elizabeth, who hid her smile behind her glass of water. They both giggled while Fiona opened the bottles.

Fiona checked her watch. "The first guests are to arrive any minute now."

"I'll go warm up," Elizabeth said, reluctant to leave the safety of her hideout. She crept into the dining room. Walter and a couple of men she didn't recognize stood at the far end with drinks already in hand. She glided across the floor quietly in her flats and sat down at her harp.

As guests started to trickle into the dining hall, Elizabeth skillfully plucked the strings of her instrument. Between songs, she scanned the room for Jude, only to be disappointed. The fact that the one man she wished to see hadn't showed left her uneasy.

Before long, the dining room was packed with people talking so loudly, the din almost drowned out her music. She played simple, upbeat pieces that evoked feelings of joy. It was still a party, even though the mood in Beauloch felt serious and heavy. Walter approached her near the end of a song. When she was done, she rested her hands in her lap and looked up at him. He gave her a wink and turned to address the crowd.

"Thank you all for coming. It's been such a pleasure to have family and friends back at Beauloch. I know you all took a risk venturing out into the cold rain, but we have a real treat for you tonight." He held out his arm toward her. "Please give a warm welcome to our musical talent for this evening, Elizabeth Ross."

The crowd clapped. Elizabeth stood up and smiled. She gave a small wave to the unfamiliar faces surrounding her. The only one she recognized was Jamie. While he was close to the man she was looking for, it wasn't *him*. As soon as the crowd quieted, Elizabeth sat back down on her bench and began to play again.

The first song was a gentle, romantic piece composed by a French harpist. It served as an introduction to her repertoire. When she finished, the crowd clapped and she continued, like she would at any other posh party she'd been hired to play at in London. Was it any different, really? She might not know the circumstances of the people surrounding her, but by the way they were dressed, she thought they were of greater means than herself. Much greater.

She repeated the process: playing a piece, pausing for the applause, then continuing again. Right before she began her last piece of the evening, she caught a glimpse of Jude leaning on the mantle of the fireplace. Had he been there the whole time?

A great relief poured over her when she finished the last song. It was the longest one she'd played, and sweat had begun to bead down the back of her neck. She stood up to take a bow, something she'd done hundreds of times before. She looked over to the fireplace again, but Jude had gone.

Walter put on some light jazz to fill the silence. Elizabeth stretched and made her way to the bar for wine, getting stopped by a couple of people who wanted to compliment her playing. She gave them a bright smile even though she felt weary on the inside. It was like Jude had abandoned her, even though the notion was ridiculous. Then again, she knew no one at this party except his brother and mother, whom she avoided after that awkward introduction.

Annie poured her a glass of wine from the bar. "That was beautiful," she said.

"Thank you, Annie. Have you seen Jude around anywhere?"

"I haven't seen him all evening."

"Thanks." Elizabeth took her glass of wine and pushed her way into the crowd to search for the elusive laird. She scanned the faces, wondering who each person was to him. About halfway into the room, a hand caught her shoulder. She turned around to see Jamie with a big smile on his face.

That's something that runs in the family then, that devilish smile, she thought.

"I have to say, that was outstanding, Elizabeth. I'm not sure I've ever heard music so divine. Where did my brother find you?" he said. The whiskey in his glass smelled potent. He took a sip and placed his other hand in his pocket, totally at ease while he awaited her response. Elizabeth wondered if this was what Jude would be like if he hadn't touched the darkness.

"Fiona invited me to come play a few weeks ago. I met the laird then."

Jamie almost choked on his drink. "He let a stranger come into his home to play for him? Well, something is chipping away at that marble exterior of his. Perhaps it is your beauty."

Elizabeth blushed, taken aback by the comment. She'd dealt mostly with posh snobs who had better manners during these types of events, but she'd also been dressed more conservatively then. She suddenly felt uncomfortable in the tight gown. "No. It is just my music he enjoys."

"I'm not wanting to diminish your talent, I was just trying to give you a compliment," Jamie said. His face turned red.

There it was, the discomfort Elizabeth had been trying to avoid all evening. She took a couple of gulps of wine and smiled. "I hate compliments."

Jamie laughed, breaking up the awkward tension that had arisen suddenly. "If I'm being honest, I hate them too. I'll be more mindful of that next time." He let out a long sigh and looked down into his glass. "When will this kick in?"

Elizabeth smirked, enchanted by the manners of the laird's little brother. She sensed genuine consideration in his tone. "It was a pleasure speaking with you." Elizabeth put her hand on Jamie's shoulder. "You'll have to excuse me though. I've not yet had dinner," she said, telling the truth. In the rush to prepare for the evening, she'd only had some cheese and a few pretzels. The aroma that had been wafting from the kitchen made her stomach grumble. She spotted a sideboard with food laid out on it.

As she took a step toward it, a man crossed in front of her. They bumped into each other with a significant amount of force.

"Excuse me," Elizabeth said.

The man was older, probably in his late fifties. He grabbed both of Elizabeth's elbows and held her in place. "My apologies," he said, flashing yellow teeth as he smiled at her. His face was flushed, and his bright-blue eyes looked her up and down. Elizabeth felt strange, like she was being sized up for something. She had to forcefully pull her arms away to get out of his grasp. Feeling uneasy, she didn't wait for an excuse or apology for his behavior and went to the sidebar where there was no one else around.

She piled some salmon tartare, bread, and cheese on a plate and escaped to a corner of the dining room. It was the best spot to not be bothered by the strange man, and also to keep an eye out for Jude.

Why had he appeared out of nowhere during her concert, only to disappear once again? Was he avoiding her in particular?

Frustrated by these questions, Elizabeth shoved the bread and cheese in her mouth, drained her wine glass, and set out to see what was going on in other parts of the castle. She approached the ballroom first and peeked her head inside, but it was too dark to see if anyone was in there. Then she went into the library. It was empty too, but the dull light from a floor lamp allowed her to sneak into the narrow entrance of the secret passageway. Walter had mentioned Jude had been wandering the damp corridors earlier, so she'd try her luck there.

The dark halls echoed with the voices of the party. Jazz music floated out into the far reaches of Beauloch, making it seem as if time didn't exist in the ancient castle. Elizabeth imagined the same music filled the rooms sixty or seventy years ago, and she liked that feeling—that some things were changeless, that they endured.

Elizabeth peeked through the fleur-de-lis-shaped grates that looked out into the rear vestibule, but the castle doors were shut. Not a single person had stepped outside to smoke. Instead of going back the way she came, she went upstairs to the Blue Room. It was just as she'd left it, with her hairbrush and makeup scattered on the vanity. She went out into the hall and stopped at the top of the stairs. She gripped the banister and peered down into the atrium.

Down at the other end of the hall, a loud *thump* caught her attention. Nothing moved in the shadowy corridor, or nothing she could see anyway. Farther off, deeper into the long stretch of the darkness were the old bedrooms, but none of them had been used in years. She only knew this because Annie gave her the full tour after Jude left to find Gran.

Maybe he's making himself scarce in his old bedroom.

She turned the knob on the first door to her left, and was surprised to find it unlocked. The room was pitch black. No one was inside. Elizabeth continued down the hall. A narrow door on her right stood ajar and a dim light escaped into the hall.

Annie never took me inside this room.

Elizabeth pushed the door open and went in. Lightning struck a few times in the distance outside a bank of tall windows, revealing a floor lamp in one corner. She memorized the room during the flashes and went to the lamp.

The yellow light revealed an impressive study, with bookshelves that went all the way to the ceiling. A large oak desk stood on the left side, its surface covered with stacks of books and notes neatly piled together. Above the desk, all manner of unique things lined the shelves of a bookcase, including an old map of Scotland, runestones, an astrolabe, tiny carved figurines, and some occult paintings Elizabeth couldn't identify the origin of.

Her wonder about Beauloch only increased at the discovery of this interesting room. She wanted to go through some of the desk drawers, but she'd already violated Jude's privacy her first night at the castle. So instead of snooping through drawers, she went over to the tall windows on the other side of the room.

Upon closer inspection, Elizabeth realized that one of the windows was a glass door. She tried the iron handle and opened it. The wide balcony on the other side was sheltered from the rain, allowing her to venture forth. It had to be the biggest balcony she'd ever been on, with fat pillars holding up a wide railing made of concrete.

Elizabeth placed her hands on the top of the rail, feeling the cold rain soak the gritty surface. Lightning struck the loch, causing her to jump. She backed away from the edge but continued to watch the storm from the shadows. The sheer force of the winds and the bite of the cold rain left her in awe. Elizabeth couldn't remember the last time she'd felt so close to the raw power of nature. It sparked something deep inside of her that she couldn't explain. Goosebumps feathered across her arms and back.

You'll catch your death if you stay out here too long.

Her dress wasn't nearly enough protection from the wild elements. Turning back, she spotted the silhouette of a man standing in the doorway of the study. Elizabeth went back inside.

"I've been looking for you," she said, stopping in front of the desk. The man entering the study wasn't Jude.

"You've been looking for me? Well, I should feel honored," the man said. His shadowy figure strode into the study with both hands in his pockets. The antique lamp revealed an older face with lines around his eyes and mouth, and slicked-back, dirty-blond hair, which accentuated sharp cheekbones and a high nose.

It was the man she'd bumped into in the dining hall. His cold blue eyes were fixated on Elizabeth as he approached. She remained in place, frozen from something that was a mixture of fear and intrigue.

"I'm sorry. Have I frightened you?" The man smiled as if he was pleased his presence had put her off.

Elizabeth straightened up her posture. "No. I apologize. I thought you were someone else," she said.

"Oh, who were you looking for?" He blocked her way to the door.

"Just my friend who came to watch me play," Elizabeth said.

The stranger approached, and Elizabeth turned and stepped back until her ass pressed against the desk. He placed himself directly in front of her.

"Your performance was astounding, my dear. How long have you been playing the harp?" He cocked his head to the side, as if trying to get a read on her.

"Oh, I think about seventeen or eighteen years now." Elizabeth braced herself against the desk with both hands. She did her best to act casual, but she knew he could sense her trepidation.

"My name is Boris, by the way. I'm not sure I mentioned it." He held out his hand. Elizabeth took it.

"Elizabeth," was all she offered.

Boris leaned in to study her face. "You're of premium stock, aren't you? Are both your parents still alive?"

"Premium stock?" Elizabeth said, astounded at the

man's words. Who in the hell was he, wandering Beauloch and cornering her like this?

"Oh, you know. I've seen many women your age who are so tired and whittled down by life, but you…" Boris stroked her bare arm. "You're in your prime. How much do you weigh?"

Elizabeth pushed off from the desk and whirled away to get out of Boris's reach. "How dare you say these things?" Her tone was direct, but there was fragility in her voice. She'd been taken aback by this strange encounter. Her heart hammered against her ribs. The cold winds rushed into the study from the balcony, bringing with it moisture that whirled around her. She must not have closed the door tightly enough on her way back in.

Boris laughed a slow and steady laugh, turning on his heels to face her. "Can I be frank, Elizabeth? I know who you were looking for. The laird has been keeping you hidden away in the castle, hasn't he?" The faint glimmer of steel caught Elizabeth's eye as Boris raised a slender knife to her neck. She backed into a bookshelf.

"Please, don't hurt me." Her body quivered with terror

"I'm not going to hurt you, but you have to learn the order of things here. I'm the laird's master. He is my dog. Do you understand? He's been a bad dog too, disobeying his master. Now I've learned he's hiding out with some bitch, and I'm wondering how to punish him so that it doesn't happen again. Hmm? Got any ideas?" Boris ran a finger from her chin to her neck, slowly tracing her collarbone and down her arm. He placed his hand on her exposed ribcage and pushed his thumb into the side of her dress and up her breast, gently stroking the soft underside.

Elizabeth turned her head and tried not to look at the pure evil that had a hold over her. With her wandering eyes she spotted a protractor on a bookshelf behind the desk. It was an old brass one, with a fine point on both ends. It wouldn't be as sharp as the knife Boris had, but it was something she might be able to use against him if she could get her hands on it.

"I'm wondering how lovely it must be to have the youth and talent like one such as yourself has." Boris grabbed her left arm and dug the knife tip into the crook of her elbow.

Elizabeth stayed quiet, trying to survive whatever ordeal this foul human might put her through. She looked on with horror as Boris got on his knees and licked the small stream of blood that flowed down her arm. He moaned with pleasure as he drank her blood. With one hand he held her arm down to her side, with the other he lifted the hem of her dress and caressed the back of her leg, running his fingers up and down her calf.

He's vulnerable now.

Elizabeth took her chance to escape and kneed Boris in the nose. He screamed in agony and clutched at his face. "Fucking bitch!" He lunged in her direction.

Elizabeth ran, but he grabbed her from behind and ripped her dress down the side. She pivoted toward the balcony, ready to jump over the railing if she must, but he seized her hand. Elizabeth tried to wrench herself free of his grip by grasping the edge of the desk to use the heavy oak as leverage. She yanked hard and pulled herself around to the back side. Boris suddenly let go and she flew back into the bookshelf. She used the opportunity to twist around and reach for the protractor. The instant she wrapped her fingers around it, an excruciating pain took hold of her right leg.

He stabbed me!

Elizabeth cried out. "No!" She whirled around and plunged the protractor into the base of Boris's neck near his collarbone. He groaned in agony. It wouldn't kill him, but it had bought her enough time to flee.

Elizabeth hobbled to the entrance of the study. She needed to get help, but her leg was in so much pain that she could only limp. Her mind raced, thinking of the best way to stay hidden from Boris. The stairs might take too long with her injury, and he could easily push her down the steps. She staggered through the dark hall and back to the Blue Room.

Once inside, she checked the lock three times and moved as quickly as she could to the entrance of the servants' staircase. At first, she thought about changing out of her dress, but didn't trust that Boris wouldn't break the door down with his superhuman strength. Her only option was to go underground. Before she made the arduous journey down the steep steps, she reached around to feel the stab wound on the back of her right hamstring. Bright crimson blood covered her hand. She knew she had to find help fast. With every ounce of strength she had left, Elizabeth staggered down the stairs in the dark.

The throb of the injury burned her from the inside out. Nausea hit her as the adrenaline tapered off.

"Fiona? Annie?" she called out. The thought of dying alone in the dark saddened and frightened her. "Hello? Anyone?"

Each step was an eternity. Elizabeth yearned to see her

parents, to hear the sound of Millie's voice, and to rest her head on the shoulder of the man who would be the first to find her dead body.

Is Jude still alive?

Elizabeth clawed up the cellar steps and onto the floor of the kitchen. She looked at her leg. Her blood had smeared across the polished wood floor. How much had she lost?

Chapter Thirteen

❧

J ude homed in on Boris from the far end of the dining hall. He'd seen the man arrive earlier, when he'd stood at the banister, taking note of everyone who had come to Beauloch. Ever since the monster had stepped foot inside the castle, Jude remained scarce. He knew Boris had come to check him out and gather more intel on his personal life, which was why he had stayed as far away from Elizabeth as he could. The last thing he wanted to do was draw attention to her.

Boris stood with a glass of wine in his hand, speaking to Jude's mother. She seemed to be laughing at everything he said to her. Jude was so distracted by this he realized he'd lost sight of Elizabeth.

He whispered curses as he searched the room for the lithe figure that had enchanted the audience with her music. In truth, he didn't feel comfortable having so many eyes on her when he couldn't claim her as his own.

He caught sight of his brother's fair head bobbing through the crowd. That was the last person he'd seen her talking to. Jude slipped through the bodies to meet him.

"Where is she?" he said.

"Elizabeth? She was just here, having a glass of wine."

"Did you see where she went?"

"Not a clue. Why? Is there trouble?"

"Come with me." Jude pulled his brother aside. They went into the hallway where it was quiet.

"One of Father's old friends is here. If he learns Elizabeth is with me, she could be in danger. I've had her in my sights all evening, until a few minutes ago."

"Why would she be in danger if he's a friend of Father's?"

"Remember how he ended up with two bullets in his skull, and we never found out who was responsible? This could be one of the men responsible, Jamie," Jude whispered as quietly as he could manage, trying to urge the point home to his clueless brother.

Jamie gazed down the long hall, still processing his words. He scratched at the scruff on his chin. "I'll take the underground passages. I spent more time in them, and I know them better than you."

"We meet back here in fifteen minutes." Jude glanced at the time on his phone. "If I'm not back by then, alert Walter to the trouble."

"Okay, Mr. Bond," Jamie snickered.

Jude shoved his brother up against the wall. "This is serious, Jamie. If you're not going to help, then fucking leave," he growled.

Jamie pushed back and broke free of his brother's hold. "Fine. Fifteen minutes."

Jude gave him one last glare and went back into the dining hall.

His mother stood beside Elizabeth's harp with her arms crossed and a drink in her hand while she spoke to Fiona. She looked uncomfortable being back here, but to Jude, this place was home, no matter how bad things got, and he'd do his damned best to protect it and Elizabeth.

He saw Annie restocking the food on the sideboard and went to press her.

"Have you seen Elizabeth?" he said, keeping his voice low.

"Not since I poured her a glass of wine a few minutes ago," she said.

Jude grumbled in frustration and went out of the dining hall to search the places she spent the most time in. He started in the Blue Room but found no sign of her. Then he went down to the library, which was also empty. He even went to the ballroom to see if she'd gone there to escape the crowd.

The idea of her waiting for him in his bed aroused him, but that thought didn't help, so he brushed it away. He went through the other rooms on the ground floor until his timer went off. Jude raced back to the hallway outside the dining room and met Jamie.

"Well?" Jude said.

"I didn't know you reopened the way into the greenhouse. How long ago did you seal it off?"

"Jamie! Focus! What about Elizabeth?"

Just then a high-pitched scream echoed from the

kitchens. Both brothers rushed in to find Annie shaking over a dead body covered in blood on the floor. Jude's heart dropped into his gut. He ran to Elizabeth and rolled her onto her back.

"I need to take her clothes off to see where she's been hurt," Jamie said as he knelt beside them. He rolled up his sleeves.

Jude barely comprehended his brother's words. His sole focus was on Elizabeth's pale complexion. There was no doubt in his mind who had done this. Those demons, the foulest things on this earth, had hurt the most beautiful, pure thing to have ever graced his presence. And now she was dead.

As he held her in his arms, she felt cold to the touch. Tears formed in his eyes and blurred his vision of the poor creature he'd brought to ruin. It was all his fault. Keeping her close to him had been selfish. He knew the danger they were in after he'd failed to take part in The Order's debauchery at his initiation. The pain and sadness was almost too much for him to bear. His whole body was wracked with sorrow as he pressed his forehead against hers.

"I'm so sorry, Elizabeth. This is all my fault. Please don't go. *I love you.*" He could barely get out the last words. He regretted not having said them sooner, and now she might never hear them.

His brother took the body away, leaving him alone to mourn. Walter and Fiona picked him up and placed a glass of water in his hands. He stared at it, thinking how useless it was to him. A familiar voice mentioned something about a trail of blood leading into the cellars.

"I'm going to follow it," Walter said.

Jude slammed the glass of water onto the countertop. He pulled out his pistol. "You'll do no such thing."

Jude had an anger in him he never knew he could feel. It was something that came from outside of him, like the world around him was all in red, and the only way to make it normal again was to destroy the evil he had allowed to thrive for all these years. He didn't care if he went down in flames with them. Devouring the demons of The Order was his sole purpose now.

Jude flipped the safety off his pistol and descended past the cellar and into the belly of Beauloch. His flashlight guided him while he tracked the droplets of blood that led up to the Blue Room.

She hadn't been in there when he'd checked earlier, so the fatal injury had to have been inflicted somewhere else. Jude crouched down to feel the blood that had soaked into the carpet. It was difficult to see since it blended in with the pattern, forcing Jude to stay low to the ground as he followed the trail out of the room and down the long hall of the second floor.

Guilt immediately struck him. He hadn't thought to look down this way since he always kept the bedrooms locked in this area of the castle. After his father had died, it had been too painful to see all his personal effects. His parents' bedroom, his old room, his brother's, and the study lay ahead.

The door to the study was wide open. Jude readied his pistol to fire and crept inside, only to be met with an eerie emptiness. Whoever had hurt Elizabeth was long gone. The door to the balcony had been left ajar and creaked in the wind of the storm. He went over and shut it.

From the windows of the study, he could see all the cars leaving. Walter must have sent everyone home after they had discovered the body. The sight of his beloved Elizabeth covered in blood continued to torture him. Of all the pain he'd endured at the hands of those monsters, none had torn at his soul like this did.

The strength he'd recovered during his time with the witch didn't seem to matter now. Nothing mattered. Elizabeth's blood stained the edge of the desk.

They slaughtered her like a helpless lamb.

Voices from down the hall drew him out of the study. He went to the Blue Room, where a small group of people had gathered.

It was only his anger that allowed him the strength to push past the people to see her. She was sprawled out on her stomach, wearing only her undergarments. Jamie was having Annie help him stitch the gaping hole in the back of her thigh.

"Must you do this now? She didn't make it," Jude said, falling to his knees in defeat.

Walter knelt beside him and placed a hand on his shoulder. "She's alive, my laird. Jamie is treating her mild shock with a sedative."

The words didn't register. Jude heard them, but the sight of Elizabeth's pale skin suggested that she was never coming back.

"Leave her be, Jamie," he said. Frustrated, Jude jerked his brother away from his task. "I said, leave her alone!"

"Jude?" Elizabeth's hand rose from the bed.

He got down on his knees and sobbed again. "You're alive?"

"Let your brother finish his work." Walter peeled him away from the bedside.

Jude knew there was no better doctor in the country than Jamie. His brother had lost himself in his studies after their father had died and graduated with honors from Stanford. Then he did a couple of tours in American hospitals located in high-violence areas. He'd seen it all, and then some.

"Let's go down and make some food and hot tea for the poor girl," Fiona said.

Walter coaxed everyone out and back down the stairs. They convened in the kitchen.

Jude paced back and forth in front of the bloodstain while Fiona and Walter washed the dirty plates from the party. "Did either of you see anything? I swept the entire ground floor," Jude said, his stomach knotted with frustration.

"Why don't you go see your mother out? She waited behind so she could speak with you," Walter nodded toward the atrium.

Jude got the message. He was being impossible. If anyone had any inkling of what had happened, they would have mentioned it. He huffed and made his way to the foyer. The doors of Beauloch were wide open to the torrential rain. A driver paced the front steps with a lit cigarette. The foul smoke wafted over Jude.

"Are you the driver for my mother?"

"No. I'm Mr. Rocoeurs' driver. Your brother, I think?"

"What about *Mrs.* Rocoeurs? Has she left? Do you know?"

"I saw her get into her vehicle a few minutes ago, I think." The driver pointed at the black Mercedes idling behind his.

Jude groaned with irritation and dashed out into the freezing rain and up to the back door of the car. He pulled on the handle, but it was locked, and a few loud raps on the glass yielded nothing. It was very much like his mother to play these types of games, especially if she felt she'd been spurned or wasn't getting her way, but he had no patience, not tonight.

Jude sprinted around to the driver's door and flung it open. Slumped over the wheel was the driver, dead from a gaping hole in his throat.

&

ELIZABETH WOKE UP, HER LEG HOT AND SORE. THE memories of Boris in the study came back to her, but they were fuzzy. Sitting next to the bed was Gran, a pair of knitting needles in her hand.

"Oh, you're finally awake." Millie put her work down and stood up to pour some hot tea into a mug.

"Gran? Why are you here? Where's Jude?" Elizabeth sat up. The Blue Room was dark and cold, with only a few candles for lighting.

"Walter came to my cave and told me what happened. I'm sad and angry that the laird allowed you to become a target like this. He's gone now."

Elizabeth took the warm cup of herbal tea and sipped

on it. She could taste the nettle mixed with the alcohol of whatever tincture Millie had added. She reached down to feel the wrapping on her leg.

"They stitched you up nicely, but I made a poultice." Millie sat back down and took up her knitting needles again.

"Where did Jude go? I thought I heard him talking to me."

"He left to go search for his mother. Whoever attacked you must've taken her to lure him back to The Order. I imagine it was you they were after, but since you escaped, they pivoted to the laird's own kin."

"Boris kidnapped Jude's mother? Where did they take her?"

"Don't know."

Elizabeth drank more tea. The rain continued to fall against the windows of her room. "How long was I asleep?" she said.

"All day. Jude's brother gave you a sedative to treat you for shock. I think it's almost dinnertime. Are you hungry?"

"I've been out that long? Gran, I need to help him. That man who attacked me is dangerous. If I hadn't stabbed him in the neck with that damn protractor..."

Millie stopped knitting. "You stabbed him? Good girl." She leaned forward to pat Elizabeth's hand.

"Gran, Jude is in danger."

"I know he is, darling. That man you stabbed murdered a driver last night. I imagine Jude may not make it back, but that will stop their interest in you."

"No, it won't! That man went on about my breeding and other weird things! He licked blood off my arm! He won't back down, even if Jude is dead." Elizabeth strained to pull herself out of the bed. She limped over to the doors of the bathroom and rang for help on the intercom. She looked back at Millie, whose face had turned downcast. "I'm sorry, Gran, but I cannot hide from them."

Annie came up through the passageways to help Elizabeth with a shower. Elizabeth gingerly stepped under the hot water, doing her best to wash off the sweat she'd accumulated during the last twenty-four hours.

"What of Jamie?" she said.

"He's napping in the library, waiting on word from Jude," Annie said with a delicate sadness in her voice.

"Take me to him."

Annie wasted no time preparing Elizabeth's things. She helped her into a pair of loose-fitting jeans and pulled a clean thermal over her head.

"You're not leaving, are you?" Millie said, getting to her feet.

"Not yet." Elizabeth gave her Gran a big hug. "I'll be right back."

"You better be. That leg needs rest." She kissed Elizabeth on the cheek with her soft, wrinkly lips. The sensation ignited old memories. The longing she'd had for her Gran all these years turned into anger. How could people be so evil? What did they really want from Jude? Or her? The vile sensation of Boris's tongue going up her arm gave her a pang of nausea. She swallowed it down. "Annie, take me to the library."

Annie took Elizabeth by the elbow and helped her down the grand staircase. All the glow from the evening before had gone, leaving Beauloch clouded by the evil that commanded it. Before they made it to the last step, a loud banging echoed through the heart of the castle. Elizabeth looked to Annie, whose face was frozen in fear.

"Annie, go get Jamie. Tell him to arm himself," Elizabeth said.

Annie darted off to find the younger Rocoeurs brother.

The noise had come from the front doors. The rapping continued, followed by a voice she couldn't quite make out. She thought it was the sound of a woman crying, but Elizabeth knew not to trust her senses. She'd heard too many stories about an evil spirit fooling someone into thinking they were a maiden in distress when it was really a monster trying to lure a victim to their death.

Jamie rushed past Elizabeth carrying a long rifle. He took aim at the door. "Annie, open it," he said.

Annie flung one of the doors open, revealing a woman soaked from head to toe. She cried out as she stepped into the castle and fell to her knees.

"Mother!" Jamie lowered his rifle and went to the poor creature writhing on the floor.

"Annie, shut and lock the door," Elizabeth said, not caring how demanding her tone was.

Jamie wrapped his arms around his mother. He tried to console her, but her words were broken up by her intense cries. "Ha-have him," she muttered.

Elizabeth noticed she wore the same dress as the evening before—a dark-grey cowl-neck dress—but now it was covered in mud, and her shoes were missing.

"They have him? They have Jude?" Jamie said. His mother nodded, her face twisted with the pain of losing a child.

"We should take you upstairs, my lady." Annie held out her hand to Irene.

Elizabeth wanted to help, but she'd never gotten the opportunity to speak with Jude's mother the previous night, before things went to shit. As far as Irene knew, Elizabeth was just the hired talent for the party.

Am I really anything more than that? she wondered.

"Come away," Millie whispered from the bottom of the staircase. They went back upstairs to the Blue Room. Elizabeth flopped down on the bed, her body tanking from the stress and fatigue of all that had happened in the last few days.

"Drink this. I'll go get you some food." Millie handed her another cup of tea and quietly shuffled from the room.

Elizabeth stood in front of the windows as she sipped her drink. The view of the loch was impeded by the dark storm clouds that continued to linger. The longer she stared, the more her mind attempted to comprehend the madness that had unfolded in her life. Jude had been part of that madness, and her heart couldn't deny she missed him. Had it all come to an end? She couldn't bear the thought of losing him so soon.

High up in the sky, the misty clouds roiled into the shape of a crone's face. A violent shiver crept up her back. Her head swam with dizziness.

"What are you doing? Get back in bed!" Millie demanded.

Elizabeth obeyed and tottered back to bed.

Millie set a tray of food on the nightstand—a simple sandwich with fruit and cheese on the side. "Eat up. We're leaving first thing in the morning, at dawn." She sat back down in her chair and picked up her knitting needles.

"What? Where are we going?"

"We need help from the gods, and there's only one place to find them."

"Where?"

Millie turned to the window and nodded her head in the direction of the loch. "Out there."

Chapter Fourteen

❧❦❧

Rain hammered across the windshield of the SUV. Boris kept a tight grip on the steering wheel as the young laird approached the vehicle. He'd been parked just beyond the front gates of Beauloch for nearly an hour, waiting for him.

The Rocoeurs bitch shrieked the moment he opened the passenger side door.

"Get in and we will let her go," Boris said.

The laird froze when he saw the pistol aimed at his mother's head. Two brothers from The Order had her subdued in the back. Jude got into the passenger seat and shut the door.

Boris sped away. He wove through the mountains for about ten minutes, then pulled off the road. He had to make sure they weren't too far from the castle when they tossed the Rocoeurs bitch out.

"Here," he said.

The brothers shoved her out of the SUV. She yelped as she landed on the hard ground.

Boris kept his eyes on the young laird to gauge his reaction. Jude didn't flinch.

No words were said as they drove. The rain had cleared, and Boris's home came into view from far down the road. The sight of his grand estate pleased him every time he saw it. It was his crowning achievement. Years of serving no one but himself had brought him all the good fortune in the world. He just had to keep it that way, and to do that, he had to rule the brotherhood with an iron fist.

Once inside, Boris sat down in a chair in the parlor, nursing the wound on his neck with fresh gauze. The feral hound sat across from him with his eyes shut. "Open your eyes, little pup. I want you to look upon the face of your master."

"This arrangement is over," Jude said.

Boris got to his feet and stood in front of the dog. Before the laird could react, he took hold of his neck. "Arrangement? You paid us in blood, and we allowed you to keep everything you have—your mother, your brother, your moldy castle, and what little money your father had. The brand on your shoulder and the oath you swore is eternally binding. No one leaves the brotherhood until they die." Boris squeezed harder with every word, forcing his hound to struggle for air.

He picked up the laird and lifted him onto his toes. Boris knew his strength was more than what Rocoeurs was expecting. His vitality grew every time he took in the young man's blood.

Boris threw him back down into one of the chairs and

sauntered over to the bar for a shot of whiskey. "You have a little something you've been hiding from us." He poured another shot, downed it, and turned around to face his guest.

"I like the beautiful English rose that has been holing up at Beauloch. In fact, I'm so partial to her that I think I'd like to see what sort of brats we might produce together."

Jude lifted his lip, snarling at Boris.

"Ah, you don't like the idea. You should have thought about that before you joined The Order."

"Well, maybe you should have thought about that before you killed her," Jude said.

Boris smirked. "I had to fight off the little bitch after she put that damn thing in my neck, but I don't think I dealt a deadly blow. You're bluffing."

"Am I? Go see for yourself. She was blue and had no pulse when I found her."

Boris drew in a deep breath. "That would be a shame. As you said, I'll go find her myself, once we are finished with you."

"Well, whatever you've got in store, let's get it over with. I'm tired of wasting my breath on you," Jude said.

Boris motioned at one of his men standing near the door. A set of hands grabbed Jude and pulled him out of the chair. Another set tied his arms behind his back. The brothers shoved him out the massive grey door of the manor at the back and down the path that led to the Harlock ruins.

It was Boris's full intention to beat the Rocoeurs dog into submission. His hands tingled with pleasure at the anticipation of what he was about to do. He stayed back as they took Jude deep into the dungeons, then called for Dr. Brenner. The doctor came to him at once.

"Prepare your instruments, Doctor. The Rocoeurs boy has defied me for the last time."

❧

JUDE'S HEART RATE INCREASED, KNOWING HE PROBABLY wasn't going to make it out of his situation alive. He hated the thought, not because he feared death, but because he wouldn't be able to protect the ones he loved if The Order snuffed him out. The sole purpose of joining the brotherhood had been to secure safety for his family.

The iron doors at the back entrance to the dungeon slammed shut behind him. Voices of the brothers talking echoed down the long corridor of the Harlock dungeons. Jude shuddered at the thought of dying in the place he hated most, and so shortly after he'd found someone whom he loved with his heart and soul. It was the one thing he hadn't contended with when he'd made plans to destroy The Order. At least, if he perished this night, she would have the opportunity to find someone she loved.

Love. He had told her he loved her, but only after he thought she was dead. What sort of monster was he? The kind that wanted, *needed* to be loved back, and he might never know if that was possible if his punishment ended in disaster.

Instead of being laid out on the granite table, the masked men led Jude to the alcove, where a set of shackles were attached to the wall. They wasted no time securing his arms above his head and locking both of his feet together with irons.

Boris entered the alcove with a large torch. He lit two more on the wall on either side of Jude, taunting him with the primitive devices that had been prepared for his punishment.

They don't want my blood tonight. They just want to torture me, he thought.

"You know, when your father tried to renege on his word, I wanted to bring him here. Other forces were at play then, and we never got the chance. It's a shame. Blood rites can be one of the most beautiful, most intimate things one can partake in," Boris said as he cut away Jude's clothes with a pair of surgical scissors.

"You seem quite strong, but..." Boris pulled the remaining pieces of sleeves and pants off Jude, exposing him to the elements of the damp dungeon. "That vitality is not yours to enjoy any longer. We are the ones who risk everything to better the world." Boris pointed the shiny silver scissors at the other men. He looked back at Jude. "I'm not sure you understand the pressure we are under, or just how taxing it is to maintain control of the world. It drains one to have to constantly make friends with billionaires, politicians, celebrities, scientists, or whoever else has money and power. The game we must play is a crass one. I mean, how tedious..." Boris sank the tip of the scissors into Jude's leg. Jude cried out at the sudden pain. "How tedious to have to be the keepers of the kingdom."

"Boris, you've done enough talking," a voice said from the shadows.

Boris ripped the scissors from Jude's thigh.

The pain echoed throughout Jude's entire body. He started panting, trying to save most of his energy for the inevitable pain to come. If he could survive this one night, he would be able to make it back home, back to Elizabeth.

"Go ahead and take what you want from him while I prepare my things." Boris left the alcove and walked to the table that normally held the sterile instruments used during the ritual.

One of the men stepped into the torchlight. Jude recognized him as Dr. Brenner, whom he'd met the night of his initiation. Dr. Brenner brought a tray of tools over to Jude and hooked up an IV catheter to remove some of his blood.

"This will go quickly," the doctor whispered, holding the bag out to inspect the blood pouring into it.

"What? No! You cannot do this, I'm a member of The Order now!"

The man looked up at him; his grey hair and round spectacles made him look like a normal fellow he'd meet on the street.

At the end of the day, these are just men, he thought.

Jude reminded himself of that fact as his crimson life filled the bag. It was quiet in the dungeon, which was eerie to him. Normally they all stood in a circle around him, chanting things in some dead language.

"I'm almost done." The doctor removed the needle from his arm.

"Good," Boris said. He sauntered into the alcove with a small iron rod in his hand. "Have you ever been to China, dog?"

"No, only to hell."

The brothers in the main chamber chuckled.

Boris rushed him and pushed the dull point of the iron into Jude's shoulder. Currents of pain coursed throughout his entire body. He fell from his feet, forcing the chains on his wrists to catch all his weight at once.

"There are points in our bodies that, when manipulated, can cause excruciating pain. The Chinese know about them because they understand our flow of qi." Boris wriggled the device deeper into Jude's shoulder, making him whimper.

Jude shut his eyes and clenched his teeth. Boris withdrew the rod and the pain subsided. A few deep huffs allowed Jude to catch his breath. He opened his eyes to Boris's yellow smile.

This monster enjoys seeing me squirm.

Boris slapped him hard across the face. "Focus, Jude. We've only just begun." Boris held up another device for him to see. It was a modern-looking needle, almost a foot long. "Don't worry. This is just the instrument to help us insert the barbs." A glistening chain dangled from the top of the needle with a shiny spike. "Charles, I'm going to need a hand with this."

Dr. Brenner appeared again from the shadows. He examined the device in Boris's hands. "Are you sure?" he whispered.

"You'll ply the skin while I do my work. Let us begin."

Jude shut his eyes, concluding then what his father must have learned all those years ago. No matter what he did, how much blood he sacrificed, Boris would never allow him to be free. Joining the brotherhood meant nothing.

These demons would use him, torture him, until there was nothing left of his body or soul.

§

The mist made it difficult to see. Elizabeth lay flat on the ground, her body pressed against the damp leaves of the forest floor. Millie lay beside her, her crooked index finger pointed at the stag that was only yards away.

Elizabeth waited for the creature to become aware of the danger he was in and dart off, but Millie had made them both practice their breathing all morning so as not to make a sound. She lowered her bony finger. The stag rubbed against an ancient yew tree and Millie signaled with her other hand for Elizabeth to raise her weapon.

Elizabeth slithered like an adder against the leaves. She propped herself up on one knee and raised the rifle. She drew in a long, steady breath and pulled the trigger. It went straight into the heart of the beast, causing him to fall to the ground.

When Elizabeth tried to stand up, Millie pulled her back down. "We don't want for his last visions of this world to be our faces. He deserves better than that."

The steam which rose from the stag's nose dwindled bit by bit, until there was no more.

"Death is so sad, so final," Elizabeth said.

Millie stood and wrapped an arm around her. "You gave him a clean, honorable death. The gods will be proud." She went up to the beautiful beast and started cutting the carcass. "Here, come help me collect a few things."

Elizabeth put her rifle aside and joined Millie, who had

peeled back the flesh of the stag to reveal the innards. "We need the adrenal glands for strength, the liver for vitality, and the heart and antlers to give thanks to the gods for supplying us with this medicine."

After they collected the desired parts from the body, they hauled the carcass up to the clearing with the flat boulder to make a pyre for the beast. It took both of them and a pulley method using branches and rope to hoist the stag onto the wide rock before they started the fire.

"What are we to do now?" Elizabeth said.

"We let the gods have their part, and we get to work on ours," Millie said.

Elizabeth followed her to the back of her cave, where daylight poured into a small section. There, an altar had been prepared for the antlers, and they submerged the heart in a glass jar with oil and herbs.

Elizabeth thought it actually looked very beautiful, with all the candles and dried flowers Millie had laid out.

"What god are we praying to?" Elizabeth said.

Millie laughed. "The old one."

Elizabeth started to get on her knees, but Millie stopped her. "No, child. This one wants you on your feet."

Elizabeth looked back up at the antlers that had been placed on the cave wall. In between them, white paint formed the face of the Cailleach. The sight of her put Elizabeth into a trance. Her mind drifted to how all the strange events of the last couple of months had brought her here, to this very spot in front of this altar.

"Come, we need to prepare for the laird's return." Millie coaxed her away from the altar and onto the cushion beside her low round table.

Ever since they'd gone into the woods, Gran had hardly brought up the subject of Jude. With every passing hour Elizabeth couldn't help but think he wasn't coming back.

Is Gran preparing me for the inevitable?

Tears welled up in her eyes.

"Oh, my dear, what is the matter?" Millie brought her pestle and mortar over to the table.

"Gran, I..." Elizabeth forced herself to wipe the dampness from her eyes so she could see. "When I was back at Beauloch, after I'd been attacked, Jude told me that he loved me. I thought it was a dream at first, but I remember it so clearly now." Hot tears dripped onto the cave floor then, and she put her head between her knees.

Millie crushed up some bloody piece of the stag they'd just killed while Elizabeth mourned. All the emotions she'd held back since she'd arrived in Scotland came to the surface. Once she finally caught her breath, Millie handed her a rag to dry her eyes.

"You know, it only hurts you so much because you feel the same way about him." Millie scraped the ruby paste into a big wooden bowl.

"What am I to do, Gran? The man I love is being held captive by an evil cult. Even if he survives, how will we ever be safe? Or have peace?"

Millie sprinkled some dried herbs into the bowl and whispered something in Gaelic. "If he survives, he may not be the same man as before. I've walked this earth for many years and have seen many things, and the evil that dwells in the Harlock dungeons is the foulest type. But take heart, my dear. Love is the strongest force in the world."

Elizabeth continued to gaze into the steady, burning

flames. "Love? What about all of this? What about this magic, this medicine? What about the gods?"

Millie smiled. "What do you think they are?"

A light drizzle swept through the crack in the ceiling and across the altar, causing the candles to dance in the wind. Elizabeth had never noticed how alive the wilderness made her feel. Maybe Gran was right about everything. Since she'd left Beauloch to go into hiding, she'd lost track of the days. The troubles of the modern world couldn't reach her so deep in the forest. Fear of men, of the brotherhood, of the unknown had dissipated on her first night in the cave, but the ache for Jude in her heart remained.

"How do I know if what I feel is true?" Elizabeth said.

Millie chuckled. "You'll never know how deep the water is until you plumb the depths of that well, and love is a vast and mysterious well."

JUDE GASPED FOR BREATH, BUT IT DIDN'T SATISFY HIS hunger for air. He tried to move, but there was no strength left in him. A darkness surrounded him like he'd never known before. When he finally saw a light, he became afraid. The blackness slowly turned into a white light, and all around him was a vast meadow. Not far off, a woman stood in the tall, golden grasses. She had long red hair flowing down to her waist, but her skin looked wrong.

The figure floated closer to Jude, and he saw that her skin was grey and lifeless, yet she appeared as alive and animated as he was. What did that mean? The woman drifted closer. She held out a hand blackened with rot. Her palm faced him, inviting him to press his against it.

As soon as he felt the cold hand of Death, Jude screamed.

The encounter forced him to jerk awake. He came to on a cold, damp floor.

Am I alive? Where am I?

Jude was so tired he could barely move a muscle. A single wall sconce illuminated the stone chamber he lay in. The flutter of a crimson red cloak brushed past the doorway to the alcove. Voices of men arguing in the distance echoed into the round room, but Jude couldn't make out what they were saying.

A set of hands peeled him up off the wet stone. They dragged him outside and into a vehicle. He dozed off and on, never knowing how much time had passed. When the vehicle stopped, he was kicked out the door and landed in a muddy spot on a road.

Jude wasn't sure if the daylight he saw was real or not. It was too difficult for him to keep his eyes open for more than a second. A flash of grey clouds covered him, and a shallow puddle held him close to the earth.

Elizabeth bent over to inspect a patch of wild rosehips growing alongside the creek. The forest had become like an old friend, a place she once knew as a child, and reconnected with later in life. Millie had brought her outside every single day, despite her injury, and taught her where to look for food and how to hunt, as well as show her some of the sacred things they could do to honor the spirits of the forest.

"Gran?" Elizabeth said.

"Yes?" Millie picked through the wet leaves on the ground.

"When I tried to escape Beauloch that first night, I was bitten by something. I'd fallen into a hole and this giant serpent slithered over me. The green eyes of this creature didn't seem real, but I can still recall the way her cold scales felt against my leg, so it *must* have been. It struck me hard on the shoulder, but when I woke up the next morning, there were no marks."

Millie laughed. "You're not the only Ross to have visions of the goddess."

"You've had them too?"

"For a time, when I was about your age. The serpents came in my dreams, preparing me for motherhood. They were often green, and nestled among wildflowers in a field in summer. Other times they bit me to awaken me to danger, like the time your father had gotten out of his crib."

Elizabeth imagined Millie in her twenties, and her father as a mere babe. Something about that image soothed her anxiety about the disturbing encounter she'd had.

Her thoughts were broken up by the static coming from Millie's utility belt. The walkie-talkie that she kept close came to life. Walter's voice echoed through the trees. Millie brought the device close to her ear. Elizabeth couldn't make out the gamekeeper's words, but his tone was dour.

"They found him. Get ready to leave." Gran pointed in the direction of the cave.

"Is he alive?" Elizabeth remained with her feet planted, frozen stiff with fear.

"For now. Come on, let's hurry."

Elizabeth and Millie rushed back to the cave and grabbed all the food and medicines they had prepared for the laird's possible return.

"Walter is picking us up on the path." Millie guided them out of the trees and into the clearing where the old trail was. Walter met them at the road on the edge of the forest. He opened the door to his Land Rover and cranked the old truck into gear.

The roar of the engine was the only sound on their way back to Beauloch. Elizabeth's knees were quivering by the time they hopped out and rushed inside the castle.

"He's upstairs." Walter led them up the grand staircase and steered them down the wing toward the bedrooms and the dreaded study where all of their troubles began. Many times, Elizabeth wondered whether if she hadn't come down this way, maybe Boris wouldn't have had the opportunity to assail her. She'd voiced her guilt one night over a fire, but Gran had dispelled her worries. Boris set out to do harm that night, and he would've found a victim no matter what she did.

An anguished cry echoed throughout the castle. They all stopped in their tracks. It was clear where it had come from—Jude's old bedroom. They stood a few feet outside the closed door.

"He's alive then." Elizabeth breathed a sigh of relief.

"Maybe you should stay back for a bit." Walter placed

his hand on her shoulder. The soft wrinkles around his eyes and mouth strained with concern.

"Why?"

"I'll go first. The medicine we made will force his body into recovery. It's what he needs right now." Millie planted a kiss on her granddaughter's cheek and opened the door to the laird's old bedroom.

As she tried to peer in, all she could see was blackness.

JUDE HAD NO SENSE OF TIME WHEN HE CAME TO. HE WAS back home, that much he knew, but the room was dark save for the flames burning low in the hearth.

"How do you feel?" a man's voice said.

Jude flinched at the sound. He turned his head to see his brother Jamie sitting beside the bed, checking an IV drip attached to his right arm.

"I met Death, and she was pleasant." Jude tried to pull the covers up, but a searing pain prevented him from getting a grasp on them. The slightest movements put him in agony. It took a moment to catch his breath. "Tell me, brother. Will I live?"

"That is up to you. The pain you're feeling is from the metal they left underneath your skin. I'll remove them once you gain some strength back." Jamie placed a small trash bin on Jude's lap.

Despite the pain it caused him, Jude's muscles contracted, and he retched into the bin. Nothing came up but some foul liquid.

"Your friend here is going to give you something for the

pain." Jamie took the bin away and pointed to the witch standing in the corner of the room. She had prepared a cup of tea on his old writing desk. He had to blink a few times to make sure he wasn't hallucinating.

Memories of his time with her in the forest brought him a sense of peace. If she could work her magic like that once, maybe she could do it again.

Millie regarded him with wary eyes when she approached his bedside. "This will help you get your strength back, but it will also make you sleep," she said, holding out the warm cup. He took it gently with both hands.

"Where is she? Where's Elizabeth?" Jude implored.

"She's down the hall. She'll see you once you're a little better."Jude reached out to grab the woman's arm. He winced in agony, the metal barbs left under his skin by his tormentors doing their job. "Bring her to me. Please."

The witch nodded and returned to the table to prepare more tonics. "You'll get your appetite back once you sleep," she said.

The sound of the fire crackling and the witch's bottles tinkling put Jude at ease.

I am home, and Elizabeth is safe.

He had survived, but he wasn't the same man as before. Trying to sort through his emotions only fatigued him, and whatever potion he had drunk put him into the deepest sleep of his life.

Chapter Fifteen

A tormented scream rattled all the windows on the second floor. Elizabeth startled at the horrific sound and dropped her tea. The cup shattered on the parquet floor, creating a hazard in the dark room. She'd stayed awake late into the night, pacing the Blue Room, waiting for Jude to come around.

Gran had stopped by once to check in on her, but she didn't know where the elusive woman had disappeared to. Before anyone tried to stop her this time, she hopped over the broken ceramic and snatched a candle from the serving tray Annie had brought earlier. She lit it with a match and darted into the hall.

Her bare feet shuffled across the coarse wool carpet. Another roar and a crash of furniture made her pause.

Something is wrong.

Elizabeth ran down the long corridor and threw the door open to the laird's bedroom.

Jamie had a scalpel in his right hand, holding off an imminent attack from Jude.

"They could kill you if I don't remove them!" Jamie said.

"No one lays a hand on me! No one!" Jude roared back.

"Fine. Have it your way." Jamie threw the surgical blade in his black bag and stepped in front of Elizabeth. He leaned in to whisper to her. "Maybe you'll have better luck. He needs the barbs removed as soon as possible before infection sets in." He left, slamming the door behind him.

"Jude?" Elizabeth said.

Jude sat on the edge of the bed, both feet flat on the ground. His head was in his hands, and his fingers clutched at his long dark hair. He didn't look up or acknowledge her.

Elizabeth stood in front of him, waiting for him to say something, anything. Without warning, he reached out and grabbed her by the waist but kept his head down. "Will you help me?" he said, his voice quiet. Something dripped onto the top of Elizabeth's foot.

Is he crying?

Elizabeth pulled her foot back. Little drops of blood had splattered onto her toes.

"What did they do to you?"

Jude finally raised his head to reveal a blackened eye and multiple cuts across the right side of his cheek and jaw. He pulled her in close and kissed her with so much force, she felt like she couldn't breathe. Sharp objects poked against her breasts and shoulders, but being back in his arms was like being consumed by fire. It overtook everything, and she melted against him.

His tongue gently prodded at her mouth. She relinquished the fortitude she'd built up during her time alone. Elizabeth let him in, allowing her senses to ignite as he tasted her. Despite his battered condition, his lips were still soft, like velvet. He threaded his hand through her hair and drew her head back, giving him better access to her mouth. Jude let out a soft moan. Elizabeth had never been handled in such a way, and the pleasure she found in it startled her.

He pulled away and frowned. Elizabeth noticed her ivory blouse was covered in blood. She stepped back. "Jude, you're—"

"Bleeding, I know. It's these damned barbs." He winced and prodded at the protrusions on his chest.

"You won't let Jamie take them out?" she said.

"It's just ... I can't stand to have anyone's hands on me right now." He sat back down on the bed.

"Not even mine?"

Jude looked up at her with a primal hunger in his eyes. In that moment, Elizabeth knew he had meant the words he'd uttered in her ear after Boris had stabbed her—he *loved* her.

"Your touch is the only one I want. It's the only one I'll ever want." He slid his hand down the back of her leg to where her injury was. "How are you?"

"I'm fine. Gran worked her magic on me."

"She was here earlier, wasn't she?" He glanced over at the herbs and tonics sitting on his old writing desk.

"Yes, she was. She said you need rest."

"It's hard to sleep knowing they're still out there." He stroked the small of her back.

"Don't think about that. Focus on right here right now. You need those barbs removed."

Jude pinned his gaze on her, and in his eyes she recognized a desperate plea to be loved. Elizabeth wanted nothing more than to give that to him. She gently nudged him back onto the bed and climbed on top to straddle him. If she hadn't put on her thick denim jeans this morning, which created a barrier between them, she wasn't sure she'd be able to focus as well as she was. She studied the four puncture wounds on both of his arms, the four on his chest, and the two down his torso. A thin silver chain protruded out of each one.

"I'm going to use these. Is that okay?" Elizabeth picked up the forceps Jamie had left behind on the surgical tray.

Jude nodded and braced himself by squeezing the tops of her thighs. "Just do it."

Elizabeth placed one hand on his arm. She pinched the silver chain hanging out of his right shoulder with the forceps and pulled. The metal barb tugged underneath his skin, creating ripples. Jude grunted and squeezed her legs even harder.

"I'm sorry. I'm sorry." Elizabeth's voice cracked. She tried to be quick. Her stomach churned at the sight of what she was doing to him, but it had to be done. She did it because she cared for him so much.

That was her only thought when the chain finally slipped out of his skin. How deep did her feelings go? Was it really love? Her heart skipped a beat. Elizabeth wondered if true love could be shared between a man and a woman. She'd given her heart to someone before. What might Gran say to help her through this?

You'll never know how deep the water is until you plumb the depths of that well, and love is a vast and mysterious well.

Seeing Jude in such horrific pain brought tears to her eyes. Elizabeth swallowed down the knot that had formed in her throat.

"Don't cry." Jude sat up to be at eye level with her.

"What did they do to you, Jude?" She dabbed his puncture wounds with fresh gauze.

"They made me realize what I care about in life. That's all." He wiped a tear from her cheek.

"Please, let me finish removing these," Elizabeth said.

Jude laid back down and gritted his teeth. Elizabeth's stomach clenched when she examined the chains protruding from his chest.

You can't stop now, she thought.

The moment she tugged on the next one, Jude clamped down on her legs. When the prickly barb was about halfway out, a deep growl escaped his lips. Blood ran from the opening, but Elizabeth didn't have time to address it. She knew that if she stopped, he might not let her finish.

The other barb in his chest was even more difficult. It tugged against his skin, remaining stuck as she pulled. This prompted an even louder yell from him. Elizabeth's ears hurt from how loud his cries were, but she continued. Her stomach lurched when the chain finally released from under his skin. He shot up and clutched at her sides.

"We have to finish," she said, pushing him back down onto the bed.

Jude panted so hard it was difficult for her to get a hold of the chains embedded in his ribs. The moment she clasped onto one, Jude shuddered. Elizabeth had to focus on his breathing as she tugged at the torture device that was doing its job perfectly.

Nausea threatened to stop her from completing the task, but she willed herself to finish. Jude moaned in agony as the barbs tore at the soft flesh beneath his skin. Elizabeth's heart was pounding by the time she reached the last barb. By then, her hands were covered in blood.

Jude screamed the loudest as she freed him of the last chain. As soon as she was done, he sat up and wrapped both arms around her. She held him close as his breathing went from labored to steady.

JUDE STEPPED OUT OF HIS COPPER TUB AND WRAPPED A towel around his waist. The draft in the ballroom forced him to seek heat by the hearth. There was a knock at the door.

"Come in," he said.

The old woman who had worked her spells on him shuffled into the room. Jude secured his towel to make sure he was decent.

She took a seat on the tattered sofa beside him. "You have an extra moon until they summon you again." She withdrew an apple from a deep pocket in her skirt and sliced it with a small paring knife.

"I know what I must do. They will not find me so ill prepared the next time we meet." He crossed his arms with determination.

The witch pulled a glass vial from another pocket and

held it up to the firelight. Jude took it from her hand. It contained a thick, black liquid.

"What is this?" Jude said.

"It is a meeting with Death. As to whose death, well, that's yet to be seen," she said, keeping a stoic gaze on the fire in the hearth.

"I don't understand. What does it do?"

"Once you drink this, you will be close to Death. Your blood will be consumed by the shadows of her realm. If one was to partake in the drinking of said blood…"

Jude couldn't imagine it to be so easy. Just a bit of this liquid would turn his blood into poison? How?

"What happens if I take the whole thing?"

"The whole bottle means you get to meet Death. It is up to her if she wants to keep you or not. I wouldn't advise it."

"Duly noted." Jude placed the bottle on the table beside the sofa. He remembered how cold and lifeless the hands of the ancient Cailleach of his dreams had been. He'd never believed in anything apart from what he knew in this world, but after his encounter with her, his mind had been changed forever.

"I still have that bog myrtle, but something tells me you don't need it," Jude said.

"No, but *you* may. Take it to this place." Millie pulled out a weathered map from inside her cloak. Red ink circled a blank spot in the forest near Harlock. "Leave it as an offering."

Jude studied the map. "I will."

"Your mother is still here. She wishes to see you," Millie said.

Jude went to his dresser. He got dressed behind the witch's back and sat down next to her.

"What do I tell her? How do I begin to explain everything that has happened?"

The old woman let out a long sigh and stood up. "I'd start with the truth." She patted him on the back and went to the door. "If you do happen to see Death again, tell her I said hello." She left.

Jude wondered what she'd meant by those words. He went into the library, where Jamie and his mother sat beside the fire looking at old photo albums. They both froze when they noticed him.

"You're a sight." Jamie beamed a smile up at him.

His mother flattened her lips and her spine went rigid.

"I came here to apologize to the both of you." Jude took a seat across from them. The low light concealed some of the injuries he'd received at the hands of The Order. His face showed obvious trauma, but his body, chest, and arms were covered by the thick sweater he wore.

"I knew those men. They were friends of your father's," Irene said.

"If those were friends of Father's, then he was not the man I'd hoped he was. For so many years, I thought he'd infiltrated some secret network of cultists, but after searching Beauloch up and down for evidence of that, I've come to the hard realization he may have been one of them."

Jamie perked up. "I always thought the same thing. When I found those letters in his drawers to some man named Arthur, I knew he was up to something."

"What letters?" Jude said.

"That old stack of letters in his study. What? You haven't read them?"

"Wait!" Irene held up her hands. "What are you two on about?"

Jude knelt in front of his mother. "When father was still alive, he joined a fraternity that dealt in blood magic. How deeply he involved himself in their affairs I couldn't say, but after he died, they approached me. They demanded a blood payment from our family. I had to join their ranks, otherwise they would've taken Jamie. They gave me no other choice but to capitulate."

Irene broke out in tears. Jamie wrapped his arm around her.

"My God Jude, how long have you been doing this?" he said.

"Maybe eight years now. Please understand, I only did it to protect the both of you."

Irene shook Jamie's arm off her shoulder. "Protect us? Look at what's happened! I was kidnapped from my own home! What on earth are we going to do now? We're lucky they haven't come and killed us all!"

Jamie tried to soothe his mother as she lost her wits. Jude got to his feet.

"I'm going to take care of The Order, but I need you both to go into hiding. That way, nothing like what took place at the party can happen again."

Jamie stared at his brother in shock, the reality of the situation no doubt setting in.

"That will be no problem. It will be a cold day in hell before either of you see me again!" Irene shouted. She lunged up from the sofa and stormed out of the library.

Jamie put his palms together, as if in prayer. He bounced his fingers against his lips. "Do you need anything from me?" he said.

Jude drew in a deep breath. "Take her and go far away from here. I'll send word when it's safe to return."

Jamie got up and pulled Jude into a hug. Then he turned to leave.

ELIZABETH STEPPED UNDER THE SPRAY OF SCALDING HOT water. Images of Jude writhing beneath her as she removed the metal bits from his skin flashed in her head. She'd fallen asleep beside him covered in his blood, and when she awoke, he'd vanished.

Maybe he wants to be alone after the ordeal.

A bar of Gran's soap sat in the holder in the shower. Elizabeth picked it up and brought it to her nose. She needed the clarifying aroma after breathing in the scent of blood, sweat, and bile the night before. The pleasant smells of rose and bergamot ignited another memory of Jude.

On the other side of the glass partition, the mermaid tub sat empty. As she slid her hand over her breasts and thighs, she remembered the way his hands had felt against her wet skin. It forced a smile onto her lips.

"What are you smiling about?" a voice said from across the room.

Elizabeth dropped the soap. Through the steamed glass, a short black-clad figure stood just inside the bathroom door.

"Gods, Gran, you scared me!" Elizabeth said.

Millie opened the shower door and handed her a rag. "Get that blood off your hands. It's bad luck."

Despite Elizabeth's efforts, her hands and arms still had dried blood on them. Her stomach roiled after being pulled from such a nice memory back to a hideous one. She forced a swallow down her tight throat. "I was just thinking about how mad things have been since I left London. It's almost funny." She scrubbed her skin with the rag.

"Funny? You have a strange sense of humor. You get that from your mother's side of the family." Millie pressed her back against the glass to give Elizabeth some privacy. "Listen..." She lowered her voice to a whisper. "Your maid is out there so we have to be quiet." She turned her head to the door, her face twisted with suspicion. "I think there's someone in the castle who is working for The Order. I'm not sure who it is, so you need to be careful."

Elizabeth twisted the handle to turn the water off. "What makes you think that?"

Millie chuckled. "Just call it an old woman's hunch."

Elizabeth stepped out of the shower and wrapped a towel around herself. She peered into the Blue Room and saw Annie lying on the chaise lounge. "I'll be more careful."

"It's not safe for me to stay. If they find out I'm alive and have been helping you, there's no telling what they might do." Millie bent down and kissed the top of Elizabeth's head. "If you need me, you know where I am." She crept out of the bathroom and disappeared.

Elizabeth quietly stepped into the Blue Room and got dressed. The maid snored lightly, never moving once as she milled around. Elizabeth often had misgivings about

Annie, but betraying Jude and working for The Order? Was the young woman capable of such a thing? Elizabeth needed more answers. She needed to find Jude.

She went down the grand staircase and past the atrium. She meandered through the castle, searching for Jude. After trying the ballroom and the kitchen, she went to the library. She quieted her footsteps as she drew near. Behind the closed door, voices echoed off the high bookshelves.

Elizabeth sensed the similarity in their deep tones; a common occurrence when listening to families speak with each other. What were they discussing? Elizabeth pressed her ear against the door.

Jude is sending his family away.

Footsteps approached the door and she dashed to hide in the shadows, but it was too late. Irene spotted her.

Elizabeth readied herself for anything. She stood under a large oil painting of an old white man, a Rocoeurs ancestor, as Irene approached. He looked down on them both, his faded blue gaze locked on the scene below him.

"You're making a mistake by being here." Irene's wild silver hair framed her angry, brown eyes. She inched closer to Elizabeth. "If you don't leave now, you're going to end up a prisoner of this place. Get out while you can. Trust me."

"I'm not a prisoner."

"You're pretty." Irene cocked her head to one side. She reached out and touched Elizabeth's lips with the back of her hand, her soft knuckles grazing over them in admiration. "He's going to destroy you, just like his father did to me." She pressed her sharp nails into Elizabeth's collarbone, driving her words home.

Elizabeth ripped the cold hand away and retreated into the tunnels near the back doors. Tears threatened to fill her eyes. She hid in the darkness of the corridor beneath the dining hall, trying to gather her thoughts. Was Irene right? She'd been held captive at Beauloch for months, and things had only gotten worse. Irene's warning was rife with fear and indignation. What kinds of things did Elizabeth not know about the laird?

Through the grates, she spotted her lonely instrument still resting in the long dining hall. She hadn't played her harp since the night of the party. Elizabeth took a deep breath and emerged from her hiding spot. She entered the dining room and stood at her harp, plucking one string at a time. The vibrations eased her mind some. If all else failed, she still had her music.

The doors to the kitchens swung open. Elizabeth tensed, until Walter appeared. He came and stood beside her.

"Want me to move it?" he said.

"I think it's best if we put it back in the library and wrap it up. There will be no more concerts, and I'm leaving Beauloch," Elizabeth said.

"When will you be leaving?"

"Soon, I think."

Walter went to fetch the dolly, loaded the harp up, and wheeled it out of the room.

Elizabeth looked out toward the shroud of mist hanging over the pines. Irene's words echoed in the back of her mind.

Get out while you can.

Chapter Sixteen

***

The door opened to the library. Walter wheeled Elizabeth's harp into the room and placed it next to the fireplace. He turned to Jude and gave him a dour look. "You're letting her leave?"

Jude got to his feet. "Who? Elizabeth?"

Walter nodded.

"No. She can't go now. Who told you she was leaving?"

Walter shrugged. "She said she was leaving soon. Thought you knew."

Jude headed for the door, angry and confused. Elizabeth knew she couldn't leave Beauloch while The Order had her in their sights. He needed to explain that he'd told them she was dead. If she left now, they would know he'd lied, and she'd be in serious danger.

He headed for the stairs, wanting to take long strides, but the pain after the removal of the barbs and the other tortures he'd endured in the dungeon forced him to slow down. When he reached the top, he glanced in the opposite direction from the Blue Room. The door of his father's study had been left open. A soft, flickering light came from that direction.

Taking out his pistol, Jude readied himself. He stalked down the hallway and peered into the room only to find Jamie poring over a set of old letters scattered across the desk. Jude put the gun away and entered.

"I've found them. They were still here, in the secret compartment." Jamie held up one of the letters.

"You think they prove father was innocent?"

Jude was skeptical. He'd gone through every document he could find after his father had died, trying to find some meaning behind his sudden death, and never turned up anything.

"They used code names. Arthur must have been our father because his signature matches Father's. Here, read this one first. It's addressed to him," Jamie said, handing him a letter from the pile.

DEAR ARTHUR,

I BELIEVE YOU ARE RIGHT TO SUSPECT THAT THE KNIGHTS *surrounding your table are riddled with corruption. I've gone over your account of the events at Harlock with someone familiar with what you described. In conclusion, there is no science behind the rituals you took part in. Eternal youth cannot be maintained.*

Have you considered this may not be their goal when taking part in this act? We cannot overlook the psychological impact of this ceremony. The constant letting of one's blood may prove a useful tool to suppress someone you wish to keep under control.

W*RITE BACK SOON.*

G*AWAIN*

"W*HO* *IS* G*AWAIN*? H*E* *DOESN'T* *BELIEVE* *DRINKING* blood made Boris powerful," Jude said.

"I've no idea who he could be. Here is the next one. Father wrote it." Jamie held out another letter.

G*AWAIN*,

I *POLITELY* *DISAGREE* *WITH* *YOUR* *ASSESSMENT* *OF* *THESE* *rituals. I've given myself up to the knights to secure a better spot at the round table, and in doing so, have witnessed firsthand the power in my blood. These frail men are imbued with strength after consuming part of me. It is shameful to allow myself to be used by such vile animals, but offering my blood was the only way to discover their secrets. How else was I to understand how they rose to power, and how they have stayed that hold for the last two hundred years? I must report back to the Merlin.*

A*RTHUR*

. . .

Jude put the letter down. A deep relief washed over him. His father never wanted to trade his soul for power. The coded correspondence suggested he'd been sent on a mission by someone else to uncover the truth about The Order.

"I haven't figured out who Gawain or Merlin is, but it's all here," Jamie said.

"Do you remember that black portfolio father used to carry around? I stayed up late with him some nights in the library and saw him remove papers from it and throw them into the fire." Jude flipped through the letters in his hand. How had he not noticed his dad had secreted something in the desk?

Jamie crossed his arms, his brow furrowed. "I don't remember a portfolio, but if it's true, father must've thought these were important enough to keep."

"Maybe he wanted to keep them in case something happened to him. He wanted us to know the truth." Jude laid the letters back down on the desk.

Jamie ran a hand through his ashy-blond hair. Jude always thought his brother took after their mother. Their temperament and disposition leaned on the gentler side, until they were provoked. Then their wrath could outmatch even his own.

Jamie paced the room, growling in frustration. "We cannot go to the authorities," he said.

Jude plopped down in the desk chair and watched his brother desperately search for a solution. He'd tormented himself in the same way all those years ago when The

Order first approached him with their demands. There was no easy way out of this.

One of his new wounds caused a pang to course through his body. He grabbed at the sore spot on his chest. "Don't worry, Jamie. I'm going to take care of these monsters once and for all," Jude said, still wincing in pain.

Jamie gave him a look of concern, then went over to the glass door and pulled it open. Jude got to his feet and followed him onto the balcony. They both leaned on the railing, gazing out at the silver moon reflected in the ripples of the loch.

"We were never allowed on the balcony when we were little," Jude said.

"That was because you tried to climb onto the railing when you were five," Jamie said.

They both laughed.

"I mean what I said. I'm going to finish what he started," Jude said.

"I know you will. Just try to come back to us alive."

"I'll do my best."

The sound of footsteps on the gravel drive traveled up to where they stood. Jude pulled Jamie back into the shadows and watched the figure move in the darkness to the edge of the trees. It hesitated for a moment, then vanished into the forest.

"Who was that?" Jamie said.

"I don't..." Jude dashed back into the castle.

THE DOOR OF THE BLUE ROOM SWUNG BACK HARD ON its hinges and slammed against the wall. Elizabeth froze. She'd been folding a sweater to pack into her suitcase.

"Jude?"

"Elizabeth, I'm sorry." He rushed to her and surveyed the clothing on the bed and in the luggage. "Walter said you planned on leaving, and I thought I saw you go into the woods just a moment ago."

Elizabeth sighed, placing her favorite cable knit sweater into her case. "That was Gran. She said it's not safe for her to stay here, and frankly, I've been wondering the same thing." She finished tucking her top into the side of the luggage that had been tightly packed and faced him. "I didn't mean to, but I heard your conversation earlier. You're sending your family away, but you are still intent on keeping me here even though I'm in danger."

Jude stepped forward and used both hands to caress her neck underneath her ears. "You're safe here with me. I promise. I'll never let anyone hurt you. Do you understand me?"

Elizabeth removed his hands. "You say that, but you don't know what's going to happen. Nobody knows what the outcome of all this may be, and I have a target on my back now. Why should I stay here?"

Jude glowered at her, visibly hurt by her rejection. "I told them you were dead. If you leave now, they may find you, and I won't be able to protect you."

"You didn't protect me when Boris licked the blood off my arm down the hall!" Elizabeth shouted. The memory of it made her tremble.

Jude gently squeezed her shoulders. "He did that?"

Hot tears trickled down her cheeks. She angrily wiped them away and nodded.

Jude's downcast eyes reflected the light from the fireplace. Elizabeth could see the fury building behind his deep, honeyed gaze. "You're right. I wasn't there to protect you." He brought his hand to his chest, fighting a grimace.

A knot formed in Elizabeth's throat. "So you'll let me go?"

Jude turned away to avoid looking at her. "Of course you may leave." A low grunt left his chest, and he walked out, closing the door behind him.

Elizabeth took a step forward, then hesitated. Her mind raced with every thought imaginable. Fear, sadness, hope, and even love wriggled its way deep into the recesses of her psyche. A tight knot formed in her chest.

True love couldn't be so unbearably painful as this.

Before she changed her mind, Elizabeth packed her suitcase. She didn't know where she would go, but she didn't care. Beauloch had become a prison and Jude her captor. Even though he had her heart in his clutches, she needed to escape to avoid what he might do if she stayed within reach. She needed to get as far away from this place as she could.

The castle was deathly quiet as she hauled her luggage down the stairs. No one met her in the foyer. Elizabeth pulled out her cell phone, but it didn't have service.

My phone is almost dead anyway.

She would have to wait until tomorrow to get a cab that could take her to the train station. Her best option was to go back to Millie's cottage for the night.

I'll have to call my parents in the morning.

Elizabeth's mother would berate her for leaving her ex-husband, and her father would guilt her for taking their money. It would only be a temporary situation, though. She could find another moldy apartment and start all over.

She yanked the iron handle on one of the giant oak doors. It groaned, announcing her departure. The night sky glistened with twinkling stars and the moon beamed down so brightly it cast a heavy shadow on the pebbles beneath her feet.

Elizabeth slipped between a pair of thick firs on the edge of the woods. With ample visibility, she strode down the footpath with confidence. The way that led to the village was still steep in certain places, but she maneuvered the pitfalls well. Before she reached the clearing with felled trees, she stopped to catch her breath. She threw her case down on the ground and sat on the hard edge. The brief pause in her escape left her questioning her decision to leave.

Should I not have heeded Irene's warning?

The snap of a twig caught her attention. She shined the light of her phone in every direction but saw nothing. Before she let herself become overwhelmed with fright, she got up and continued to haul her case down the path.

She'd only taken a few steps before the sound of an animal closing in on her forced her to release the handle. The moment she turned, the wild beast had her in its clutches. She cried out in fear, but the palm of a hand closed over her mouth and muffled her screams.

"Be quiet," Jude said.

Elizabeth squirmed to break free, but his hold on her was too tight. He pressed them both up against a pine tree.

She tried to speak, but he tightened his grip on her face. "Someone is waiting for you on the other side of the hill," he whispered.

They stayed in that position for a few minutes, without saying a word, until Jude pulled out his phone. He sent a message, then put it back in his pocket. Not long after that, a car approached, and they peered through the trees. They couldn't see the vehicle, but the headlights shined through the forest, moving slowly, as if the driver was looking for something. The lights passed them by and continued on.

Jude released her from his grasp. He checked his phone again. "We're all clear."

Elizabeth gasped for air. "What the fuck is going on? Did you follow me?"

"I did follow you. I made a promise to never let anything happen to you, and I'm keeping that promise," he said, his intent clear.

Jude snatched her back up and kissed her, but she pushed him away and bent over to retrieve her case.

"Why are you angry with me?"

"I want to be alone," she said. Elizabeth lumbered forward and stopped a few feet into the clearing. The lack of tree cover made her feel more exposed, but going back wasn't an option. Jude grabbed her case by the handle.

"Tell me. What have I done to make you angry?" he demanded.

Instead of responding, Elizabeth pulled hard against his grip. Her hand slipped from the handle and she fell on her ass into a pile of wet leaves. "Fuck!" she said, clutching the tender spot on her leg where she'd been injured. Jude quickly got down on his knees.

"Are you hurt?" he said.

"No. I'm fine." She tried to get up, but Jude pinned her arms against the foliage, forcing her back down. He straddled her with his massive legs.

"Good. Now tell me what I've done to make you leave," he said.

Elizabeth tried to wrench herself free but couldn't gain a single inch against his hold on her. Jude was easily twice her size, and even with his wounds, was stronger than she could ever hope to be. She drew in a deep breath. "Please," she begged, but his grip didn't weaken, and his gaze remained on her, shadowed only by the dappled moonlight dancing on the ground around them. "I'm just scared," she admitted. It wasn't the full truth.

"You're in more danger if you go back to the cottage. You know that. What else is there?"

"I'm scared of *you*, Jude."

That earned her release, even though she hated the feeling when he let go of her. He offered her a hand up and she took it.

"I think you should come back until we can clear the area in the morning. Then I'll have Walter take you to the train station. Where you go from there, it's probably best I don't know," he said, and picked up her case.

She followed him on the path in silence until they were back at the doors of Beauloch. Walter waited for them both in the foyer.

"I've called the boys out to help me do perimeter

checks. We'll sweep it again at dawn, and I've alerted Millie. She's the eyes of the forest."

Jude gave him a nod. Elizabeth walked with Jude back to the Blue Room. He left her case beside the bed without saying a word.

Once he was gone, Elizabeth felt too defeated to do anything else but sit down on the edge of the bed and cry.

JUDE PACED THE ROOM. HE'D ALREADY KNOCKED OVER two piles of books and thrown an old ashtray at the wall, leaving a dent in the wood panel. His arms shook with rage, but he knew deep down that his anger was just a mask for his true feelings. Elizabeth couldn't stand to even look at him. The pain she'd had in her eyes when she told him she wanted to be alone revealed her true feelings.

I'm just a hideous monster to her.

The ballroom was stifling. Jude ripped his shirt off, and the gauze covering his wounds along with it.

"Annie!" he shouted. Outside, another storm had fired up. The north winds blew against the castle, creating a whistling noise. Jude couldn't stand to hear it. He walked over to the radio and turned the local station on. The instant he heard the music, he froze.

The beautiful sound of a Celtic harp filled the room. Jude collapsed on the floor in defeat. He sat with his arms flung over his knees, his head down. Someone opened the door.

"You called for me?" Annie said, her timid voice echoing off the high ceilings.

"Has my mother left?"

Annie took a step into the room. Jude raised his head to see her cowering in the corner.

"They're packing their things now."

"Make sure they don't leave without Walter escorting them. He's out right now, but it's imperative they wait for his return. There's been some activity on the road near the village."

Annie waited for a moment. "Is that all?"

"Have you brought my tonics down from my bedroom?"

"I put everything on the table over there," Annie gestured at the end table by the fireplace.

"Good. I'll take my bath, whenever you get time."

"Of course. I'll bring the hot water."

As soon as she was gone, Jude sauntered over to the table and opened the small leatherbound book he'd seen the witch jot things down in during his time in the forest. He searched for the notes she made about his sleeping tonic. Jude needed something strong to help him forget about Elizabeth but he struggled to read her scrawny handwriting.

Annie and Fiona came back with the cart full of pots of hot water. The two women poured the steaming water into the tub, just like they always did. It was a scene too familiar to Jude, and he almost couldn't stand it. Too much had happened since that first night he was bathing in the tub and heard the most beautiful sound he could imagine.

The harp music on the radio came through a little crackly because of the high winds. Jude felt like that old hag, the harbinger of death, was taunting him.

"There. It's ready," Fiona said as she finished off the bath with some herbs.

Jude undressed and sank his tired body into the water. He tried to distract himself with the witch's spells but tossed the tome aside, unable to focus on anything except Elizabeth. Every waking moment he couldn't help but think of her. Even the recent discovery of his father's letters was eclipsed by the thoughts of her beauty, her music, and especially the way her lips felt against his, how her body felt so soft and supple against his horrendous form.

Jude clawed at one of the newer wounds. They still ached from the nasty barbs Elizabeth had pulled out of him. A tiny trickle of blood ran down his chest and into the water. He watched it in a trance, thinking about how his scars would forever be tied to her, to that memory.

The wind blew even harder, whistling over the sound of the harp still playing. Jude sank down deep into the water, muting all the damn noise he didn't want to hear. Beauloch was too hollow, too empty sounding.

If it wasn't for the throbbing of his healing wounds, he would've stayed in the tub indefinitely, but his blood craved the medicine the witch had brewed to patch his soul back up and strengthen him to fight again. His body would be sound, even if his heart was now a gaping hole.

After he took his potions, he went to the radio and slammed it against the floor, shattering it into a thousand pieces.

Chapter Seventeen

❧

Elizabeth had dozed on the chaise lounge and was awoken by the wind. It howled over the castle like a demon in flight. She quickly got up and changed out of her clothes she'd thrown on for her escape and slipped into a sheer nightgown. Something roiled in her heart like a violent tempest building over the ocean, and for some reason, she longed to be in the eye of the storm. All of this running had gotten her nowhere.

I need to face him. I must tell him how I truly feel before I implode.

Elizabeth moved quietly into the hall and saw the door to Jude's old bedroom half open. A rustling noise came from inside.

Steeling her nerves, Elizabeth gently pushed the door open and found Jamie packing up the last of his medical supplies.

"Oh, Elizabeth. Did I wake you?" Jamie said. He looked

at her revealing garb and blushed. He cleared his throat and quickly looked away.

Elizabeth crossed her arms to try and cover her exposed breasts. "No. I was just going downstairs to speak to Jude, to apologize."

"Ah, I'm sure you've done nothing wrong. This entire ordeal has been trying for everyone. That's why I need to take my mother far away. She has a weak constitution." Jamie placed the bloody forceps and other surgical tools in a sterile bag.

"I understand," Elizabeth said and picked up one of the barbed chains she'd pulled out of Jude's arm. They both stood there for a moment in silence, looking over the hideous torture device. "It amazes me how one man can endure so much, and still be as kind as your brother." Tears began to form in her eyes.

Jamie chuckled. "He is kind, but don't underestimate him. Jude is strong, and you, my dear, only make him stronger." He caressed her hand and laid a gentle kiss atop it.

Elizabeth held back her tears as Jamie turned to leave but as soon as he shut the door, she let them burst from her eyes. It took her a moment to gather herself. She sat on the edge of the bed as she caught her breath. Strong winds tore through the glen and rattled the windows of the room.

You must find him and tell him the truth.

Elizabeth finished wiping her last tear with her sleeve and went downstairs. Halfway down the steps, she stopped to wach Walter escort Jamie and his mother into the Land Rover. When he shut the front doors, the wind slammed them against the threshold. Elizabeth glanced at the grand-father clock in the atrium. It was past midnight.

He may be sleeping.

After she descended the remaining steps, she sidled through the shadowy hall and crept up to the door of the ballroom. If Jude was indeed sleeping, she didn't want to disturb him. With a gentle fist, she knocked on the door. No sound came from the other side.

Instead of knocking again, Elizabeth went into the room. The fireplace had naught but a dull flame and glowing embers that flared every time the wind came down the chimney. A single lamp illuminated the debris that had been thrown to the floor in a rage. She tried to go around some of it but stepped on something sharp.

"Ouch!" She lifted her right foot and pulled something from her heel.

"Elizabeth?" Jude sat up in his bed and held out his hands to her.

She edged closer and sat down beside him. They locked eyes. In that moment, nothing existed but the two of them. Every doubt she had burst forth like a strained dam that held too much rain. Her walls came crumbling down, and she leaned in to kiss him.

The moment she opened her mouth to let him in, he growled. Elizabeth climbed on top of him and laced her fingers through his hair. Being so close, she could smell the familiar, pungent herbs Gran used to heal deep wounds. She pulled away for a moment and opened her eyes to see Jude gazing up at her like a ravenous wolf.

There's no going back now.

He gripped her waist and neck as he forced her mouth

open to his a second time. Elizabeth let go, allowing herself to feel the wild urges that flooded her senses. He trailed his mouth down her jaw and onto the tender spot beneath her ear.

She swallowed down the knot in her throat. "Jude, I'm scared because..." Jude sucked on the nape of her neck and used gentle fingertips to slide her nightgown off one shoulder, exposing her left breast. "I'm scared because ... I love you, Jude."

Jude tightened his grip on her neck and clamped down lightly onto her nipple with his mouth, causing her to cry out. Elizabeth gasped and clutched the back of his head as he kissed and sucked her taut flesh. She could feel his fingers undoing the ties on the front of her gossamer gown. He ripped it off, caressed her back with both hands and looked up at her with his hungry eyes.

Elizabeth ran one hand along the red spots on his chest. First, she traced an old, raised scar and followed it down to the spot where she had removed a barb. The newer wound was more inflamed. Jude gripped her hips then worked his way down to her ass with one hand and gave it a firm squeeze. He sat up and whirled her around on the bed like she weighed nothing. She landed softly on her back, with mounds of blankets and pillows underneath her.

It took him no time to take his shirt and pants off and throw them aside. He loomed over her, running a hand from her jawline down to her waist, taking in every inch of her. Elizabeth shifted, a little embarrassed at first. She tried to cover herself up, but Jude pinned her hands to her sides.

He lowered his head to kiss her sternum, and her entire

body to shook from the sensation of his wet lips touching the thin skin over the bone. She let out a slight moan. Jude worked his way over to her right nipple, which was puckered up, ready for him to devour. This time he was a little more gentle as he suckled her breast, cupping it with his soft palm.

Elizabeth's face tingled from the pleasure. Jude released his hold on her wrist, only to use it to give her other breast a firm pinch. Elizabeth grasped the sheets beneath her. Jude trailed his kisses to her navel and sat up, watching her writhe with pleasure.

He placed one hand on the delicate lace covering her womanhood. The fabric had soaked through with her arousal. "You're very wet," he said and continued to pinch her nipple while he massaged in between her legs.

Elizabeth flushed red, tortured and helpless underneath his touch. "I'm sorry," she said.

Jude laughed and gently removed the damp undergarment. He seized both of her wrists and held them above her head. The silk of his lips barely brushed against hers, as if taunting her. Elizabeth fell apart at his very touch.

Jude ran a finger along the outside of her sex, feeling the wetness of her desire. His soft grazes forced a whimper from her mouth. She tried to close her legs, but Jude forced them open with his thighs. She clutched onto the sheets above her head, anticipating his entrance, but he continued to torture her, gently running his hand through her folds, over her swollen bud, and across her entrance.

She bucked in response, but he held her down, his strong hands grasping at her waist to steady her. He moved down on her and kissed her inner thighs, giving her a tiny bit of relief before he placed his mouth on her rosy apex and kissed it over and over again. More blood was drawn into her delicate flower.

Elizabeth's left leg tensed and moved inward, but he caught it in his hand. He raised his head and flashed that damnable smile, revealing his sharp canines. Jude gracefully climbed back over her to feast on her neck.

"I lied too," he whispered into her ear, nibbling on the soft lobe. "Because you're never leaving here."

Jude plunged himself deep inside her, prompting her to cry out. He rocked back only to go deeper a second time and then a third, using his hard cock to claim her as his. Jude gripped her behind the knee and forced her open wide as he pushed himself deep and hard. She never knew her body could accommodate such a large man, and felt her insides give way to his rock-hard member.

Elizabeth was helpless underneath him, and she loved every second of it, tearing at the sheets and moaning as Jude kept a steady pace. She never knew fucking could feel so good, and lost herself in the rhythm as Jude didn't hold back.

He groaned with pleasure as he kissed her. His strong lips seized hers, and his palm claimed her breast, grabbing and pinching it until every part of her body belonged to him. Elizabeth's senses flooded with ecstasy and a desperate whine escaped her. It grew louder as the earthquake in her began.

Jude clamped down on her breast with his mouth. Elizabeth yanked him by the hair as they both erupted like Mount Vesuvius. She cried out as her body rippled from its core, and he groaned low as he drove himself inside her.

The muscles in her womb continued to spasm until she collapsed and released her hold on him. She lay back, paralyzed with satisfaction.

JUDE KISSED THE TOP OF HER HEAD AND CAREFULLY GOT out of bed. It was late morning, and he needed to shift his focus back to The Order. He drew in a deep breath, wondering if she knew how serious he'd been when he told her she'd never leave Beauloch. The moment had been heated, and he'd accidentally said his thoughts out loud.

She's almost gotten away twice now.

Elizabeth had beguiled him when they first met, and his loneliness had forced him to attack her, because that was the only way he knew how to get close. Last night was different. She'd attempted to escape the bond they'd built over the weeks. Instinct told him he should tread carefully, but his heart had a mind of its own.

Jude left the ballroom, picked up breakfast in the dining hall, and took it upstairs into the study. He ate while he pored over the cryptic letters between his father and this other man who called himself Gawain. He couldn't glean any new information from their contents. He sat back in his father's chair and watched light rain fall over the loch as he ruminated over what he wanted to do next.

Would she accept his proposal? Deep in his heart, he wanted nothing more than to tie her to him forever. It might be a desperate ploy to do so, but after last night, after she'd opened herself to him and allowed him to taste and touch every inch of her, after he felt the loving bliss they shared, he had to try.

A pang of loneliness forced him to his feet. He needed to be next to her, to feel her soft skin, hear her voice, and admire the beautiful creature he'd managed to capture all for himself. He went back to the ballroom, but she'd left his bed.

Is that a bad sign?

His heart dropped, but he didn't give up. Much to his relief, the inflamed wounds on his chest and arms didn't ache as he ambled up the grand staircase. It was like their union had healed a part of him. At the top of the steps, he caught Annie leaving the Blue Room with an empty tray.

"Oh! You can't go in there. She's not decent," Annie said, her gaze earnest.

Jude laughed, but his housekeeper's face remained serious. "Is she unwell?" he said.

"No! She's having her bath right now. You'll have to come back later."

Jude did his best to hide his smirk. He nodded at her and went back downstairs. In the ballroom, Fiona was sweeping up the pieces of the broken radio, her mouth in a flat line.

She's disappointed in me again, he thought.

"Let me get that." Jude tried to take the broom, but Fiona yanked it back.

"I know you're an angry man, Jude. I'm just waiting on the day things might return to normal. It's all I can hope for." She bent down and swept the pieces into a dustbin. He stepped back and studied the disdain she wore on her sleeve.

His heart sank and a sense of guilt threatened to over-whelm him, only because he knew she was right. Things needed to get back to normal, whether he was alive to see it happen or not.

The first thing he did was go back upstairs. He started down the dark hall where the main bedrooms were located and stopped at the last door on the left. His hand hovered over the handle for a moment. A sadness threatened him until he pushed it back with better memories; memories of Elizabeth.

He entered the large bedroom, taking in the details of the floral wallpaper that his mother had put up all those years ago. The green and yellow hues brightened as he switched on a lamp. Of all the rooms in the castle, this one had always been his favorite, even with all the pain it stirred in his heart.

He approached the vanity in the corner and opened the top drawer. Inside was a wooden box with a pile of lavish jewelry he never thought he'd look at again. None of it had interested him until he'd met Elizabeth.

He lifted the tray of rings and bracelets to gain access to some of the older pieces that had belonged to his mother. He'd had his mind on one particular ornament and the moment he laid eyes on it, his heart skipped a beat.

Knowing she'd been married once before, Jude didn't want to give her an ugly, old ring that probably wouldn't fit. Instead, he opted for a silver necklace with a dazzling emerald pendant. Everything about it reminded him of her. He couldn't wait to see the look on her face when he gave it to her.

She had to say yes to his proposal. It was his only plan

to keep her at Beauloch. Even if he wasn't to survive his next meeting with The Order, he wanted her to remain on the estate. She deserved all the beauty and grandeur the old castle held within its ancient walls. Whenever she played her music, it brought life back into the old stones. He couldn't explain it, but he felt in his soul that this was where she belonged.

ELIZABETH HAD JUST FINISHED PUTTING HER CLOTHES ON when there was a knock at her door. Jude opened it and came in, that grin melting her heart all over again.

"Are you ready?" he said.

When he stood in front of her, Elizabeth remembered how tall and imposing he could be. She had to tilt her head back to look up at his handsome face. It was the face of the man who'd made the most intense love to her. She blushed

"Ready for what?" Elizabeth said.

"I'd like to stroll around the gardens with you. They're probably not much to look at right now, but the sun has come out. We should bask in it while we can." He stepped up close and laid a gentle kiss on her lips.

"If you say so," Elizabeth said. She'd fought so hard to calm her nerves in the wake of her surrender, but she couldn't shake the uneasiness she felt. She tried to hide behind her smile. It was easy enough because part of her really was happy. If not for Boris and The Order, she would be living a dream.

Jude took her hands. "Have I done something wrong?"

Elizabeth was taken aback. Never in her marriage had

her husband detected her unease. She thought she could mask it.

"No. Of course not. I'm just still a bit frightened by everything."

Jude pulled her in and embraced her fully. For Elizabeth, it felt like all the pain and worry melted away when he held her. She gripped his sweater and put her forehead against his chest. They stayed there for a minute.

"Okay. Let's go," Elizabeth said.

Jude interlaced his fingers with hers. He held her hand until they reached the gardens.

Behind Beauloch, low stone walls surrounded the grounds that had been cultivated to grow numerous types of flora. Moss-covered flagstones created paths that meandered into different sections. Jude led them down a way lined with thick bushes. The path crossed a narrow footbridge at the bottom of a waterfall. The frigid waters gushed over black stone, spraying them with cold mist.

Where is he taking me? she wondered.

Many plants had gone dormant for the winter, but a patch of pink cyclamens spilled over onto the path. Elizabeth stopped to admire them.

"It's nicer in the summer," Jude said.

"It's beautiful, even now."

"Do you ever play your harp outside?" Jude leaned against the stone wall. They'd reached the far end of the garden.

"I do when the weather is nice. I just have to be careful not to get it wet or anything."

Jude looked around. "I'm sure we could have some paving stones placed back here."

Elizabeth looked at him, watching how he was turning things over in his head. What was he planning? She remembered the words he had said when they were in the throes of lovemaking, but they couldn't be true. Could they?

"Come." Jude took her hand and pulled her under an arched trellis covered in ivy. On the other side, the stone wall encircled a beautiful rowan tree.

They stood underneath it, the sun and wind greeting them like a playful child.

"Do you like it here?"

"You seem so worried that I'm offended by nature, but I think it's beautiful no matter the time of the year." Elizabeth took in a deep breath of the fresh Scottish air. She shut her eyes and listened to the song of the waxwing perched on a high branch of the rowan.

"I just want you to be happy here, with me," Jude said as he placed something in her hand. Elizabeth opened her eyes to an exquisite silver necklace in her palm.

"This is beautiful."

"Let me." Jude moved behind her. She handed the necklace to him, and he fastened it around her neck with ease. He placed himself in front of her, his figure towering over her, making her feel small again, but in a good way. He smiled. "I meant what I said last night. You should always be here."

"Is that a demand?" Elizabeth chuckled.

"No. It's an offer. One that I hope you take." Jude lowered his dark, chocolate eyes to her face, searching for what she felt.

Elizabeth's face flushed red again. "What? Like a proposal?"

"Yes. Would you honor me?" Jude said, his voice almost a whisper.

Elizabeth froze, stunned by the sudden shift in his tone, his manner. She never knew he could be so direct, yet so tender. He stepped closer and kissed her, breaking her free from the sudden shock she felt. His tongue eased her mouth open. Elizabeth pulled back.

"That's not fair," she said.

"Life's not fair. I'm not going to stop until you give me an answer." He kissed her again.

Elizabeth had no control. Her body softened in his arms as he laid gentle kisses on her lips. His touch was full of pure affection, not once pushing for anything more than the words that could only be said with a kiss. Elizabeth knew what she and Jude felt for each other was real. Despite all that had happened since she'd arrived at Beauloch, she was happy.

She wrested herself free from the deep kiss. "I don't know, Jude. It's a lot to take in right now. Please don't be angry with me."

Jude took her face in his hands. "I'm not angry with you, but I will have my answer soon, even if I have to yank it from the depths of your heart." Jude kissed her again, more deeply this time, backing up the force of his words with his actions. Elizabeth resisted at first and tried to wrench herself away, but he held firm, not allowing her to escape his arms.

A moment later he gave Elizabeth a break, allowing her to come up for air. He kept her firmly wrapped in his arms.

"You're a beast, you know that?" she said.

Jude grinned, clearly pleased by her words. "Am I?"

Elizabeth's stomach rumbled loudly, breaking the tension. She held a hand to her belly. "Sorry. I'm pretty hungry."

"Why didn't you say so?" Jude scooped her off her feet and held her in his arms. Elizabeth yelped and clasped her hands around his neck for stability. "Don't tell me to put you down. I've been wanting to do this for a very long time."

"What's that? Carry me around like a doll?" Elizabeth teased.

"That and feel my own strength again. If it wasn't for you, Elizabeth, I'd still be locked up in my room, the ghost of the man I once was." Jude tilted his head down. Their foreheads touched.

"Just give me a little bit of time. I promise I will have an answer for you soon," Elizabeth said.

Jude carried her back to the castle.

Chapter Eighteen

❦

From his chair, Boris leaned into the dull lamplight of the parlor room. His unbuttoned shirt hung off his shoulder, displaying the place where the bitch had stabbed him.

"It's healing well," Dr. Brenner said.

"Good." Boris stood up and went to the bar. He poured two glasses of whiskey. "What should I do with the girl?" He set one glass down in front of his friend.

Boris had known Dr. Brenner for many years. The rogue physician had been the one who'd aided him in the mechanics of the very first blood ritual. Dr. Brenner often dabbled in strange areas of study, like cloning and eugenics, but his real interest was the female body.

"You should do whatever you want with her. Where is she now?" Dr. Brenner sipped his drink.

"She's alive and well, according to my source at Beauloch. I've sent out a hound to collect on the debt Jude owes us for his transgressions. The hound will report back to me on her current condition after he's had a bite out of her. It's the only way she will learn to behave."

Boris pressed against the new flesh that had formed over his stab wound. He still couldn't believe someone as delicate as Elizabeth had attempted to maim him. Never in his life had a woman attacked him. He was going to make sure it was the last time.

"You'll keep her here then." Dr. Brenner put his medical supplies back into his bag.

"She's the real prize, doctor. I didn't believe such beauty and talent could exist out in the wild. Her face, her lips—they radiate good genes, good health. I couldn't dream of a better woman to continue my lineage."

Dr. Brenner cleared his throat. "Looks can be deceiving. We should test her before—"

"Test her we will, my friend. I know you have your science, but I'm certain of what must be done. It all starts here." Boris smirked, tapping his temple.

Dr. Brenner nodded. "Of course."

Boris stepped in front of a painting he'd brought back from America. It was a grotesque scene of a demon violating a fair maiden. He'd bought it at auction at a high price, and needed it near to remind himself that there were only two kinds of people in the world: the strong ones, like him, and the weak ones, whose only purpose was to serve him.

Jude stretched out on the sofa in the library while Elizabeth sat nearby and played the harp. He couldn't take his eyes off her as she moved her hands over the mysterious instrument. The resonance of the harp put him into a sort of trance. He'd never believed in magic or enchantments until he'd heard her perform that first night in the ballroom.

When she was finished, he stood up, and offered her his hand. "Sit by the fire with me," he said.

Elizabeth took his arm, and they sat down together on a thick woolen blanket in front of the roaring fire. Outside, the winter winds dashed against the turrets. The sunshine they'd enjoyed a few days earlier had faded quickly, and the Cailleach had reasserted her dominance over the land.

Jude placed a second blanket around her, hoping to keep her warm. "I wanted to talk to you about something."

Elizabeth peered up at him with those dazzling green eyes. They were what had inspired him to give her his mother's emerald necklace. Elizabeth's beauty stole the breath from him, only because he couldn't believe such a perfect creature could ever love someone so damaged as him.

"I know you don't have an answer for me, but I'd like to make some arrangements for you in the meantime. I'm in the process of adding your name to the deed for Beauloch. That way, you will always have a safe place to go."

Elizabeth's eyes widened. "I'm not that poor, I can look after myself."

"It's not about that, Elizabeth." Jude was at a loss for what to say. The last few days had been so wonderful.

I wish I could freeze time and stay with her forever in this moment, he thought.

Elizabeth sat up straight, her eyes suddenly on him.

"You're doing this because you think you may not live," she said, her words soft but harsh. "Is that what your plan is? To give your life to The Order?"

Jude shook his head. "No. It's not my plan, but things don't always go the way we want them to." He leaned in to kiss her, trying to rid himself of the thought of leaving her behind. It was too painful to bear, and the touch of her lips only made it worse.

"You haven't told me what your plan is. Gran helped you with something, that's all I know."

"Maybe it's best I don't tell you." Jude wrapped his arms around her and flipped her around to face the fire. Elizabeth reclined back against his chest. The flames in the hearth danced erratically from the northern winds that entered through the high chimney.

"I think someone has been spying on us," Elizabeth whispered.

They both turned their heads toward the grates near the floor.

Jude laughed. "Maybe Annie just likes to see you when you're without your clothes," he whispered in her ear. The temptation to touch her took over, and his hand went up her sweater and cupped her left breast. Elizabeth laid her head back on his shoulder and looked up at him, her sultry gaze lighting a fire deep within him.

"Why must you torture me like this?" she said.

Jude pinched at her nipple through the thin lace of her bra. "Because I want to hear those words again," he said, giving her a single kiss.

"What words?" she said.

"You don't remember?" Jude said, taken aback at first.

"Remind me," she said, turning around to lie back against the blanket.

Jude climbed over her. "Let's see. You had come to me in only a bit of silk."

Elizabeth laughed. "Is that all?"

Jude removed her sweater and bra. "You said something while I was right about here." Jude placed his mouth over her right nipple, devouring it with greed. She shifted underneath him.

"My memory is fuzzy though." Jude unbuttoned the front of her pants, feeling the wetness on her panties. A heat flared in between his legs. "You were apologizing for *something*." He rubbed her apex vigorously and she started panting, making him rock hard with her perfect sensuality.

"What was it?" He forced his hand past her cotton panties and pushed his finger inside of her. She threw her head back and moaned deeply, letting go of her inhibitions.

Blood started to course through Jude like a raging river. His cock throbbed against his jeans. Every aspect of Elizabeth turned him on like he was a hormonal teenager. He rocked his hand back and forth, prodding around until he found the spot that drove her wild. She trembled beneath him like a helpless victim, trying her best to muffle her cries of pleasure.

He kissed her open mouth. "That's it. Come for me," he whispered.

Elizabeth's body spasmed as his finger stroked her wet insides. She collapsed on the blanket, breathing hard.

Jude kissed her neck but she quickly sat up. "Must've slipped my mind," she said, smiling. She straddled him, ready to kiss him, but he denied her.

"I never heard you say it," he said.

"Tell me what I said." She placed her hand on the bulge in his jeans and quickly unzipped his pants and took his cock in her hand.

Jude let out a helpless groan. He reached out to stroke her thighs, but she slipped free, inching her way down to position herself in between his legs.

"Elizabeth..." Jude murmured. Elizabeth gently wrapped a hand around his cock and put her soft lips against its throbbing head. "Fuck..."

He lost his composure and fell back on his elbows as she teased him with her tongue.

"What were you saying?" she said, before she slipped half of his manhood into her mouth.

Jude squeezed one of her breasts as she continued to suck him, using her hand to guide him deep into her mouth. He was helpless against her lips and tongue. His mind left his body for a few moments as he watched the beautiful goddess make love to him. Her hair fell around his waist in glossy brown tendrils. He couldn't help but reach out and sink his hand into it.

"Elizabeth, I'm going to..."

His warning only gave her confidence as she focused her mouth on his head. He exploded with pleasure, losing control as he yanked on her hair.

He expected her to back off immediately, but she remained in place and her tongue lapped up every last ounce he had. The moment he let go of her hair he fell onto his back. Elizabeth released him and crawled up to spit out his semen onto his chest. She smiled, dipped her tongue into it, and swirled it around.

"You're a beast, you know that?" Jude said, trying to catch his breath.

"I thought I was the beautiful lady that had gotten lost in the woods," she said, lying at his side. She took a spare napkin from their dinner tray and wiped him off. Jude followed her hand across his torso and ran a hand through her hair.

"You really tugged hard back there," Elizabeth said.

"I'm sorry. I couldn't control myself when you were doing that," Jude said.

Elizabeth laughed. "Let's see, we've fucked in the bathroom, the ballroom, and now the library."

"Fucked? We've only fucked once, and I should have been more careful." Jude sat up. He placed his thumb against her lip, needing to feel the soft flesh that had just made love to him.

"Why? Because I haven't said yes to your proposal?" Elizabeth said. She sat up and reached for her sweater, tossing it on without her bra.

"No, because of The Order. My father was completely subjugated by them, and once he was gone, they went after me. If I don't succeed in destroying them, I might sentence an innocent child to a lifetime of hell."

Elizabeth furrowed her brows.

Jude immediately regretted his words. "Don't worry, my love. I won't do that to you again," he said, and kissed her hand over and over. "I will use protection if I cannot control myself."

Elizabeth smiled. "As long as we are in a proper bedroom. Why are you so avoidant of the second floor, by the way?"

Jude released her hand. "It's where all the old memories are. Our old bedrooms are there. And when I grew weak from the rituals, I couldn't make it up the stairs so I just started sleeping in the ballroom, and I thought..." He paused to look at her steady gaze.

"You thought you could never make it up the steps again after they were through with you."

He nodded.

"Did you take the escorts into the old rooms?" Elizabeth said.

"What?" Jude was taken aback by the question. There was only one person he could thank for regaling the details of his past to her.

"I mean the women you paid to—"

"I heard you, but what? No. They never went upstairs. Elizabeth, please don't think I'm one to go off with random women. Most of them came to keep me company. A lot of the time they watched me sleep or stayed up late to talk with me."

"And the other times? I'm genuinely curious. I've never personally met someone who's bought an escort. What was it like?"

Jude blushed, remembering the two women he'd bedded. They had been physical affairs, nothing more. "It was very dull. The first one I took to bed was nice, but she never spoke much. I can't even remember her name."

"It was that long ago?"

"I'm not sure. Maybe it was six years ago? Anyway. The other woman was very kind. We got along well, and our lovemaking was very quick. I even liked her enough to allow her to stay for days at a time. She fell in love with me though, which didn't feel right. After I ordered her to be sent away, I felt like I'd done something terrible, and vowed to never do it again."

Elizabeth remained quiet, her eyes on the floor.

Jude picked up her hand again and squeezed it tightly. "Please don't hold my past against me. I did those things before I knew you existed. Could you ever find it in your heart to forgive me?"

She looked up and smiled. "There's nothing to forgive."

Jude held her close and tight to his chest, dreading every minute that passed, because it meant he was one second closer to having to release her. He knew he had to make every moment count.

It was early afternoon the next day and Elizabeth stepped out of the scalding hot water in the giant mermaid tub. As she pulled her towel over herself, she heard light footsteps in the Blue Room. She peeked in and saw no one, but a note had been laid on the edge of the bed. She padded across the room in her bare feet and opened it up.

Meet me here.

-Jude

· · ·

A SMALL MAP HAD BEEN DRAWN UNDER THE WORDS. Elizabeth turned the paper upside down, realizing the drawing was of a footpath she had once taken when she was out in the woods with Gran. She wondered why Jude might want to meet her there. She'd been bold the other night when she'd pleasured him in the library. Even now, her face blushed at the memory. He came completely undone underneath her touch. She would give anything to feel him shudder like that again.

Elizabeth got dressed, pulling on her wool coat and scarf. There was no more wind, but the temperature had dropped in the last few days and required her to bundle up.

She looked at the map one more time, then went downstairs and out the back door. She surveyed the landscape for any sign of him when she got to the gardens, still curious as to what Jude might want to do in this wretched cold. Even the slightest breeze caused her to shiver.

The path into the woods was easy to spot since all the plants had died. Elizabeth brushed past some of the debris as she wandered into the trees. A sudden flurry of air caught her off guard, forcing her to wrap her scarf around her neck an extra time. When she made it to the spot on the map, there was nothing there except a large boulder.

"Hello?" she called out.

No one answered.

Elizabeth held up the map again and turned it upside down. Maybe she'd gone the wrong way. As soon as she lowered it, a man appeared in front of her. She shrieked.

"Who are you?" she said. The realization she was in danger set in. The man was young, maybe in his mid-thirties. His beanie hat and hunting jacket indicated he was well prepared to endure the cold. His face was slightly red, and his black beard was trimmed nice and neat. On the surface, he seemed like a normal guy, but something deep in his eyes gave him away. Their icy-blue stare hinted he would soon commit a violent act.

The note wasn't from Jude. You're a fucking idiot.

Elizabeth's heart raced. She knew she had to run. It was her only choice, but her damned coat was weighing her down. The moment she grabbed the front to begin to shed it, the man hoisted a hunting rifle he'd been carrying over his shoulder.

"Don't move," he said, pointing the barrel at her head. From his stance, he seemed intent on pulling the trigger. Elizabeth didn't dare move a muscle. The trauma of being stabbed by Boris sent a bead of sweat down her neck. Her throat went dry. She held her hands up.

The man slowly approached her. Elizabeth never looked away from him. The hatred behind his pupils was so palpable that her legs started to shake. The man smirked, threw his rifle back over his shoulder, and grabbed the front of Elizabeth's coat. He pulled it open. At first, she thought he might be looking for weapons, but his gaze had a hunger in it.

"Let me go," she pleaded.

"Not today, love." He released the lapel of her coat and squeezed her by the throat. The force he used was so violent, she thought she would lose consciousness. He slammed her back against a tree.

"You're a pretty little bitch, aren't you?"

Elizabeth tried to wrest his hand from her neck with her tiny fingers, but his grip wouldn't budge. The man reared his head back and smashed it against her face. A flash of white blinded her from the impact.

"Cunts like you need to learn some respect," he snarled.

The man threw her to the ground. She scrambled to get up, but he placed his boot on her back, and pressed down hard with his weight.

Elizabeth clawed at grass and mud with both hands, desperate to break free. From behind, the man yanked her hair. His deep laugh resonated through the trees as she yelped from the pain. After what felt like an eternity, he let go and knelt beside her. Elizabeth went limp. He rolled her over and placed the heel of his boot on the right side of her chest, just beneath her breast.

An unbearable weight bore down on her.

Elizabeth gripped the muddy hiking boot in an attempt to heave it off her, but her hands slipped.

He's going to kill me.

The man slowly dug his heel into her ribs. The breath went out of her, and black spots filled the edges of her vision.

A sudden relief from his crushing force made her open her eyes. The man had stumbled backward, holding his throat. Elizabeth was in too much pain to sit up, but she saw a figure in front of him.

Another henchman?

She rolled onto her stomach and looked down the path in hopes of escaping, but a familiar voice brought her attention back to the activity behind her.

Jude had the man in his clutches. Now it was the henchman who was pinned against the tree. Blood spewed from the man's neck. He grasped at the wound with both hands, trying desperately to stem the bleeding. He choked and gurgled as he gasped for breath. Elizabeth crawled backward to put some distance between her and the two fighting men. Her eyes followed Jude's hand as he ripped open the henchman's hunting coat with a large knife he had drawn from a sheath on his belt. With strength she didn't know he had, Jude shoved the blade deep into the gut of his victim.

The man convulsed, using the last of his strength to grab Jude by the shoulders. Jude removed the knife and threw him down on the ground.

Elizabeth flinched as the limp body fell into a shallow puddle. She clung to the trunk of the yew tree and shook from fright. The surge of adrenaline started to taper off until Jude pulled out his pistol and fired three rounds straight into the man's face. The loud gun blasts made her ears ring and sent a new shockwave through her nervous system.

Elizabeth had to avert her eyes from the carnage. Her throat tightened up and tears started gathering in her eyes. The pain in her face flared where the man had assaulted her.

"Elizabeth? Are you all right?" Jude bent down beside her.

She opened her eyes to see his face darkened with rage. She flew into his arms, needing to feel the warmth, the safety of his embrace. It was like magic, how the fear and panic dissipated so quickly from her mind. He held her for a minute or two, caressing her against his giant chest.

"I think he's dead," she said.

Jude kissed her on the top of her head. "Come on. You

shouldn't have to see this." He led her back to the castle. Elizabeth stopped at the steps in the back garden, clutching her side.

"Are you hurt?" Jude said.

"He, um..." Elizabeth swallowed the knot back down in her throat. "He tried to break my ribs."

Jude's eyes grew wide with rage. He scooped her up in his arms and carried her the rest of the way.

"Jude, I can walk," Elizabeth said, but he didn't heed her words and kept her in his arms until they were all the way up the stairs and back in the Blue Room. He eased her down onto the bed.

"I already said I'm okay," Elizabeth said.

"Why did you go out into the woods?" Jude sat on the edge of the bed and brushed his thumb over her swelling cheek.

"This was on my bed when I got out of the bath." Elizabeth pulled out the piece of paper she'd stuffed into her coat pocket. Jude took it and held it under the lamplight. His brows creased and his mouth turned down.

"Someone was in your room." He hopped up to inspect the panel that acted as a door to the secret passages. It was shut tight.

"Gran warned me that someone at Beauloch was spying for The Order. Do you think Annie or Fiona could've left it while I was in the bathroom?" Elizabeth said. She instinctively touched the spot near her eye where the attacker headbutted her.

Jude scowled and rushed back to her bedside. "You said you weren't hurt."

Elizabeth could feel inflammation setting in. "I'll be

fine." She covered the tingling spot with her hand. "That man was clearly sent by the brotherhood. I must've angered Boris when I stabbed him in the neck."

Jude tucked a few strands of her hair behind her left ear. "Let me deal with The Order. The next full moon is in a few weeks. Once they're gone, we can figure out who's been helping them. In the meantime, you're never to leave my sight. Do you understand?"

Elizabeth cocked her head. "How did you know I went into the woods?"

Jude drew in a deep breath. "That's what I mean. It's been difficult keeping an eye on you when you're off on the other side of the castle. You need to stay close, so I can at least get some sleep."

Elizabeth nodded. Jude gently caressed her face with one hand and kissed her lips.

That evening, they dined in the ballroom. Elizabeth pored over the books Jude had stacked on the far side of the room. She pulled one from a pile and brought it to the spot they'd made in front of the fireplace.

"This is interesting. It's a book about old Viking settlements in the Highlands," Elizabeth said as she flipped through the pages.

"My father loved Scottish history," Jude said and kicked back on a pillow. He held out one arm, inviting her in. Elizabeth lay back with the book and snuggled in close. When he closed his arm around her, she winced.

Jude sat up again and gave her a stern look.

"I think it's just tender from falling," Elizabeth said.

"Show me." Jude took her hand.

She knew he wouldn't let up until she showed him her

ribs. Elizabeth lifted her sweater, easing it over the purple and blue bruises that had formed on her side. Jude looked upon her with fury.

"It doesn't hurt," she said.

Jude pulled her sweater back down and stroked her cheek with his thumb.

"I'm going to kill every last one of them. Every man in The Order will be exterminated by my hands. I promise you this."

Elizabeth nodded as the memory of Jude shanking her attacker in the woods resurfaced. The same hands that loved her so tenderly were also the hands that had destroyed a man. She didn't doubt his words for a second after seeing the resolve he'd had when he wanted to end a life.

Chapter Nineteen

❧

The following day, the solicitor arrived at noon. Jude welcomed him in the study with scones and tea. For the most part, it was a dull affair; going through stacks of paperwork that said the same things over and over again. Jude signed his name probably twenty times before they were all done.

Jude shook the man's hand and showed him out when they'd finished. He thought his anxiety would lift, but he still had to tell Elizabeth that she was now to inherit Beauloch and all the land reaching far past the loch and the hills to the north if anything were to happen to him. He couldn't delay it any longer. It was his last evening at Beauloch before he went to face the demons. There would be bloodshed, and things would never be the same after that, for better or for worse.

He went into the library and found her there, playing something on the harp. It sounded just as beautiful as it did the day they'd met. Watching her hands move over the strings put him into a trance. All the pain and fear he'd been harboring melted away as the music carried him from the room, up the glen, and to a far distant land where there was peace.

Elizabeth finished the song and glanced up at him. "Do you like it?" she said.

"Of course. It's beautiful. What's it called?" Jude came back down to earth.

"It was something I made up when I was out in the woods with Gran," she said.

Elizabeth came to him. Jude wrapped his arms around her and kissed her.

"I have a special dinner planned for this evening. Did Annie mention it to you?" Jude said.

"She did. I have something special planned myself." Elizabeth gave him a mischievous smile.

Jude's heart fluttered. She still hadn't given him an answer to his proposal. In the last couple of weeks, he'd constantly wondered if she wanted to reject him, but kept putting off asking so she wouldn't break his heart before he was sent to his doom. Granted, he'd have to be alive for them to wed, but that didn't change how he felt about her.

"I hope this plan comes with an answer to my proposal."

"I might just be making a proposal of my own," Elizabeth said as she trailed the tips of her fingers up his spine

Heat flared in his blood. The herbs that the witch had given him made him feel stronger and more alive than he ever had. That, along with holding the light of his life in his arms, made it seem like there actually was a benevolent god or goddess looking down on him. If he survived, he thought he might become the happiest man alive. Jude knew he had to tread carefully with that sort of thinking though. Many times he'd had hope, only for it to be dashed by people who were only around him to drain him like vampires, whether they were part of The Order or greedy socialites trying to manipulate their way into his life.

Elizabeth was different. She'd never once asked for anything and had given her heart and soul to him in the most beautiful ways—by playing music, by seeking out medicines in the forest for him, by holding him and kissing him with her soft lips. Jude knew she'd been unsure at first, but she'd opened up to him like the beautiful roses that once bloomed in the gardens at Beauloch.

Later that evening, Jude checked himself over in the mirror a few times, wondering if his black suit was too fancy for the evening he'd planned. It was a dated choice, but he knew Elizabeth would rather he be his genuine self than put on airs during what could possibly be their last night together. In the end, he liked the way he looked.

Jude climbed the stairs and knocked on the door of the Blue Room, trying to be patient. His stomach was all aflutter until Annie opened the door.

"We're ready," Annie said, and stepped aside to reveal the most beautiful creature Jude had ever laid eyes on.

Elizabeth wore a bright-green dress the color of blooming shamrocks in the spring. It was long, going all the way down to the floor, and had a silver tie that cinched at the waist. The neckline was wide, accentuating her strong shoulders and the emerald necklace he'd given her when he'd asked for her hand.

"You look amazing," he said, but his words embarrassed him. Amazing? What was he, twelve?

Elizabeth approached him and offered her hand to him. "You look quite dashing yourself."

Jude took her by the arm and walked her down the stairs. They took their time, going slowly through the main hall and into the dining room. Jude sat her down in the chair next to his, the one at the head of the table.

Fiona and Annie brought out French onion soup for the first course. Jude ate it, relishing the taste. He wondered how much of his life he'd wasted on cold meals in the ballroom, eating alone as he tried to recover. Now he had a chance to make up for all that lost time, with Elizabeth at his side, which put a smile on his face.

"What are you thinking?" Elizabeth said, lowering her spoon.

"I'm just thinking about how happy I am with you," Jude said.

Elizabeth got up and held out her hand. "Dance with me?"

"What? Now?"

"You put this amazing piano music on. We can eat afterward."

Jude got up, took her hand and pressed his palm on her lower back. They rocked back and forth to the slow rhythm. Outside, the moon was almost at its peak, shining down over the treetops and through the glass windows. The silver beams glowed on the wooden floor at their feet. It was like a taunting spirit, reminding him that his time was limited, which made the moment all the more precious to him.

"I need to tell you something," Jude said.

Elizabeth looked up at him, her eyes dazzling in the moonlight.

Jude had to clear his throat. "I met with my solicitor earlier. Beauloch and all my assets are now in your name. If something—"

"Stop talking," Elizabeth said, and placed her head back on his chest.

They continued to sway to the music until the growl of her stomach broke the tranquility of their dance. They both laughed at the noise.

"Let's eat now," Jude said, taking her back to the table.

Fiona and Annie brought out two piping-hot steaks covered with a balsamic glaze, served alongside mashed potatoes and a roasted vegetable medley. It was Fiona's specialty she'd perfected over the years as the head cook. The taste brought back memories of birthdays, celebrations, and other holidays. Jude missed the time when Beauloch had been full of life and laughter. If he came back in one piece, he was going to make it his mission to see his home that way again.

"Now it's my turn to ask what you're thinking," Jude said.

"I was just wondering. If dinner is this good, what's for dessert?"

Jude laughed.

"No, really. The anticipation is killing me!" Elizabeth smiled.

Jude made sure dessert wasn't delayed, prompting Fiona and Annie to bring out two plates of chocolate lava cake with homemade vanilla ice cream on top. It was the same dessert Fiona had made when he'd completed his schooling. The distinct memory of the first time he'd bitten into the hot and cold, gooey, creamy goodness had never left him. He watched Elizabeth put a spoonful in her mouth. Her eyes shut and she let out a low moan of pleasure.

Jude studied her reaction to the indulgence. The way she licked the ice cream off the spoon fascinated and aroused him. She stopped eating when she caught him gawking.

"Aren't you going to have some?" she said.

"Of course." Jude flushed red and sunk his spoon into the cake.

Fiona brought out a special herbal tea blend to help them digest their food. It was a recipe the witch had talked about in the leatherbound book he'd been flipping through at random times.

"The chamomile may make us sleepy," Elizabeth said.

"I doubt I will sleep at all tonight." Jude blew on the hot liquid.

"Will you meet me upstairs? There's something I want to show you."

Jude put his cup down, intrigued. "What is it?"

Elizabeth scooted her chair back and stood up. "Come upstairs once you've finished your tea." She leaned over to give him a kiss and started for the door.

ELIZABETH PACED THE MASTER BEDROOM. IT HAD BEEN Jude's parent's room when his father was still alive, and even though the changes she'd made with the staff's help hadn't been overwhelming, they were enough to make it obvious the space had been worked on. While she'd kept Jude away, Walter had brought in men to paint the wainscot, replace the carpet, and hang new curtains. Fiona helped buy a new duvet and had some of the benches and chairs reupholstered with modern tartan textiles, and Annie snuck in some of Jude's clothes and hung them in the closet. The fresh smell of paint and new carpet made Elizabeth's stomach do a flip.

Maybe we should have left things as they were.

Her heart skipped a beat when Jude entered the room. She stood by the bed, waiting.

"What is it?" Jude said, oblivious to the changes.

"We made some updates in here. Do you like it?" she said.

Elizabeth watched his gaze go to the walls, where she'd put up brighter paintings of the Scottish Highlands, featuring green mountains and thick blooms of yellow gorse. Then he turned his eyes to the bed, which had new linens. The old ones had been grey, but these were a light green that matched the leaves on the wallpaper. Between that and the different plants and candles she'd lined along the windowsill, she thought the difference would be obvious.

"It's nice," Jude said. He placed his hands around her waist. "Is this all you wanted to show me?"

Elizabeth stood up straight and rested her hands on his shoulders. "I'd like to stay here tonight."

"Any reason?"

She shrugged. "It's the nicest room in the castle. You only stayed downstairs because you were trying to recover. When you return from your last meeting with The Order, we should both sleep here."

Jude brushed over her mouth with his thumb. "If that's what you want."

Elizabeth spun around and held onto one of the bed's wooden posters for balance. "Help me out of this?"

Jude came to her with hunger in his eyes. He took his time pulling down the zipper on the back of the dress. Elizabeth twirled to face him. She eased the silken green dress off her body, revealing the scandalous number Annie had helped her into just before dinner.

It was a black bodysuit with sheer lace that barely covered her breasts. Solid panels of fabric accented her waist. A floral design guided his eyes down to her most sensitive parts. She leaned back against the poster to display her curves.

"Take your shirt off," she said.

Jude removed his jacket and unbuttoned his shirt. Elizabeth closed the gap between them, leaning in so her breasts touched his bare skin, thin lace the only barrier between them. She wrapped her arms over his shoulders.

"Kiss me," she said.

Jude grabbed her waist, his long fingers running over the places where her skin was exposed. He dipped his fingertips down into the lace panels and kissed her vigorously, forcing her mouth open with his. Elizabeth let him in, feeling the power of his body as it pressed firmly against hers.

Jude pulled back suddenly. "We have to be careful."

Elizabeth kissed the scruff on his cheek. "Maybe I don't want to be. Would it be so bad if you left something behind?" She took his hand and lowered it to the soft curve of her hip. "What if we make a deal? I'll agree to marry you, if you don't hold back tonight."

Jude's eyes darkened. Elizabeth knew what he was thinking because it was the same thought she'd had all evening. This might be their last night together. Things had already gone bad with The Order once, not to mention the appearance of the man who had tried to maim her in the forest. Her ribs were still a little tender, but the feel of Jude's hands on her numbed any pain she had. Jude moved his hands to her bare ass. He felt for the string of her thong and gave it a gentle tug, causing her to gasp.

"If I do this, you'll marry me?" Jude gripped her ass cheek and gave it a firm squeeze.

Elizabeth nodded. "Yes." She kissed him.

A deep rumble vibrated through his chest. He picked her up and lifted her onto the bed. Elizabeth sat up on her elbows, watching as Jude removed his pants. He was naked in no time, crawling over her like an animal about to devour his prey.

He kissed her, forcing her down flat on her back. Elizabeth reached out and placed her hands on his chest, but he quickly grabbed them and pinned them above her head. She realized she wasn't going to get any control in the situation, but that excited her even more. The look in his eyes as she tempted him with her scandalous lingerie was stuck in her head as he kissed her neck, biting and nipping at the thin skin near her throat. His love would no doubt make bruises, but these would be from pleasure.

Jude prodded her sex with his hardened head. His hard dick pressed against the delicate lace that barely covered her. He squeezed her breast, then pushed the cup aside to expose it. He placed his mouth over her, biting down hard on her nipple. Elizabeth shrieked with delight. He then softened his lips to suck her tender flesh. Blood rushed to the surface of her skin, and down the valleys of her waist and into her dripping sex.

Jude slowly pulled on the black lace, moving it down to her navel. Elizabeth reached for his shoulder, but he quickly subdued her again, and held her arms against the bed. He trailed his tongue down the dips of her curves, biting and nipping every now and then, leaving her moist and red from his mouth.

Elizabeth was helpless underneath his hands, her mind going wild with every touch and every kiss. He suddenly ripped the rest of her garb off and placed his mouth over her sex. Elizabeth gasped as he ran his tongue through her folds and over her swollen clit. She wanted to claw at the sheets, but he continued to dominate her by keeping her arms still. Elizabeth arched her back for relief as he sucked and teased her. She couldn't help but cry out with pleasure as the heat in her rose.

When he let up, she was panting with ecstasy.

"Turn around," he said, his tone demanding.

Elizabeth was unsure at first. She studied his devilish eyes before she flipped over onto her stomach. Her heart raced, not being able to see him anymore. What was he going to do to her?

Jude raised her hips and entered her with full force. His grip on her was maniacal and his thrusts were so strong she could feel it in her spine. Her ribs started to hurt but the pleasure she felt as his cock filled her small crevice took over her senses completely. Jude paused for a moment to push her legs wider. He gained even better access and Elizabeth felt his head reach the entrance of her womb.

She cried out louder than she ever had, unable to contain herself. Jude took his time, torturing her with hard, steady thrusts. He squeezed the back of her neck as he continued to hammer into her.

When he pulled out, she scrambled onto her back. At first, she thought he had paused because she'd done something wrong, until she saw the darkness in his eyes.

"I want to see your face when you come," he said, going back down on her. This time he put his finger into her, prodding around as he licked her over and over again. Every time she moaned, he slowed his pace, kissing her sex to bring her back down to earth. Then Jude paralyzed her with his tongue, dragging it across her bulging clit, causing her to cry out.

Right before she exploded, he entered her again, moving his cock slowly back and forth inside her. He placed his thumb against her clit, gently pressing it as he went in deep. Elizabeth's vision blurred as Jude made divine love to her. She groaned, her entire body pulsating from the pleasure he drew from her.

He sucked her nipple, overflowing her senses, and she felt her nerves light on fire from his touch. She whimpered, then lost her voice, indicating the imminent flood of her release. Jude gripped her legs above each knee, forced them apart and went in fast and deep, all the while keeping his hand on her hot bud.

Elizabeth screamed and clutched onto Jude's forearms. He tried to stabilize himself from the earthquake they both felt as she convulsed around him. Her womb dipped and his hard cock pushed up against her. Jude pushed himself as deep as he could go, the explosion of passion making both of their bodies tremor.

The spasms lasted even longer than the first time they'd made love. Elizabeth had never experienced a climax like this. She continued to come until her muscles gave out. Her head fell back and she collapsed.

Jude gently pulled himself out and laid down beside her. "Did I hurt you?" he whispered, and stroked her cheek with the back of his hand.

"Oh, no. You didn't hurt me," Elizabeth said in between deep breaths.

"I couldn't control myself." He raked his gaze over her naked body.

Elizabeth threw her hands over her head. "You should never control yourself."

Jude turned onto his side and laid a hand across her torso. She felt like a goddess then, like every ounce of her had been dipped in golden ichor.

"You know, when you were out in the forest, I got very lonely one evening," Elizabeth said, looking up at Jude's rich, chocolate eyes. She ran her finger along the stubble of his jaw. "Annie had told me which room was yours, and I snuck in there. After a couple of glasses of wine, I imagined you were with me, kissing me, touching me like you did tonight, and I pleasured myself in your bed." She smiled, relishing the memory.

Jude ran his hands down her waist. "I wish I could have been there to see it."

"I could show you when you get back."

"No. You'll show me now."

Chapter Twenty

✦

Jude stood in the doorway of the master bedroom, admiring Elizabeth's beauty from afar. The way her brown hair caught fire in the morning sun nearly stole his breath away. Her delicate hands lay above her head, surrendering to her dreams. Her head was turned to one side, resting deep in the feather pillow, and her lips were parted ever so slightly. If Jude hadn't known her like he did, he wouldn't have thought she was human. Every inch of her glowed from the inside out.

He cleared his throat and forced back tears as he tried to burn the image of her into his mind. Jude shut his eyes and turned away. He went downstairs and into the ballroom, where he took the last of his tinctures from Millie. The fireplace crackled from the rushing wind that came in from the north. It howled like an angry ghost.

Annie filled up his copper tub like she always did, and Fiona brought in fresh clothes from the laundry. After he bathed and dressed, it was a little past noon.

Fiona brought in a rich and creamy potato soup with a beef pie and fruit salad. She set the tray down on the coffee table in front of the fireplace.

"Is there anything else you need before you go?" she said.

"Everything you might need is with the solicitor." Jude stood in front of the woman whom he'd known his entire life. She'd always been so patient and kind to his family. Fiona's wrinkles were pronounced as she tried not to cry. Jude took her in his arms and gave her a firm hug.

Not only had the witch's herbs strengthened him, but they also brought a deep sense of ease. He was like an unyielding oak tree when he released her.

"Elizabeth will probably sleep most of the day. Don't wake her."

Despite her efforts, Fiona wept.

"It'll be okay," he said as she wiped her tears on a rag.

"You come back to us. Even if it's not in one piece," she said, dabbing her eyes. She took in a deep breath. "Eat before it gets cold." Fiona left the room in haste.

Jude sat down and enjoyed what might be his last good meal. Meat pie was his favorite food, ever since he was little. As he ate, he snatched up the bottle of poison from the side table and flipped it upside down to study the contents. The witch had warned him not to consume the entire thing.

I'll need to be careful tonight.

He did his best to pass the time by eating and resting, but thoughts of what came next tormented him until the last light of day faded away.

After he took a final bite of the beef pie, Jude went out

the front doors of the castle, where Walter had pulled the Land Rover up to the front steps. He threw his duffel bag onto the passenger seat and turned to the gamekeeper.

Walter leaned against the front bumper with his arms crossed. "How long do you think you'll be this time?" he said, his gaze fixed on the gravel at his feet.

"What Millie gave me to take should work quickly. If I'm not back by the morning, you'll know I've failed," Jude said.

Walter looked up at him. "Give 'em hell."

Jude laid a hand on Walter's shoulder. "I promise I will, but if something happens, take care of them." He tilted his head at the castle doors.

Walter gave him a firm nod. Jude released his grip on the old groundskeeper and got into the vehicle. Jude got into the Land Rover and took off for Harlock. Instead of his usual route, he took the marked road on the map the witch had given him.

Jude headed out to find the secret place she'd marked in red ink. At first, he thought she might be daft, because he could find no indication of the road she'd marked on the map, but he was soon proved wrong. The Land Rover bumped and jostled over the pitted ground as he turned down an overgrown lane. The forest surrounding him grew dense. Tree branches slapped against the windows. He stopped in a small circle clearing and got out.

There in the grass, multiple rings of stones surrounded a large statue at least six feet tall. The black metal figure standing in the center was that of an old hag. Underneath her feet, a pile of skulls had been carved into the base of the statue. In her left hand she held a staff. He was sure it was the same woman he'd seen in his visions the last time he'd been at Harlock.

Jude entered the stone ring and approached the effigy. He laid the bog myrtle at the foot of the statue and prepared to pray. This was the first time he'd done so in many years. The last time, he'd simply recited words he'd been told to speak. Now he searched deep within his heart for the right thing to say. He still wasn't sure what he believed in, but he knew his brush with death had been real, and he wanted to reach out to her, the one whom the witch called the Cailleach.

"We met not very long ago," he said. Talking to an inanimate object made him feel strange. Jude paused to look up at the face of the woman. What was he expecting? For her to come to life and talk to him? He barely believed there was anything divine at all in the universe, and reaching out like this was a real stretch for him.

Jude cleared his throat and continued. "I'm about to go to a very dark place; I think you know where I'm headed. I'm not sure what's at the end of this road, but if you're there to greet me, I welcome it. I'm not afraid, but I wish to return to the waking world because there's someone I love here. She's more than I could ever ask for. She's better than this world. She's like you, beautiful and strong. If it wasn't for her, I wouldn't be here right now, standing before you. Take me to the underworld if you must but spare her if you can. Let her live a long and happy life, even if I'm not here to see it."

Jude stood in silence for a moment and went back to the Land Rover. As he sat in his seat, a snowflake whirled around in the air and landed on the windshield. The approach of the angry winter storm meant it was going to be cold in the dungeons. Jude zipped his coat up and drove down the road to the Harlock ruins.

When he pulled up, heavy sleet came down like ice shards being hurled from the sky. Jude grew worried. If the weather was this bad, everyone in The Order might not show up to take part in the final ritual, which would derail his plan to destroy them. If even one member remained alive, his family would be at risk.

I cannot let that happen.

Jude raced through the freezing downpour and hauled the trapdoor open. Once inside, the angry wind slammed it shut behind him.

He took his time going down the stairs, hoping not to alert them of his presence just yet. If he could remain in the shadows, he might hear some of their plans for the evening. Despite his initiation, Jude knew Boris and his friends would find a way to steal his blood.

I'm counting on it.

When he made it to the bottom of the stairs, he paused to listen.

No candles had been lit on the walls, and no noise came from the main chamber. He could still hear the storm outside, but the sound was faint. He took cautious steps up to the iron door, a light flaring inside his heart. No matter what happened tonight, he was never coming back to Harlock ever again. The excitement caused his blood to race, and he tried to quell the sensation with thoughts of what lay ahead.

Just take one step at a time.

He did just that and pushed the door open to set foot

inside the main chamber. It was pitch-black inside. Jude pulled out a lighter from his coat pocket and lit a candle on the wall. He approached the table that held the medical devices. Boris wanted to drain his blood.

Good.

A noise from down the hall caused Jude to turn his head. A figure emerged from the shadows. Boris was already dressed in his ceremonial robes. He lit a candle he held in his hand and placed it in a sconce on the wall beside the altar. Jude kept his distance, making sure the granite table stayed in between them.

"You're early," Boris said.

"I wanted to head out before the storm hit," Jude said. It wasn't a lie.

"That was smart thinking, my young pup. In fact, I have something special planned for this evening, so I'm glad you're here early. As we wait for the brothers to arrive, why don't we have something to warm us up?" Boris went to a small cabinet by the back entrance of the dungeon. He pulled out a couple of glasses and a bottle of whiskey. Jude watched him pour two drinks.

Boris handed him a glass and Jude reluctantly took it.

"It's been difficult for you to come to terms with your new position. It may take time, but first, you must finish your debts to the brotherhood. You are still in thrall to us for what you have done. There will be no more harsh punishments, as I believe you have learned your lesson, but there is a bit more that we need from you, to see us through this nasty winter. Three days of ritual have been planned to take us into the new year. I hope you are well rested."

"Three days? What will I do during this time?" Jude said, his heart racing. He didn't know what Boris had planned, which made his decision about what to do next very complicated.

"You will do as you have always done. The moon will not come out in this dastardly cold, therefore its pull is weak and won't imbue your blood with power. We require extra. Prepare yourself, young laird." Boris turned and left the chamber.

Jude waited until he couldn't see Boris's outline, and quickly withdrew the witch's potion from a hidden pocket in his coat. He drank the entire contents and stuffed the empty vial back in the secret compartment. He wasn't taking any chances. Millie had told him the effects wouldn't be pleasant, but he would still have his wits about him for many hours after he consumed it. Jude did his best not to dwell on the pain that was to come, and instead thought about the sweet release once it was all over.

When Boris returned, Jude kept images of Elizabeth fresh in his mind. Memories of her naked body beneath him allowed him to escape to a place of pleasure. That, alongside the magical sounds of her harp, eased him back from the cliff of dread he was teetering on.

"Let us begin," Boris said, lighting another candle.

"What about the others?" Jude said.

"They will come soon."

Jude sensed there was something Boris was hiding, which made him nervous. He tried to remain calm as he took his coat and shirt off and laid back on the granite table. The cold rock stung his bare skin. Jude let out a long huff, his unease more apparent than he liked.

When Jude stilled, Boris stuck a needle in his arm. Scarlet blood flowed out of his vein, through the plastic tube, and into the groove carved along the edge of the table. As his blood flowed into the narrow trails and made its way around the table, Jude tried not to think about how things could go wrong.

Boris moved to the other side of the altar. He dipped his finger into the granite furrow slowly filling with toxic blood. Jude's eyes followed Boris's hand as he brought it up to his mouth. Boris stuck out his tongue but quickly withdrew it before tasting the liquid and took hold of Jude's neck.

"You think you could kill me so easily?" Boris's eyes turned black. If demons were real, Jude was facing one down right then. The man had too much strength to be human.

I've given him this power, Jude thought.

He fought to release the grip Boris had on his throat, but the monster held him in place with too much force.

"You'll stay here until every bit of your blood has drained from your body. Until there is nothing left of you." Boris snarled. He unsheathed a knife and dug it into Jude's other arm to release a spring of blood.

Jude's vision started to tunnel. Bile burned at the back of his throat. His muscles grew weak with every passing second. Were these the effects of the poison, or had Boris slipped something into his drink? Elizabeth was right. Someone in his home worked for The Order and had tipped Boris off about the poison, and that fact hurt him more than all the pain he'd endured during his time in the Harlock dungeons.

He fought with every ounce of strength he had, but Boris held fast, choking him with superhuman strength.

Everything went black.

❧

THE STORM FROM THE NIGHT BEFORE HAD BECOME stronger. Icy rain pelted Boris's windshield of the black SUV as he pulled up to Beauloch castle. He got out and rapped on the giant doors. A small, blonde-haired woman inched open one of the oak behemoths.

"Who's there?" she said.

Boris kicked the door open the rest of the way, and the young maid fell onto her back. "Where is she? Where is the little bitch? Tell her that her dog is dead!"

"I'm right here," Elizabeth said, standing at the landing on the grand staircase.

"The Laird of Beauloch has betrayed The Order. A debt is owed!" Boris shouted.

Elizabeth descended the stairs with the same grace which he'd seen her do everything else. The spot on his neck still ached from her magnificent wrath. Ever since he'd laid eyes on her, he knew she was the real prize. Now that Rocoeurs was gone, he was free to indulge himself in her as he saw fit.

"Take me to pay the debt. Just leave the staff alone." She stopped directly in front of him.

Boris could tell she was frightened, but it didn't explain her sudden submission. "You come so willingly. Why?"

Tears formed in the young woman's bright-green eyes.

"If what you say is true, if the laird is dead, then I have no reason left to live." She shook with grief as she spoke.

Boris led her to the vehicle waiting out front. He tied her hands together with a coarse rope and gagged her for the drive to his manor, where he would begin the necessary steps to prepare the harpist to bear his children. It would take little effort to break her down; less effort than it had to overcome Rocoeurs, but still it needed to be done. Humiliation was always key to making women subservient to their masters.

Once inside the manor, Boris stood in front of the lithe figure. He slapped her across the face.

"That is for the dog's behavior. His decision to betray me cost him his life. Don't make the same mistake," he said. Boris inched closer to her. "We're going to do wonderful things together, you and I. As soon as this storm lets up, the brothers will get to meet you." Boris ran a finger across Elizabeth's cheek and wiped the single tear that fell from her eye. "But we will have some time before all that. You're going to play your music for me tomorrow. I want to hear it again."

Boris ran his fingers through her silky brown locks, remembering just how good she'd tasted. He fought to control his impulses. His mouth watered at the thought of ravishing her while he drank the youth and vitality from her veins.

I must be patient.

She was his now. The harpist belonged to him, and she would stay under his control forever.

❧

ELIZABETH DIDN'T STRUGGLE AGAINST BORIS AS HE pulled her by the hair. He took her to a sparsely furnished bedroom with only a bed and a small wooden table beside it. As soon as he shut her in and she was alone, Elizabeth fought against her restraints, trying desperately to break free, but the bonds around her wrists were too secure. The door opened again, and a short man with curly hair and round glasses entered. He set a black medical case down on the edge of the bed and pulled out a pair of scissors.

"I'm going to remove your gag, and cut this rope." He peeled the duct tape from her mouth and slashed the rope with a box cutter.

The moment she was able to, Elizabeth spoke. "Please, you have to help me!"

The man took her by the shoulders and forced her to sit on the bed. "Quiet, lest you bring him back to torment you further. Your best bet is to obey his every order from now on. Do you understand me?"

Elizabeth nodded.

"My name is Dr. Brenner, by the way." He reached into his bag again, removed a stethoscope, and took her vitals.

Elizabeth took in a few deep breaths. She had to stay calm.

Boris must be holding Jude captive somewhere else in the house, she thought.

Her heart didn't truly believe he'd died. The mere thought of Jude's life coming to an end threatened to pull her under a wave of despair. If she believed it now, she would never be able to come back up for air. No matter what had happened to Jude, Elizabeth knew she had to find him and bring him home.

Dr. Brenner removed the lid from a bottle of pills, dumped two into his hand, and held them out to her.

"What are these for?" she said.

"They are just for sleep. I promise."

Now wasn't the time to fight. The Order had her well in their grasp. She needed to wait and learn the lay of the rooms, the schedule of the cleaning staff, and other critical details. She took the pills and threw them back.

"You look like you're in good shape. I'll see you tomorrow," the doctor said. He picked up his kit and left the bedroom, locking the door from the outside.

Elizabeth ran to the window. If she could slip outside and gauge the size of the manor, she might get a better idea where the other rooms were. She pulled back the curtains, but a large metal grid shadowed the other side of the frames.

The window is covered with iron bars.

Elizabeth took a step back in disbelief. Defeated, she sat on the edge of the bed. The drugs started to take hold.

THE STILL AIR FELT COLD AGAINST HIS SKIN. JUDE HAD been here before. All around him was a colorless, grey terrain. He stood on a wide, meandering path that cut through dormant trees and dead, brittle bushes. Under his bare feet, ashen sand left footprints as he walked. Up ahead, he spied a faint orange glow near the edge of the path.

Jude approached a man sitting under a green yew tree, the only flora he'd seen alive until this point. His face looked old and wan as he stared into the flames of his small fire in front of him.

"Hello?" Jude said.

The man didn't acknowledge him, so he moved on. Not much farther down from the man, another yew tree sheltered a small encampment. Beside the glowing embers of a fire, a young woman lay on a pallet of blankets. The pallid skin on her face made Jude think she might be very sick.

A distant cough tore his attention away. As he continued down the trail, Jude passed another small clearing where a young child sat. The blue-faced boy held a stick over the weak flames of his fire, cooking something.

None of them said a word.

In the distance, a vast mountain range rose into the sky. Its peaks were covered in an icy frost that Jude knew was unlike any that existed on earth.

What is this place?

Overhead, a bright, blue moon shone, providing light as he made his way through the frigid landscape. A slight breeze blew over Jude's bare arms. He looked down and noticed the skin on his hands appeared frightfully pale.

Have I always been this way? No, I don't think so.

Jude continued along the dusty walkway until he came to a lake. It was completely black, with ice forming at the edges. All around it were trees covered in green moss. They didn't look quite alive, but they weren't dead either.

On the far side of the lake, a figure emerged from the shadows. A woman with long red hair that flowed around her arms and past her fingertips appeared in a pure-white dress. She moved to the water's edge, collecting something from the ground and placing it in a basket hanging from her arm.

Jude waved his hands high above his head to get her attention, but she was too busy doing other things to notice. Then he tried to yell, but no sound came out of his mouth. He tried over and over to get the woman's attention by screaming, shouting, and making other noises, but to no avail. The only sound he heard was the frigid air dancing over the icy mountains.

Chapter Twenty-One

Elizabeth woke wearing a long red dress. Someone had brought the garment to her some hours earlier, but the sedative had distorted her sense of time. She knew a day had gone by since she'd arrived, but not much else. She approached the window. If she had to guess, the sun had set a while ago. In the darkness, Icy snow blew through the iron bars to tap against the window panes.

Dr. Brenner entered the room.

"He's almost ready for you. Come, sit." He pointed at the bed and Elizabeth sat down.

"Turn around."

Elizabeth put her back to him and he pulled a bristle brush through her hair.

"Ow," she muttered.

The doctor didn't relent and yanked out a few strands at the root. "So beautiful." He paused to bury his face in her hair. The tip of his nose brushed the back of her neck.

"What time is it?" Elizabeth said.

"It's late in the evening. You slept all day," he said, and stood up. Dr. Brenner walked out of the room, pausing in the doorway. He gestured for Elizabeth to follow him.

Elizabeth's stomach twisted into a tight knot. She hadn't realized the sedative would be so strong as to knock her out for almost twenty-four hours. She had hoped to come up with a plan while she lay awake in bed, but that opportunity was long gone.

The doctor led her into a gaudy parlor room. In the corner sat her lever harp. Someone had brought it from Beauloch. Boris sat on a tufted leather couch on the opposite side of the room from her instrument. He stood as she made her entrance. Dr. Brenner exited the room and locked the door behind him.

"Food is over there," Boris said, pointing to a silver tray with small hors d'oeuvres laid out on a table in one corner of the room.

Elizabeth sidled up to the table, putting a little more distance between her and Boris. The memory of him pinning her against the bookshelf and licking her blood almost made her gag. She fought hard to forget it and forced herself to eat. If she was going to find Jude, dead or alive, she would need her strength.

Boris sipped amber liquid from an ornate glass, and his eyes never left her while she took her time nibbling different cheeses, fruit spreads, and pâtés. Trying to break his gaze, Elizabeth poured herself a glass of water and pretended to inspect the harp.

Her actions must've intrigued him, because the moment she plucked a string, he got to his feet and approached her. She tried to create more space between them by retreating to the table in the corner again and putting her glass down, but he followed her. Elizabeth looked away from him, her eyes glued to the floor as he combed her hair with his fingertips.

The dress she wore was somewhat modest, except for the plunge in the back, which went all the way down to her ass, revealing copious amounts of skin. Boris ran his fingers along the hem of the long V at the back of her dress, starting at the shoulder and ending at the very bottom of her back, causing her to tremble with fear.

"I want to hear you play," he said.

Elizabeth took that as her cue to sit behind the harp. She felt a little bit better with the large instrument in between her and her captor. Before she could begin playing, she had to tune it. Elizabeth took her time, listening to each string, hoping to wear him out before the evening was over. If she could keep him drinking his whiskey, she might be able to put him in a trance.

After she tuned the last string, Elizabeth glanced in Boris's direction. He sat at one end of the oversized couch, one ankle resting atop his other knee. It was difficult to distinguish his features in the dim light, but she could still make out his grey-streaked hair, gelled into a perfect swoop.

His face was deceiving because he appeared a lot younger than he was, but Elizabeth could see past the glamour he tried to put on. In the darkness, she might not be able to see his prominent crow's feet or his yellow, stained teeth, but she knew they were there.

Elizabeth started to play. She began with simple pieces

she'd known forever. They were almost dull, but she emphasized them enough to pique his interest. Her hands danced over the harp like two swans frolicking in spring. After about eight songs, she paused to look at Boris.

His gaze was still on her, boring through her like the cold knife he'd stabbed her with that night at the party. Her leg still ached from the trauma. As she ended another classical piece, Boris got up and poured himself another drink at the bar. She finished the song beautifully, but the fear of what he might do next made her mind go blank. What could she play now? While she lowered a few levers, Boris came up behind her. He took a strand of her hair and breathed in her scent.

"Don't stop," he said.

Elizabeth waited for him to release her hair, but instead of letting go, he grabbed a handful and yanked her head backward.

"You'll stop when I tell you to." He released his grip on her, allowing her to get into position again to play.

This time she was nervous, so she played the pieces she knew best. They weren't difficult, but her fingers slipped a few times. Still, she gave it her all, knowing Boris would be upset if he thought she was defying his orders. While she played, he ran his knuckles gently along the nape of her neck, and every hair on her body stood on end. He slid his hand down to the exposed skin on her back and brushed his fingers up and down along her spine.

When Elizabeth finished the song, she heard Boris breathing heavily and his hand fumbling inside his pants. She quickly started another piece, so as not to anger him.

All the while he stood mere inches from her, pleasuring himself to her music.

Elizabeth didn't think about what type of music might be appropriate for such an occasion. She just hoped it would be over soon. As she played, his breathing turned into moans of pleasure. He continued to stroke himself just out of her view.

At the end of an arpeggio, he finally came. Boris squeezed the back of her neck as he grunted with relief. It took every ounce of her will to finish the song and not try to run from the room.

Elizabeth finished her piece and Boris relented his hold on her. He went back over to the couch, taking his whiskey with him. He picked up a small remote and pressed a button. A ring echoed outside the door of the parlor.

Dr. Brenner reentered the room.

"Success?" he said, facing Boris, his back to Elizabeth.

"It was a great success. I'll notify you after the next round," Boris said, handing something small to the man.

Dr. Brenner walked up to the floor lamp and examined the ejaculate in the plastic cup under the yellow light. "This looks very good," he said.

"When will we be able to start the process?" Boris said, tipping his glass back.

Dr. Brenner turned to Elizabeth and smiled. "As soon as I examine the lovely lady, we can begin the fertilization process."

Elizabeth's blood went cold. She had to hold onto the harp to keep from fainting. Dr. Brenner approached her and placed his warm hand on her back.

"I'll conduct the exam later this evening. Not to worry, darling, it's nothing."

Elizabeth was too distraught to comprehend anything he said after that. As the evening wore on, the songs she played became a jumbled blur. She wasn't sure which ones she'd played and which she hadn't. Boris continued to masturbate late into the evening.

It wasn't until Dr. Brenner came in to fetch her that she finally snapped out of her daze. He led her back to the bedroom that was now her prison cell.

"Here, take this. It will make things easier for you," he said, holding out a pill and some water.

"No. I can't take anything else," Elizabeth said.

"It isn't as strong as what I gave you last night. Please, otherwise he will send people in here to force you to submit."

Elizabeth took the pill with a shaky hand and choked it down.

"I'll be back in an hour," Dr. Brenner said.

Elizabeth stood by the window, desperately trying to look outside, but saw nothing but freezing rain falling on the winter landscape around the hellhole of Boris's mansion. The stomach acid she'd been pushing down during her performance threatened to come up.

Dr. Brenner returned with a different medical kit.

He urged her to lie on her back. The drugs had begun working, but her legs still trembled as she opened them for the old man. She felt a familiar prodding. Memories of countless doctor visits surfaced in her mind. They'd determined she'd been healthy, but that was not what worried her.

When was the last time I bled? she wondered.

"We're done," Dr. Brenner said. He tapped her knees and she closed her legs. "See? It wasn't so bad."

Elizabeth sat up. "Where is Jude?" she demanded.

Dr. Brenner pulled his gloves off with a snap and gathered his things to leave. Elizabeth seized him by the shoulders.

"Where is he? Where is Jude!" she screamed.

Dr. Brenner removed her hands from his arms. "We've been over this. The boy is no longer with us."

Elizabeth flew into a rage. She pushed the old man against the wall and gripped his lower jaw, digging her nails into his crepey skin.

"Take me to him right now!" she shouted.

Someone else came running into the room and removed her hold on the old doctor. She kicked and screamed, demanding to know where Jude was.

"I don't believe you! I don't believe he's dead!"

Jude was everything to her, and they knew it. Her entire will to live depended on him being alive. What else would she fight for? What other reason did she have to live?

A poke and a sting in her ass forced her to sleep.

JUDE WADED INTO THE COLD WATER. HE NEEDED TO reach the woman on the other side. Something told him she would be the key to his salvation. It was the only thought he could muster from his tired brain.

You must reach her.

Jude swam as hard as he could but made little progress. There was no use in crying out, so he kept going until he grew so tired he sank to the bottom.

Blackness surrounded him and the biting cold made every inch of his skin feel numb. The water around him began to freeze, and the last bit of air left his lungs, but somehow, he didn't need it anymore. His lips started to crack from the ice, but he felt no pain.

Why can't I feel anything?

The image of a beautiful woman carved into stone flashed across his blackening vision. She broke free from the rock she'd been chiseled from and mounted a brown stag. The beast trampled through a blizzard, carrying her away somewhere. A loud shrill made Jude's ears ring. He wanted to shut his eyes, but the illusion overpowered his will. Fear gripped his chest until the maiden and the beast broke through the storm and emerged in a viridescent glen.

The light of the dale warmed his skin. All around, the ice that had formed so quickly started to melt. Jude heard a voice but couldn't make out whose it was. The surrounding frost melted as the amber light glowed brighter. The voice grew louder.

A thirst like he'd never experienced before hit him. Jude tried desperately to part his lips for a drink, but it was almost impossible.

"Drink, drink, drink," the voice above him said. Was it the harbinger of death who taunted him?

Death. I had forgotten about Death.

Jude struggled but eventually broke through the surface of the icy lake. On the horizon, a beautiful sunset illuminated the grey, barren landscape he'd been wandering for what had felt like ages. He drew in a deep breath, letting the warm light of the sun fill his lungs.

ELIZABETH CAME TO ON A SHOWER BENCH. WARM WATER sprayed over her face and chest. Someone lathered shampoo in her hair from behind.

After she'd been bathed, the elderly woman who'd scrubbed her down helped her into another red dress. Once she'd been put into the silky gown, Elizabeth sat down on the edge of the bed. The woman knelt in front of her and took one foot at a time to put thick, warm socks on her feet.

"Can you help me?" Elizabeth pleaded as the crone got to her feet.

"Quiet!" the woman snapped.

Her stomach growled, but she was too frightened and weak to ask for food. If she acted out, they might sedate her again.

After she'd had her hair brushed and makeup applied, which she only noticed because she sat in front of a mirror as it was being done, the glowering woman marched her into a large dining hall, where a group of old men sat at a long table.

They all stood up and looked at her, their faces eager. Elizabeth tried to ignore their hungry eyes, but they were everywhere. Dr. Brenner helped her into the seat at one end of the table and placed some food in front of her.

"You must eat," he whispered, and urged a fork into her hand.

Elizabeth nibbled at the baked chicken on her plate. She ate, but she was a world away. Wherever Jude's soul was now, was where hers had gone also. The men in the room spoke about her, but she didn't comprehend what they were saying until Boris rose to his feet.

"It is time for dessert, my friends. Tonight, we have but one item on the menu," he said, his words drawn out with sarcasm. The other men laughed, their aged baritone cackles filling the room.

Someone took Elizabeth by the shoulders and forced her out of her chair. She snapped back to reality. The sedatives had been soaked up by whatever crumbs she'd managed to eat and the anxiety of her situation set in again.

"The road is too icy. We'll have to walk," someone called from behind her.

Elizabeth was led out the back of the house. A frightful wind and pellets of ice blurred her vision. Wet mud soaked through her long socks as the men of The Order dragged her into the dark night. They laughed and talked as if everything was normal.

Where are they taking me?

After they curved around a low hill, Elizabeth could make out a clearing up ahead. Crumbling walls of stone jutted up through the violent snow. The men stopped beside a retaining wall lined with old rocks.

The sound of an iron door creaking open grated on her nerves. Elizabeth suddenly recalled the details of the place Jude went to during his monthly rituals. He rarely spoke about it, but the image of a crumbling castle and the extensive dungeon preserved underground never left her. They'd brought her to Harlock. Her heart beat wildly against her ribs. She struggled against the stinging grip of her captors, but that only forced the men to dig their fingers deeper into her arms.

The brothers hauled her into the pitch-black corridor. The damp earth muffled the sound of the storm raging outside, but their voices echoed deep into the Harlock dungeons. The flick of a match lit a torch in front of her. Boris guided them down the passage with it.

When they entered a large chamber, Boris lit the sconces on the wall with the flame he carried. Elizabeth's eyes darted to the faces surrounding her, now covered by hideous masks of animal skulls. She ripped her gaze away and peered around the dungeon, hoping to spot a door or window she might escape from.

Then she saw him.

Jude lay on a table in a small alcove. A single overhead light illuminated his body. His skin looked pale, and his face was bruised.

Elizabeth tried to break free, tried to go to him, but she didn't have the strength. "Jude!" she screamed.

A hand smashed into her face, nearly knocking her out.

"Lay her on the altar," Boris commanded.

Two men picked her up and hoisted her onto a black stone altar. Elizabeth looked around for a way out of this hell, but the men of The Order had her surrounded. Each wore a blood-red cloak, creating a crimson wall which prevented her from leaving. They tied her wrists to the table with thick leather straps.

Boris walked to the head of the altar and pulled out a knife from underneath his cloak. The men began to chant in a language Elizabeth didn't recognize. She struggled for breath, tears choking her airway.

"Jude, Jude!" she said again, but deep in her heart, she knew it was no use. Wherever he was, he couldn't hear her.

Panic threatened to set in until Elizabeth remembered Boris planned on using her for breeding purposes. She would survive this night, at least, but for how long after that?

The cold blade sank into the soft flesh of her forearm and Elizabeth cried out in pain. When she looked at her arm, she saw a steady stream of blood rush into a groove carved in the stone. The scarlet liquid slid down a narrow sluiceway and into a silver chalice not far from her fingers.

"Taste the essence of the finest beauty to ever grace your presence, gentlemen," Boris said as he passed the cup around to the men of The Order.

Elizabeth became lightheaded, but she couldn't look away from the horror of the men reddening their lips with her blood.

Boris wrapped a cloth around her arm to stem the bleeding. He tied it off tightly and moved to the end of the table to stand at her feet. "The strength of our everlasting Order will be secured tonight!" Boris said.

The men started up their chanting once more. Boris climbed onto the altar and straddled Elizabeth. She fought hard to slip her hands out of the leather bands, but they were too tight.

Someone handed Boris the silver chalice. He held it up high and poured its contents over the front of Elizabeth's dress, covering her neck and chest in her own blood. It splattered onto her face. She could taste the copper liquid.

Boris leaned down and licked the blood from between her breasts. Elizabeth was forced to turn her head to the side, so as not to see the terrible thing that was about to happen to her. There was a small gap between two men, through which she could see into the alcove where Jude lay. Next to him stood the hooded figure of Death.

Elizabeth felt Boris's hand crawl up her skirt.

"Take me with you!" Elizabeth shouted to the cloaked figure standing over her lover.

Boris's hand drew farther up her legs, past her knees and to her thighs.

"Hey! Who's there?" a man shouted, breaking the beat of the chant.

Everyone stopped to look in the direction of the alcove, where the grim cloak of Death stood. With blackened hands, she pulled back her hood, revealing a sunken face with cold, green eyes.

"Death treads here," she said, her voice an icy whisper.

❧

JUDE DRANK IN THE WARM SUNLIGHT. IT FILLED HIM instantly, satiating his thirst. With his strength returned, he swam to edge of the lake where the beautiful woman stood. One side of her face twisted with lines of black from the aura of death that she exuded.

"You don't belong here," she said.

"Don't I? I've been your companion for some time now," Jude said.

Death held out one hand to him. He felt again her icy,

dead fingers. The flesh was still intact, but the skin was crepey and rippled against his palm.

"I must go now," Jude said.

"You'll be back," Death said.

"Of course I will, just not for a long time," Jude said, releasing Death's hand.

When Jude opened his eyes, the old witch stood over him. She was pouring a potion into his mouth. He drank it all down, knowing it was what had brought him back from the barren land that Death reigned over.

What he drank now wasn't like her other potions. This one felt like it was made of real magic. Every muscle in his body tingled. His blood soared with life. His lungs filled with something more than air.

A commotion came from the main chamber. The witch turned to the men in red cloaks.

"Death treads here," she said, before placing a long dagger into Jude's hands.

Jude rose up from the table. He didn't wait for them to say anything before he unleashed his rage. He took the first brother of The Order who came at him the old-fashioned way, plunging the dagger into the man's gut and up into his ribs to penetrate his lungs and heart. After the man fell to the floor, Jude saw why they had been congregating around the altar.

Lying on her back, being held against her will, was Elizabeth. She'd been bound with the old straps they'd used on him during his early days in The Order. Fresh blood painted her chest and neck, and Boris lay atop her licking it up while his hand roved over her hip.

A savage animal awoke in Jude. He stepped behind the

man closest to him and grasped his hair. Without hesitating, Jude sank his dagger into the side of the thug's neck, then pushed it through his throat, ripping it out and spraying blood over the entire dungeon.

Panic ensued, and two men raced to the iron gate that led to back passage, but it was locked. The witch stood just on the other side, dangling the keys in the air, laughing. Jude chased after them, stopping to pick up an iron skewer from the rack on the wall. He raised it high above his head and brought it down with all his weight, sinking it deep into the eye of the man on his left. The man screamed in agony. Jude ripped the rod back out and the man fell to the floor, a pool of blood gathered at his feet.

"Hey, dog!" a voice called from across the room.

Jude looked up to see Boris holding a knife against Elizabeth's throat. The remaining five men stood behind him, cowering in fear.

"Another move and I will cut her throat!" Boris snarled.

Jude approached anyway, throwing the skewer onto the stone floor, the clatter echoing through the chamber. "Let her go and I might let you live," Jude said.

"Stay back!" Boris said, pulling Elizabeth closer to him. The tip of his knife dug into the delicate skin at her throat and drew a bit of blood.

Jude held up his hands in defeat, even though the monster in him still raged. He could see his hot breath in the air, like an aurochs huffing in the frost.

"Grab him!" Boris shouted. The men crept up to Jude and with sudden speed grabbed his arms. One of them took some rope hanging on the wall and bound Jude's hands together tightly. Boris smiled, his lips still stained red from blood. "So the dog came back from the dead, just in time to see his little bitch get fucked by the wolf pack."

Elizabeth squirmed beneath Boris's grip and whimpered in fear.

"You'll watch while I taste her sweet flesh." Boris lifted his knife from Elizabeth's throat and dug into the top of her shoulder.

A small tinkling noise came from behind Jude. He looked back to see an empty bottle rolling toward him from the iron door. The witch sat in a crouch but quickly stood up.

Jude looked at the small potion bottle at his feet, up at the witch, then turned back to Boris and Elizabeth.

Boris opened his mouth and placed it on Elizabeth's shoulder. He moaned and sucked blood from the cut. Terror was painted all over Elizabeth's beautiful face.

It took every bit of control Jude had not to lunge for Boris, but he knew he had to be patient. Boris took a breath, went in for seconds, and pulled himself away again.

Boris swallowed, but instead of latching onto her shoulder again, he struggled for breath.

"Elizabeth, run!" Jude said.

Boris released his grip on Elizabeth and placed his hands around his throat. He stood stunned and confused for a moment, then choked and vomited blood. Every gasp for air he took seemed to be futile. His muscles began to spasm as the poison took hold of him.

The other brothers in The Order approached him to see what was wrong. By then, blood was seeping out of his eyes and nose and the sounds he made were those of a man dying in agony.

"Here, child!" the witch said, holding the iron door open. Elizabeth climbed down from the altar and rushed to the gate. Once Elizabeth was through, the witch locked it back up.

Boris fell from the altar and propped himself up on his hands and knees. He sat up on his heels to let out a final cry of pain. Then he burst into flames.

Jude used the moment to his advantage, ripping himself free of the ropes that bound him. The remaining men in The Order were so distracted by Boris, they hadn't seen him free his hands. Jude took a hammer off the wall and sunk the sharp end firmly into the temple of the man closest to him.

He snatched his next victim by the back of the head, gripping his short hair. Jude planted the man's face into a rusty old sawhorse. He dashed it against the stand a few times for good measure, then threw him to the floor.

The remaining three men stood at the iron gate that led out to the Harlock ruins, trying desperately to get it open.

"You fools. There's no escape from hell!" Jude picked up the dagger Millie had given him from the floor and rushed the last three men.

He pinned one of them up against the iron door and sank the dagger into his belly. The man screamed and Jude ripped him open, his innards now hanging out of a horrible gash. Jude tossed him into the growing fire that once had been Boris.

The last two men were on their knees. One pleaded for his life, which enraged Jude even more. He forced his dagger up through the man's jaw and into his head, silencing him for good.

The last man cowered under the table that held the devices they'd used to torture Jude the last time he'd come to the Harlock dungeons. He recognized the man as Dr. Brenner. Memories resurfaced of the doctor helping Boris use special techniques to inflict maximum pain without killing him.

Jude grabbed him by the throat and lifted him up in the air. His strength came from a place that felt otherworldly, somewhere outside of himself. He was no longer Jude, but the monster The Order had created over the years, and that monster was angry. Jude carried Dr. Brenner to a massive spike protruding from the wall. He pushed the doctor against it until the sharp iron point protruded from his guts. Screams of pain and horror filled the chamber.

"Don't let him suffer, Jude!" Elizabeth cried out.

Jude looked at the beautiful creature who had brought him back from the brink of death, now giving him orders and guiding him on his vengeful journey. He stabbed Dr. Brenner in the heart, finishing off the last member of The Order.

"Go on! Get out of here quickly!" the witch shouted at Jude. She pulled something out of her pocket and sprinkled a thin liquid across the dungeon floor and Boris's flaming corpse. The liquid hissed and the fires rose up to the ceiling.

Jude ran to the gate where Elizabeth waited for him. She took his bloodied hand, and they raced out of the dungeons, running as fast as they could.

WALTER WAITED FOR THEM DOWN THE ROAD WITH THE Land Rover. Without hesitating, they hopped into the vehicle. Walter threw the truck into gear and sped away.

"Wait! What about Gran?" Elizabeth said.

"She told me not to wait for her," Walter said.

Elizabeth held on to the seat in front of her as the Land Rover dipped and banked over the rough country road. Jude fumbled with the seatbelt but managed to get it over her head and buckle her in.

"What's that behind us?" Walter said.

Elizabeth twisted in her seat and saw a bright-orange glow light up the night sky where they'd just come from.

"I think she set the whole place on fire," Jude said.

"We have to go back!" Elizabeth cried out.

"I promised her I wouldn't stop until you were both home safe," Walter said, putting the pedal to the metal.

Jude wrapped his arms around her and held her close as she cried. Elizabeth had missed Gran all those years, wondering if she'd met some horrible ending. Now, looking back at the rising flames, it seemed like it would be a miracle if Millie made it out alive. Being burned to death in that awful place was worse than any fate Elizabeth could've imagined for her Gran when she was missing.

"We'll come back for her. I promise," Jude said, kissing her on the head.

Elizabeth was in a daze most of the way back. By the time they arrived, she was so fatigued from the whole ordeal that she nearly collapsed on the front steps of Beauloch.

IN THE DAYS AFTER THE FIRE, JUDE LOST TRACK OF TIME. Fiona and Annie brought them their meals in bed, and Jude and Elizabeth slept in each other's arms day and night. The violent winter storm returned to unleash another fury of ice and rain in the glen, blurring the hours between day and night.

It was early one evening, while the freezing rain lashed at the windows, when they finally had enough energy to reflect on their ordeal.

"Do you want to talk about what happened?" Jude said, holding Elizabeth's delicate hands in his own. Even after everything she'd been through, she was still beautiful.

"They gave me some sedatives, so the details are a little bit fuzzy. Boris made me play the harp for him. Oh!"

Jude squeezed her hands. "What is it? What did he do?" Guilt wracked him and his gut twisted into a knot. He'd promised to protect her and had failed to do that one simple task. If it wasn't for the witch, they might both be dead.

"My harp was in the house when it burned down," Elizabeth said, tears gathering in her eyes.

"I'll buy you a new one. A better one. Elizabeth, look, if Boris did something to you—"

"No. I'm okay, Jude. I promise. The worst of what he did was let that creepy doctor examine me. That's it."

"Are you sure?" Jude said, sensing something else in her voice.

Elizabeth paused for a minute, looking down at their

hands. "Well, Boris pleasured himself many times while I played the harp."

Fury surged through Jude's veins. He scooted closer to Elizabeth and ran his hand through her hair. "Boris is long gone now, along with Dr. Brenner and the others."

Elizabeth frowned. "I know. I was there. It's just ... the memory is so horrifying. I'm not sure I want to go near the instrument ever again. Isn't that strange?"

Jude squeezed her in his arms. "No. It's not strange." They sat there for a long time, holding and comforting each other.

"What about you, Jude? Are you going to be okay? I thought you were dead. What happened to you?"

Jude sat back, trying to recall the events that led to his journey into the underworld. He himself didn't even understand it all. "I'm not sure what happened exactly. Everything was going as planned, but somehow Boris had gotten word about my plan to poison them. The next thing I knew, I was dreaming, but it didn't feel like dreaming. I was in this shadow land with a bunch of sick and dying people. A woman with the hands of death oversaw this realm. I'd seen her a few times before, when I was very sick. Then I woke up to your grandmother standing over me, giving me some sort of tonic. The rest is, well, you know, very bloody."

Elizabeth kissed Jude. It was the first time Jude felt they were completely safe from The Order. All the worries in his life were gone. He was free to love without any restraint. He pulled her in tighter, but she broke free from his grasp.

"I know who has betrayed us, and I have a plan," she said.

Elizabeth stood by Jude in the dining room. They held hands, waiting for everyone to arrive. Walter came in last; he'd removed his boots, and his dungarees looked damp from the rain that continued to pour.

"Has there been any sign of Millie?" Jude said.

Walter shook his head.

"We will keep looking. In the meantime, it has come to our attention that one of you has betrayed my trust. Correspondence has been found between someone in this house and a former member of The Order—that same order which is now a pile of ashes. Annie? Come forward."

Annie's face was frozen with fear. She took a step forward.

"Would you like to say something before we lay out our case against you?"

"Case? What? I've done nothing wrong!" Annie shrieked.

"You are the only one who knows the secret passages better than I do. That is the only way I could have lost sight of Boris that night he attacked Elizabeth. You've been helping him all this time. Maybe he was the one who sent you here to spy on me!" Jude roared. He stepped forward to intimidate the small housekeeper.

Annie ran away crying.

Walter and Fiona looked shocked and dour at the same time.

"No one is to speak with her. I'll escort her from the grounds myself," Jude said, following the maid.

When he left the room, he didn't head for the staff's quarters. Instead, he went into the underground passage. He kept quiet as he crept toward the door that had been boarded up. It was now perpetually ajar, the boards stiff and stuck in a divot on the stone floor. He slid through the opening and up the stairs to the conservatory.

Jude crouched down, peering through the narrow window of the basement office that butted up against the greenhouse. He waited and watched until someone came into the room. The window was open just enough for him to hear someone trying to make a phone call.

Whoever they called didn't answer. The person was leaving a frantic voicemail when Jude decided to burst through the window.

Fiona screamed as Jude made his dramatic entrance.

"Boris won't be able to reach his voicemail because he's dead, Fiona. How could you do this? How could you betray me and my family?"

"I-I'm sorry! Please forgive me!" Fiona said with fear in her voice as she held the landline telephone in her shaking hands.

"Give me one good reason I shouldn't end you right now for what you've done. You almost got me killed, and almost condemned Elizabeth to a lifetime of horror! And for what?"

Fiona dropped the phone on the floor. "I was just trying to help. You were going to end your life and I couldn't bear it! You're like a son to me. We're kin. Please, you must understand."

Jude sensed the fear in the old woman. "How would betraying me help?"

"Boris told me he would let you become a member of The Order if I could find someone to replace you. Someone young, of good stock. Please! I didn't know you'd fall for the girl!"

"It wasn't going to work, your plan. Boris never would have let me go free. Pack your things and leave, before I change my mind about what to do with you." Jude picked up the phone and slammed it against the receiver.

ELIZABETH STRETCHED OUT ON THE CONCRETE BENCH beneath the yew tree in the Beauloch gardens. She watched as a pair of men brought the new harp outside and placed it next to the rose bushes, which were in full bloom all along the old stone wall. The flowers were a bright yellow against the dark-green leaves. Once the men left, Elizabeth admired how beautiful the instrument was.

Jude paid the men and came down the back steps of the castle to meet her in front of the harp. "Maybe if you're outside, you won't feel so confined," he said.

Elizabeth sat up and Jude planted a soft kiss on her lips.

"I don't know. I'm probably going to play horribly now."

A rustle in the tree line caught their attention, and the small figure of Gran walked up to them. She had on her usual hag attire—a tattered cloak and utility belt—but she looked even older than before, like ten years had passed. They'd had no sign from her since that night she burned

Harlock and Boris's manor to the ground, and that was almost four months ago.

"Gran! Where have you been?" Elizabeth rushed to embrace her grandmother, who squeezed her back as she always did. It was a relief to know she still had her strength.

"I've been out, living with the fairies for a bit. You know how I do. Walter was supposed to let you know I was alive," she said. Her green eyes appeared faded, but they still twinkled with magic.

"He mentioned you were around, that was all." Elizabeth placed her hands on Gran's shoulders.

Millie lifted her right hand, revealing three shortened fingers. They'd been cut and sutured at the first joint and were scarred over. "Harlock took my hand from me, but I survived. I'm moving back into the cottage this summer, when the ground dries up. It'll make things easier for me."

"That's wonderful news," Jude said, placing his arm around Elizabeth.

"Here, I want you to have this," Millie said, holding out a small book. Elizabeth took it and flipped through different herbal recipes Millie had crafted just for her. The first one was a tea to help recover from snake bites.

"You think I could get bitten by another snake?" Elizabeth said to Millie.

"Oh, I think it's a distinct possibility. I've seen a few around the castle." Millie rocked back on her heels and admired the shiny new harp.

"Why are you being so cryptic?" Jude said.

Elizabeth looked up at the man she'd once feared but

now had come to love. His dark-brown eyes searched hers, his brows furrowed with concern.

"It's nothing, Jude," Elizabeth said. She flipped through a few more pages containing drawings of stags and red-haired maidens.

Jude looked at Millie, then back at Elizabeth.

"Enough of that! That grimoire is gonna cost you," Millie said, stamping her cane on the ground.

"What do you want for it?" Elizabeth said.

Millie pointed with her cane at the new harp sitting among the roses. "Play me a song."

Elizabeth smiled, pulled Millie into a tight emrbrace, and kissed her on the cheek. "Anything for you, Gran."

Jude placed a chair next to the harp. Elizabeth sat down and took a deep breath. She looked around at the beautiful flora surrounding her. The spring sun glorified the beauty of the earth. She stretched out her hands and began to play.

Epilogue

New glass windows had been installed in the conservatory, allowing the July sun to beam down on the late blooms of summer. Jude followed Millie around the vast room with a watering can as she inspected the lemon trees and special herbs she had planted.

On the other side of the lush greenhouse, Elizabeth reclined on a lounge chair with the small lap harp he'd bought for her as a birthday present a few weeks earlier. The delicate sound the strings made echoed around the room.

A year ago, Jude would've never dreamt he could be at peace like this. After going to hell and back, he supposed he deserved a tiny slice of paradise. Not everything had gone according to plan, but they'd survived, and he and Elisabeth had each other. That was all that mattered to him.

"You're thinking about something serious," Millie said as she added potting soil to a small container.

Jude set the watering can on a nearby worktable. "I've often wondered if it was your intention to send me to Death in those dungeons."

The old woman laughed. "You were going to meet your end in Harlock whether you wanted to or not. Boris was going to make sure of it. At least with my help, you came back."

Jude nodded and picked the can back up. After spending so much time with the witch, he didn't doubt her wisdom. "It's over now, and she's safe. That's all I care about." He glanced over at Elizabeth, still plucking away on the harp. Her hair looked gilded in the sunlight, and her hands seemed to be infused with magic as she played.

"Is anything ever really over?" Millie said.

Voices came from beyond the set of French doors leading out to the Beauloch gardens. Jude recognized one of them; his brother had arrived. Millie took the watering can from him and nodded in the direction of the back patio.

Jude went up to Elizabeth and placed a kiss on her forehead.

She stopped her playing. "Is your brother here?"

"I'm going to greet him. Don't get up," Jude said.

Elizabeth went back to plucking the harp. Jude took one last look at her and stepped outside. Jamie and his mother stood beside Walter, who had been filling them in on the improvements made to the gardens. They hadn't been back since Jude sent them away for their protection.

He wondered if his mother would ever return to Beauloch after everything that had happened this past winter.

"You made it," Jude said.

Jamie didn't hesitate to pull him into an embrace. Once he was released from his younger brother's grip, Jude set his eyes on his mother.

Irene appeared as distraught as always, except the lines around her eyes were a little deeper, and her stance seemed frail.

"How are you?" Jude said.

Irene shrugged but managed to pull her lips into a weak smile.

"Can we talk upstairs?" Jamie asked, placing a hand on Jude's shoulder.

"I'll show your mother around the gardens," Walter said. He took Irene's hand and led her down the back steps and onto the freshly paved path that led to the waterfall.

Jude followed Jamie to the upstairs study. The room was dark when they entered. Jude turned a lamp on and sat down on one of the tufted leather chairs in front of the tall windows looking out onto the driveway.

"Mom is getting worse," Jamie said. He stood rigid, looking out the windows with both hands in his pockets.

"Is there anything we can do to help her?" Jude said.

"She developed some PTSD from the night Boris abducted her. We are on our way to see a specialist in France one of my old colleagues recommended."

Jude leaned back and rubbed the scruff along his jawline. "I'd be traumatized too if I were her. You think this specialist can help?"

Jamie tore his gaze away from the clouds dotting the

sky and looked at him. "It's the best thing I can think to do right now. I considered staying in France for a little while. Maybe Mom would enjoy the warmer weather."

Jude nodded. God only knew he could have used a break from having endured the bleak Scottish weather all these years, but he didn't believe sunshine and warm weather would fix the wrongs that had been done to his mother. "Do you need anything from me? You still have money in the Roceours trust."

"I'll be fine. I think I can get certified to practice family medicine in the countryside. My friend said they're in need of good doctors." Jamie paced the room, leaving his hands in his pockets.

Jamie had born the burden of their mother's illness for a long time. Jude would have helped if The Order hadn't kept him in their clutches for so long. The sacrifices he'd made to protect his family had worn him down over the years. Despite being free from his tormenters, white hairs had announced their formal arrival in his shoulder-length hair and beard.

"Where did you both go after I sent you away?" Jude said.

Jamie let out a long breath. "We stayed on an island in the Orkneys, way up north."

"Damn. That really is a remote place."

Jamie glared down at him. "I did as you asked." His blue eyes were shadowed by the darkness of the room. Jude stood up and placed a hand on his brother's shoulder.

"You kept her safe, Jamie." Jude knew his brother needed confirmation that what he'd done was the right thing. It hadn't been an easy choice. His brother could have been helping save lives in the trauma department of any hospital of his choosing, but he'd kept true to his word. If their mother's health declined, it wasn't because of something either of them had done. "Let's go back outside. I'd really like for you to see the rest of the gardens."

As soon as Jude turned to the door, he spotted a letter sitting on the desk. "Did you bring me this?" Jude said, picking up the envelope. He'd come up to the study just that morning and cleared everything off the massive desk.

"No, we just arrived," Jamie said.

Jude flipped over the unmarked envelope and tore it open. Inside was a single sheet of paper with a one-line handwritten message:

WE MUST FINISH WHAT YOUR FATHER STARTED.

"IS THIS SOME KIND OF JOKE? TELL ME YOU DIDN'T PUT this here!" Jude said in a raised voice.

"What does it say?" Jamie snatched the letter from his hands, read the note, and looked back up at him. "Who wrote this?" he said, his face twisted with confusion.

Jude huffed. "How the hell should I know!" He threw his hands in the air then raked his fingers through his hair.

"Could it be someone from The Order?" Jamie said, trying to keep his voice low.

Jude stood directly in front of his little brother. "Everyone in The Order is dead. I'm sure of it."

Jamie backed up and read the letter again before flipping it over and searching the blank envelope for clues.

"Maybe this is one of father's old contacts from the government."

"I don't care who it is. They're done using this family." Jude tore the paper out of Jamie's hand, crumpled it up, and threw it into the wastebin behind the desk.

"The letter didn't magically appear, Jude."

Jude got up in Jamie's face. "I'm done with all this," he snarled. Before he lost his temper, Jude walked out of the study and slammed the door shut behind him.

JAMIE WAITED UNTIL HIS BROTHER'S FOOTSTEPS FADED away. He walked over to the wastebin and pulled the letter out. The handwriting looked similar to some script he'd seen before. Jamie reached into a drawer and popped open the secret compartment. His father's letters still lay undisturbed in the hidden nook.

He held up one of the old letters the man who called himself Gawain had sent to his father and compared it to the crumpled one. Some of the strokes on the letter from Gawain looked similar to a few on the anonymous note. Could they have been written by the same man? He would need more time to examine them in detail to be sure.

Before his long absence became suspicious, Jamie slipped all the letters into his jacket pocket. He started for the door, but as he reached for the handle, another thought hit him.

He went back to the desk and unlocked the bottom drawer with the spare key he'd had forever. Long ago, Jude had told him to keep it so they'd each have one, just in case either of them needed it someday.

Today might be that day.

Jamie carefully withdrew the pistol from the drawer. He checked the chamber to see if it was loaded, made sure the safety was on, and locked the drawer back before slipping out of the room.

Author's Note

The harp is a mysterious instrument. Different versions of the Celtic harp, also known as the lever harp, have existed for a very long time. Variations of the harp have had a place in numerous cultures all over of the world and their existence can even be traced back as far as ancient Egypt! They could have existed for longer, but we cannot know what history didn't record.

For most professional harpists, the lever harp is the launching point to the bigger, more versatile, pedal harp. With rotating mechanisms on the top to change the pitch of each string, the range of a modern pedal harp is vastly wider than her smaller sister. Serious musicians go on to learn classical music on the pedal harp and often play in orchestras or churches. (I'm not a serious musician. In fact, I'm more of a hobbyist.)

Like many people during the COVID lockdown, I itched to fill my time with some novel pursuit, something I hadn't ever done before. With encouragement from my husband—you could call it nagging, even—I began taking lessons in early 2022. Learning the harp helped me through some dark times in my life. Whenever I felt low or stressed, sitting down to practice for as little as thirty minutes helped ease my anxiety. For the most part, I played for myself, but as I progressed and began to perform for family and friends, my outlook on music as a healing tool changed.

The first time I took the harp out of my house—moving a floor harp is a feat of its own, by the way—was when I went to play for my great uncle in an assisted living center. The residents and staff adored the music, and it felt amazing to bring them joy, even though I wasn't playing masterpieces by Bach or Mozart. My uncle has since passed, but that day is still one of my favorite memories of performing.

After seeing firsthand the happiness harp music could bring, I knew I had to include it in my first book. As you know by now, *Harpist for the Beast* has many dark themes, which is why I needed something that could imbue the spirit of the book with hope to counter the many horrors my characters would face. I also drew on Celtic symbolism regarding Millie and the Cailleach too, which helped solidify my choice of instrument. To my thinking, if you were to wander the Scottish Highlands and happened to come upon a fairy plucking an instrument in some remote glen, it would most certainly be the lever harp. (Just make sure to watch from afar so as not to offend them! Real fairies are fickle creatures.)

If you ever get a chance to hear the harp live—lever, pedal, or other—I urge you to take it! Feeling the resonance of the soundboard while the musician is at work is not something you'll forget anytime soon.

-Summer Hayes

Acknowledgments

This book wouldn't have been possible without the help of some amazing friends. The first one I'd like to thank is not just a friend but a mentor, Lauren Smith. Ever since we met in a writing workshop in 2023, Lauren has been a vital part of getting this book from being an idea in my head to the final product you're reading now. Not only has she encouraged me from the beginning, but she's also been an immense help when it comes to navigating the self-publishing world. Thanks Lauren!

The second person I'd like to thank is my friend Kyleigh, aka Glitchy. Glitchy helped me during those late-night writing sprints when I needed someone to hype me up for this crazy story. Those memes we sent back and forth right before bed helped me laugh through all the pain I endured during the first draft. I'm looking forward to the upcoming GIFs we find for book two!

The next two people I met when I joined the Oklahoma Romance Writers Guild back in the spring of 2024. Kate Minty and Gabby Schuffert were the ones I went to when I panicked or got into an editing rut. Through countless screenshots, emails, and many other forms of correspondence, Kate and Gabby helped keep me on track to meet my deadlines.

Of course, behind every good book is an even greater editor. Andrea Neil from Two Birds Author Services has been an outstanding contributor not only to the book, but to my writing. I learned more in the few months it took me to revise *Harpist for the Beast* than I did in the previous years trying to go at it on my own.

I also need to thank not one, but two harp teachers. The first, Lorelei K. Barton, was not only an amazing harp teacher, but also a dear friend who laughed at all my sarcastic jokes during my lessons. She taught me all the core skills I needed to succeed at playing the harp, and I'll be forever grateful for her.

My second harp teacher, Julie Norman, provided the special arrangement of "Dies Irae" I've included in the audio version of this book. Julie is an amazing soul and an excellent instructor who challenges me to be a great harpist. I think the universe meant for us to find each other.

Finally, I'd like to thank my mom, who taught me how to read at a very young age. Thank you for instilling a love of books in me and taking me to the library every summer when I was a little girl. Love you!

About the Author

Summer Hayes lives with her husband and two spoiled cats in Owasso, Oklahoma. Whenever she isn't writing thrilling tales, she loves to play the Celtic harp and streams under the Twitch name BBandPhil. She also loves to stargaze and catch the Perseids every year with her close friends. If she has time, she likes to try new recipes and crochet.

**You can finder her at:
summerhayesbooks.com**

Socials: @summerhayesbooks